CECE RIOS

and the

QUEEN OF BRUJAS

Also by Kaela Rivera

Cece Rios and the Desert of Souls
Cece Rios and the King of Fears

CECE RIOS

and the
QUEEN OF BRUJAS

KAELA RIVERA

HARPER

An Imprint of HarperCollins Publishers

Library of Congress Control Number: 2023933829
ISBN 978-0-06-321396-8

Typography by Catherine Lee
24 25 26 27 28 LBC 5 4 3 2 1

First Edition

For all those who have been victims of hate.
May light and hope carry you out of the darkness.

Call of the Desert

Orange light burned across the desert as I waited in the open cerros for my enemies to pounce.

The afternoon sun sank toward the horizon, and sweat streaked my face as I turned in a circle. Brush and cacti surrounded me, and boulders and stone and hills disguised the sounds of breaking twigs and the distant clattering of claws. I couldn't see them. I was weaker than them. But I had one thing they didn't.

Río Fuerte was the only river near Tierra del Sol. And fortunately, it was only a few steps away. If I could make it there before they struck, I could show them what I was really made of. I could show them I was just as strong as the river.

An echo of distant orange—confidence, focus—streaked through the air. Someone's soul was close. And they were sure they'd land their next blow.

I leaped away just before sharp teeth clamped down on

me. The enemy was just a blur of multicolored hair and red clothes. I swung back, listening to the pulses of their souls, their intentions—before sinking my feet deep into the river.

"You think you're ready?" the angry blur cried.

Three more criaturas vaulted out from their hiding places, claws ready, eyes burning bright in the ripening sun. The cool water swept around my feet. I closed my eyes.

Let's dance, I whispered to the river with my glowing turquoise soul.

I swirled around, and the water followed my movements, surrounding me in a great cyclone. The first criatura slammed into the wall of liquid. I whipped my hands sideways, and they went spiraling off toward the cerros. It was working. The river's current moved almost in time with my heartbeat. A twig cracked behind me. I turned just in time to see another couple of enemies sneaking up behind me, hunched behind rocks, eyes glittering. I shifted my feet to face them. With my movement, the water surged forward and slapped them both away. They cried out as they skated off across the desert, kicking up dust as they went.

I panted, sweating, but I couldn't let my guard down. There was one left. And they were the deadliest of all. I searched the landscape. Where were they hiding?

Help . . .

I froze. Had I just—heard something? I searched the desert landscape, but there was still no one else in sight. Slowly, a rumble moved through the ground, rattling in my knees. The same voice climbed my bones:

Help me, por favor . . . I'm dying . . .

The voice trailed off on the wind, distant like a ripple through the water. My insides clenched. The voice's sorrow echoed in the ground. Who was that? I turned, hoping to find some clue—and stilled when claws curled around my throat.

"Close, Cece," a familiar voice said. "But you left yourself open."

I tilted my head back. Ocelot stood over me, her nails catching the light of my glowing water. Their deadly edges traced the skin of my tender throat.

"Sunsets, not again." I slumped over.

The water splashed down around me. The river returned to its proper flow, steady and strong. Ocelot chuckled as she pulled her claws safely away. Over her shoulder, Metztli popped out from behind a boulder.

"I keep reminding you, curanderita," she said, as she scribbled in the notebook Mamá had given her. "You must always stay focused."

"Sí, Metztli. Sorry, I thought I heard something." I pouted. I'd been on such a roll too. I kicked my toe into the bed of the river.

The water gurgled.

"Oh, lo siento," I whispered to it.

Coyote skated into place beside me. His hair was soaked from the cyclone spin I'd sent him on earlier, but he was grinning. "But that was so good, Cece!" he said. "You actually got me that time! The training's working. I think you could go toe-to-toe with any of the old curanderas now."

"You really think so?" I straightened up, beaming.

For the past three months, Metztli, the moon curandera, had been training me in my ocean curandera powers. There were only six months until the door to Devil's Alley opened, so after we'd escaped Tía Catrina's takeover of Devil's Alley, I'd been putting every spare moment into making sure I was ready to face her again. I hadn't been strong enough to fight Catrina then. Juana had had to carry me out of Devil's Alley. So the next time we faced Catrina and her forces, I wanted to fight alongside my criatura friends. Especially since she would be more powerful than ever, with Quetzalcoatl—once El Cucuy, the king of Devil's Alley—under her control.

Lion suddenly landed on my other side and sent water

splashing over the three of us. I coughed and spluttered as he harumphed.

"Don't be so soft on her," Lion snapped at Coyote. "Cece, you're still too slow if you're not in the water, and you're going easy on us because we're your friends. You've got to take this seriously. You're not going to be fighting people you can reason with this time."

I frowned at him. Lion was always the hardest on me, but I could tell it was because he was worried. Lion only knew how to care about people aggressively.

I clasped my hands together and beamed at him, pouring out all my love, and care, and gratitude through the air so it wrapped around his soul, where it dangled around his neck. He scowled.

"Okay! Fine!" Lion folded his arms and huffed. "You're . . . getting *better*, Cece."

I stuck my fists into the air. "I got a Lion compliment!"

"Whatever! Don't get complacent!"

"Sí, sí."

Metztli met us on the bank of the river as we all waded out. Kit Fox was waiting there beside her. His large blond fox ears perched atop his head as I approached, and he grinned, but his cheeks were scuffed from where I'd sent him flying.

"Aw, Kit!" I rushed to him and checked a little scratch

on his cheek. "Did I hurt you? I'm so sorry! I'll be more careful next time—"

The scrape healed right before my eyes. I settled back. Oh, right. Criaturas healed a lot faster than humans—but I still felt bad. My friends had been helping me train because no one else could withstand the blows. Sometimes I helped Juana train too, but even then I was careful not to hit her too hard. Metztli said curanderas used to train with each other to develop their offensive powers, but she was the moon curandera, so she didn't have physical powers. Though her ability to play with minds and memories certainly seemed powerful enough to me.

Kit snickered and brushed my hand away. "I'm fine, Cece. I'm not a little kid, you know."

I smiled weakly. Kit was actually a year younger than me in this life, but he'd also lived thousands of years in his previous eight. I guess he was right.

Metztli cleared her throat, so we all looked to her. "Muchas gracias, Coyote, Kit, Lion, Ocelot. Your help has ensured our curanderita is improving steadily." Her mouth softened, and the ever-present dots of lights in her eyes glowed a little. "But, Cece," she said, and her face dropped, "Lion is correct. Water, like the desert, is a heavy element, and you are still too slow in moving it. You must learn to account for that in battle. We have only six months until we face the wrath of Devil's Alley."

"Sí, Metztli," I said.

She was right. When the door to Devil's Alley opened again, its new queen would come for our heads.

"For now, we need to return to town before sunset," she said. "Your people will be suspicious if they see you returning later, even if the criatura months are over."

My town was suspicious of most things I did, so that was a good call. Tierra del Sol was my home, and I was preparing to defend it against an army. But they didn't know that. And they couldn't. I didn't want to find out what they would do if they found out I was a curandera, like the ones they hated of old, on top of being someone they already shunned for having saved a criatura when I was little.

The thought sobered me as I turned to my friends. "Will you come back to the house tonight? Or do you want to go hunting?"

They did that sometimes. Mamá was grateful because they often returned with rabbits and other meat to help us afford food. But I was really hoping they'd come home tonight. I wanted to eat enchiladas and cuddle so they knew how much I cared about them—even when I had to throw them around with cyclones.

"Sí, we're going to go hunting," Coyote thumbed back to the desert. "Tu Mamá's food is getting a bit scarce.

We'll sneak back to your house with something good to eat a little after dark." Coyote's eyes glittered as he smiled at me.

The sun shone on his cheeks, and my stomach fluttered like it was filled with moths. I bit my lip. I didn't know why it was doing that lately. Coyote's smile was always warm and comforting. But lately looking at it made my soul swell with tingly pinks that felt . . . different.

"Just leave the window unlocked so I can sneak in from the roof," Lion grumbled. "Unlike you all"—he glared at Kit and Coyote—"I have to sneak back in human form."

Coyote muffled a snort. Coyote and Kit often crept home in their animal forms because they were more inconspicuous. But Lion turned into a six-foot black lion with flaming red eyes—which was pretty much the opposite.

I grinned. "Of course! Juana always leaves the window open for you now."

His face softened a bit.

"Speaking of transforming! Cece, look!" Kit jumped in front of me and shook out his head. Slowly, the gold ends of his ears smeared, settling down into his hair. By the time he stopped shaking his head, his hair settled—and his ears were gone.

"Holy sunset! Kit, you did it!" I jumped on him with a hug.

Kit looked pleased with himself, with a curling grin and pink cheeks.

Lion stalked past us, arms folded. "Yeah, let's see how long you can hold them in."

Kit pouted, but I squeezed him extra hard so he knew I was proud of him. Kit was on his last life, which made transforming fully from one form to another extra hard for him. He'd been working on it for a while, and his practice was finally paying off—just like mine.

Metztli put a hand on my shoulder, and I released Kit.

"Get home soon, young ones," Metztli said to my friends. "Remember, we are waiting for word from Damiana and the Court of Fears. If all bodes well, Damiana should return late tonight with word on Catrina's allies and the brujas remaining on the surface. Don't be late for that, ¿sí?"

Damiana and the Court of Fears had spent most of the past three months scouting across Isla del Antiguo Amanecer. Tía Catrina might have been sealed away in Devil's Alley for another six months, but she was smart. I hadn't thought they had a way of communicating across the worlds—but after we returned from Devil's Alley three months ago, and we'd found Envidia had been evacuated, we knew that something, or someone, had warned them.

"They must be communicating with their queen in

some way," Metztli had said, when we'd searched Grimmer Mother's old house. It had still smelled of smoke, but it had been swept completely clean, with no signs of the bruja's animal skulls or candles or obsidian blades.

"I have searched with the Moon's light, but she has not seen where they went. They must hide themselves in the shadows at night, so their works cannot be seen by the Moon. They are planning something. That does not bode well."

The comment had been ominous, and it settled on me again as I looked to the later afternoon sky. I hoped Damiana made it home soon. And safely.

"We'll be back in time for the meeting," Coyote said, as he caught Lion and Kit by their collars and pulled them northward. They both swatted at him. "I want to hear what they've found too."

Coyote halted just as quickly as he'd turned away. Lion and Kit looked up at him questioningly. A wince moved through his body and soul at the same time. I stiffened. Coyote released them and gripped at his left forearm.

"Coyote?" I whispered.

He glanced at me over his shoulder. Stress pulled at his forehead. He swallowed hard. His hand covered his forearm, still squeezing. I thought I'd caught a small white stripe between his fingers before he shook out his arm.

He smiled at me tightly. When his arm finally hung loose again, whatever I thought I'd seen was gone.

"Get home before it gets dark, Cece." His face dropped as he looked up at the orange-lit clouds. His eyes narrowed. "Something's . . . off." He rubbed the veins in his arm.

Could he feel something too? Our eyes met one last time before he sprinted off into the desert, Kit, Ocelot, and Lion following like streaks of wind into the cerros.

"He's right," Metztli said. "Let's get home quickly, before Señora Rios worries."

She scanned the sky, her brows pulled together with suspicion. Did she feel something as well? The frightened voice from earlier prickled back up in my memory.

Metztli met my eyes again, and there was something sharp in them. "We should not leave ourselves vulnerable in times like these."

2
Before the Storm

Metztli reviewed my progress as we headed home.

"You have reached expertise in most offensive water moves, an excellent thing in times like these." She flipped her notebook. "We should start moving toward more advanced moves, like healing and mastering lightning."

Whenever I called a storm, lightning usually came with it, but I had no control over where it would strike. Metztli had said it was easier for ocean curanderas to master lightning when they could train with a desert curandera too, since lightning was the energy of a storm reaching for the energy of the earth. There were apparently a *lot* of tricky moves—both offensive and defensive—that curanderas had to train together to use properly. Things like summoning lava, creating lightning, and healing were difficult for even experienced curanderas to master. Especially, she'd said, back in her day, when El Cucuy had picked off curanderas one by one to prepare for the great battle of Tierra del Sol.

We passed into the ruins, and Metztli's eyes grew distant as she stared out at Tierra del Sol, where it waited for us on the other side. A gray-white feeling floated out from her soul, filled with old, remembered fears and tender nostalgia. I wasn't as familiar with Metztli's soul as I was with my friends'—I'd carried theirs once, and that made our connection stronger—but I had enough experience with soul language now to know Metztli wrestled with these colors often. Sadness. Apprehension. Grief.

"Are you okay?" I whispered.

Metztli blinked, like she was coming back to today. She glanced around the ruins as we closed in toward the edge of town. I'm sure she remembered what these buildings had looked like before they'd been destroyed. I wondered if she ever felt like a ghost, wandering through a time that wasn't hers.

"Sí, Cece," she said, as she took a rousing breath. "Consuelo often told me I sink too deep into my mind, both my great strength and deep weakness." She looked to Tierra del Sol. "This place has been at the heart of many wars. I only hope we rescue it before it is all ruins." She shook her head. "The brujas' sudden disappearance troubles me. For what are they gathering?"

I squeezed my hands to my chest. "Maybe they're just running away from us?"

She pressed her lips together. That clearly didn't satisfy her. We slipped toward the town square, which led to the road to my house, and my chest rushed with all Metztli's anxieties hanging in the air. Maybe I should tell her about the voice I thought I'd heard back at the river—the one calling for help. What if it was important? I placed a hand over the tear-shaped lump of my soul, where it hid beneath my shirt. It hadn't been the voice of the water. That I knew. But what if I was just picking up on the souls of . . . plants or something? Did they even have souls? I frowned to myself. I wasn't practiced in soul language, and it was the one thing Metztli didn't know how to help me with. I didn't want to make her more anxious than she already was.

"I have never heard of such a thing," she'd said, when we'd talked about it late at night after returning from Devil's Alley. "But . . . I did not have as much time to train as the other curanderas. There were so few left at my time, so many had been picked off. But Consuelo did once say that it is a mistake to assume we know everything about our world. She said there are always deeper ways to understand the nature of souls and the gods who made them."

Metztli and I reached the town square. We headed to the road that would lead to my house, trying to appear as casual as possible and not like we'd been fighting with criaturas out in the desert. Sometimes I was worried my neighbors would smell it on me, but most people didn't even bother to look at me as we moved by market stalls. That was, except for one pair of intent eyes.

I paused my stride and looked across the square. About ten feet away, a woman wearing a large sombrero stared at me under its gray shade. She leaned against the wall by Rosa, the woman who sold tortillas, though Rosa didn't seem to notice her. I checked behind me, but her gaze didn't move an inch off me. Not even as I met hers directly. The longer I stared, the more her eyes seemed off too. Like there was a hint of orange in them, but the shadow of her hat made it hard to tell. A shiver climbed my spine. Something about her looked familiar. Had I seen her before?

"Ey!" Someone's boots stomped our way. "You!"

I jumped and whirled around. Metztli put a hand on my back for comfort. Across the square, the chief of police strode toward us, eyes narrow, scanning Metztli up and down. I didn't know Señor Reyes very well, but he probably knew a lot about me, so that wasn't a great start. I stiffened but tried to keep my face calm as he made his way over.

Mamá had been relieved when he became chief of police. "Finally," she'd said. "Someone who cares." And he'd been the one to get everyone to listen to me and search for Juana on the night El Sombrerón captured her. Maybe that meant he was at least fair, somewhere beneath his hard eyes and tough, broad, barrel chest.

The chief stopped before us, eyeing Metztli. "I haven't seen you before," he said. "Are you a merchant?"

Merchants were the only people who really traveled to Tierra del Sol, so it was a good guess. But he still looked suspicious because the same merchants came every spring, and Metztli definitely wasn't one of them.

"No," Metztli said calmly, and outstretched her hand. "But it is good to meet you, Señor Reyes. I assume you protect this town in place of its ancient guardians?"

Sweat dripped down the back of my neck as Señor Reyes's eyebrows crunched down. I'd gotten so used to the way Metztli talked, I forgot how obviously out of time she was.

"¡Oh, mi prima! ¡Hola!"

All three of us looked to the west, where Mamá came rushing with her large arms wide open. I let out a sigh of relief as she swarmed in and buried Metztli in an unexpected hug.

"Señor Reyes, have you met mi prima? She lives in Costa de los Sueños, but she's here to visit!" Mamá beamed at him.

His eyebrows pulled together, more confused now than

harsh. Probably because Mamá wasn't usually so—um, bubbly? But she stroked Metztli's bewildered head so naturally that Señor Reyes finally let out a gruff smile beneath his thick mustache and settled his hands on his hips.

"Glad to see your familia has come to support you, Señora Rios," he said softly. "If you ever need extra help, you let me know, ¿sí? And remember, you can just call me Santos."

"Sí. Gracias, Don Santos." Mamá started herding me and Metztli away. "It's getting late, so we should be off, ah?"

"Sí, sí." Santos watched us go with a small wave. "But ey, señoras, if you notice anything suspicious, let me know, okay?"

Mamá stopped pushing us and straightened. "Why?" she asked. "Is something wrong, señor?"

He tilted his head. "Not exactly, señora. We've just been noticing some unusual people in and around Tierra del Sol." He squeezed his belt. "Criaturas may mostly be back home now, but brujas are like rats. Difficult to flush out."

My stomach tightened at the same time as Mamá's face. I cast my eyes around the square, but the woman I'd noticed before was gone. I squeezed Mamá's arm.

Mamá recovered and nodded. "We'll let you know if we notice anything. Gracias, Santos."

Mamá turned and started hauling Metztli down the road that led home. I ran alongside her gratefully, but our hurried movement wasn't enough to shake off the weight of Don Santos's words from my mind.

"You do not wish me to speak to your townspeople," Metztli said, in a low voice, to Mamá. "But we cannot hide forever, Axochitl. We will need the aid of all who can band with us to vanquish the queen of Devil's Alley, including the people of Tierra del Sol."

Mamá sighed. "Metztli, you speak like mi bisabuela." She herded both of us to the front door of our house. "You don't understand. This town is scared, as much as it is scarred." She opened the door and gestured us inside. A couple of neighbors walked by, and she smiled and waved at them, whispering to us between her teeth. "They hate curanderas and criaturas. I am not sure they would help, even with their lives on the line."

My stomach dropped. I had the same fear. Across the street, our neighbors left for their homes, and Mamá pulled our door shut behind us. She let out a stressed breath. I took her hand. She paused, her face softening, and kissed my forehead. All the tension from the day melted away with the warmth of her familiar touch.

"I didn't mean to say that," she said softly. "Of course their hearts will soften. But—we must be careful." She looked up at Metztli. "You understand, ¿sí?"

Metztli's brows only pulled tight. "We cannot wait much longer, señora. When the door to Devil's Alley opens in six months, we must be ready with an army. Otherwise, we will not survive long enough to pry Quetzalcoatl from Catrina's grasp," she said. "It is essential. With our numbers, even with the Court of Fears included, we do not stand a chance against all the brujas and brujos, animal criaturas and dark criaturas, and Quetzalcoatl under her control."

Mamá pressed her lips together. She knew it as well as I did. But that still left us with an impossible question:

How could we convince Tierra del Sol to side with us in six months, when they'd spent two hundred years being against all we stood for?

Plus, the fact that they already hated me didn't help.

I shrugged off my old green coat and caught my thumb in a hole in the sleeve. It ripped wider, and I frowned. Great. Another hole to mend.

Mamá cleared her throat and shuffled into the kitchen. "Cece, that old jacket is practically rags. Don't you want a new one?"

I smiled. "It's okay, Mamá. I don't want to ruin a nice one with training." That's why I didn't wear any of my crocheted shawls to practice in either.

"Well, I think it smells like oil," a small voice piped up from the kitchen.

Axolotl sat at the kitchen table, poring over some of my early elementary-school books, her feet swinging from her chair. Mamá ruffled her pink hair as she walked by, and Axolotl looked up and huffed.

"Señora Rios!" she whined. "This is too hard! I don't want to learn to read."

Metztli and I shot each other repressed smiles. The first thing Damiana had wanted Axolotl to do, once they moved in with us, was to learn to read. I think it was just to distract her—Damiana had to go on scouting missions and didn't want to risk Axolotl. But Mamá had decided to learn too, since she'd never been able to go to school like Juana and I had.

Mamá leaned over Axolotl's shoulder to look at the book. She sighed wearily. "Ay, why's it all so complicated?" She clucked her tongue and squinted at the sentence. "We'll get this, Axolotl, no fear, mija."

Axolotl didn't look afraid. She looked annoyed, and she pouted over at us hopefully, like we might rescue her.

"It's not so hard once you practice," I tried to comfort her. "You've already got the alphabet down!"

Axolotl let out a groan and dropped her face to the book. "I miss mi mamá. When's she coming?"

Mamá patted her shoulder and went to the sink.

"Damiana should be back late tonight, mija. Don't worry." She looked my way. "You must be thirsty, working so hard, eh, Cece?"

I wiped my dirty face with the back of my hand and tried to smile more confidently than I felt. "Metztli says my powers are almost as strong as Consuelo's now! I even defeated all my friends—er, except Ocelot."

Because of that voice that distracted me: a cry for help, reverberating through the ground. Something about it still bothered me. I might have thought it was Mother Desert, but I'd only ever heard her once, in Devil's Alley. And she hadn't sounded like a frightened child.

"Good job, mi vida," Mamá said, and placed the water glasses on the table. "Here, come, drink." She moved to the stove. "Where's Coyote y tus amigos, by the way? Out hunting again? Juana said she wants to go with them the next time, can you believe? Ha! She should be on her way back from the fields soon . . ."

I sat down at the table in front of my glass. But I froze mid-reach for it. The liquid inside it rippled. It pulsed in its ceramic container, bobbing up and down, and a low rumble carried through the ground. Distant sounds picked up through our walls. Sounds like shouting. Like running. Like panic.

I stood up. Axolotl looked at me with her bulgy pink eyes. Mamá stopped when she saw my expression. Metztli's gaze cut to the window. Her face hardened.

"Mamá," I breathed. "Grab your emergency bag."

We'd prepared supply bags when Metztli recommended it months ago, but I hadn't thought we'd need to use them for a while yet. Mamá ran and grabbed hers immediately. I pulled my hole-ridden jacket back on. Axolotl hopped off the chair as Metztli scooped up her notebook and her satchel.

"Hey!" She pulled on my sleeve. "What's wrong? What's going on?"

I wasn't sure how to answer. But just then, a knock came at the door. Metztli unlocked it and pulled it open.

Damiana stood on the front step, tall, thin, with bruises on her collarbone, a claw mark bleeding on her cheek, and a hat that was meant to hide her magenta bruja eyes but instead just cast shadows across her panicked expression.

"The bruja army," she panted. "They're here!"

3
The Army of Grimmer Mother

From my street, you could just see the top of the dome of the Sun Sanctuary, where it stood at the center of town. Normally, it brought me a sense of solidarity and companionship, since we often met secretly in the back laundry room with Dominga del Sol to discuss our plans.

But as Mamá, Metztli, Axolotl, Damiana, and I sprinted down the street, pushing through a growing, panicked crowd fleeing from the center of town—I could see the Sun Sanctuary's roof now covered in the silhouettes of criaturas and brujas. The smell of oil and burning hovered in the air.

The town square came into view as we charged from the south. We'd been here only half an hour earlier, but already it looked almost unrecognizable.

The market stalls had been ripped up and piled onto the northern-leading roads, creating barricades. Police officers and crowds waited behind them, calling out in panic. They tried to clear the wood and adobe, but it would take a while with the amount of debris.

The whole area reeked of fuel. The Sun Sanctuary rose on our right, unharmed as far as I could see, but the orphanage next door had its front doors partially broken off their hinges. Claw marks riddled the floor and scraped down the steps, leading directly to where the children now huddled together, eyes wide and frightened, at the center of the square. Kids as young as four and as old as me clutched each other desperately. They weren't alone, but nearly. Only a handful of Sun Priestesses, including Dominga del Sol, were left in the square to protect them from a ring of animal criaturas—Gray Wolf, Rattlesnake, Black Bear, and Iguana—pressing in toward them.

Damiana clutched Axolotl to her chest. "They've taken the children hostage."

Metztli scanned the scene with flickering lights in her eyes. "But why? Surely they would not risk themselves only to attack children. They have nothing to gain."

"¡Hola, Cecelia Rios!" a voice called.

My heart turned to ice. I pushed through Mamá and Metztli, stepping up to the edge of the square. Brujas lined roofs around the square, but one in particular crouched on the edge of the dome of the Sun Sanctuary. She wore a large sombrero, and as I looked up at her, she lit a match. The flame painted gold light across her face and revealed her orange eyes. My heart dropped. It was the woman I'd seen earlier.

"So there's the ocean curandera we've been looking for!" she called. She grinned, and all of a sudden, I remembered where I'd thought I'd seen her before. She'd been the one talking with El Silbón on the first night of the Semana de la Cosecha. "Let's see if you still want to fight for Tierra del Sol so badly when it's nothing but ashes."

She laughed and dropped the match.

When it hit the ground, fire leaped up and raced toward the children.

"Stop!" I screamed, and charged forward.

Thunder rose up inside me. A noise that shook my bones and crackled with the promise of a storm. I dashed forward, barely outrunning the flames as they raced to cover the oil-slick ground. No, I wasn't going to be fast enough on my own. Everything slowed around me, as the fire lit up the square, as my people trapped on the northern roads cried out, as the children screamed.

I had never used my powers in front of my people. I'd hidden them away for safety, just as much as we'd hidden Metztli. But there was only one way I could hope to put out oil fires like this, only one way to face off this many criaturas. I had to expose myself to all of Tierra del Sol, for Tierra del Sol.

I rushed forward, stretching out my hands. Rain clouds gathered, blotting out the light of the afternoon sun. The fire roared up toward Dominga del Sol. She flinched—and I pulled down the rain.

"Leave my people *alone!*" I cried.

A deluge stormed down on Tierra del Sol.

The water hit the ground with the impact of hail. The fire hissed and drowned in the power of the rain. It left a scorched circle in the ground, smoke trailing upward in big gray and black clouds. I ran toward the group.

"You're okay now!" I called, spitting out rain. "But you have to move fast—" I reached out.

All the Sun Priestesses, besides Dominga del Sol, flinched at my approach. Some of the kids gasped and hid from me. My heart winced. My hand lowered. I was here to help—but all they saw was a girl they already thought was cursed with a soul like water, now using impossible, frightening water powers. They looked at me the same way they'd looked at the brujas.

"¡Excelente, Cecelia!" Metztli said. "Hermanas, we must help the children escape!"

With the fire clear, Mamá took up my right, Metztli on my left, rushing in for the Sun Priestesses and the children. I swallowed the hurt down as Damiana, Mamá, and Metztli began directing the children and Sun Priestesses back down south, the way we'd come, for escape.

Damiana swung Axolotl around. "Hang on, mija."

Axolotl clung to her mom's back as Damiana took out her obsidian blade. Her magenta eyes flashed, and the Sun Priestesses gasped. Dominga del Sol's gaze saddened as she clutched a couple of kids' hands and hurried them south.

The four brujas' orange, black, yellow, and emerald-green eyes glittered down at us from above. As my familia rushed with the kids toward the southern road, the criaturas that had been focused on me suddenly lunged for them.

I didn't want to hurt criaturas. But I wouldn't let them hurt anyone else either.

The criaturas aimed right for the heads of the children. I slammed my feet into the mud, the wet droplets splattering across my coat as I turned in a circle. The water rose up from the ground. I rolled it forward in a breaking wave, batting away any blows directed for the fleeing party. Rattlesnake hissed as I sent him flying back across the square, then turned and made a small wave, pinning Gray Wolf against the nearest house. Mamá called out directions to the Sun Priestesses and kids. Damiana carried many on her back. Metztli brought up the rear, ensuring the children stayed together.

"Why have you come here?" Metztli demanded of the brujas as she drove the rest of the escape.

The orange-eyed bruja spread her arms wide. "Isn't it obvious?" Her grin turned on me.

The Criatura of the Black Bear slammed into place behind Metztli. She roared, swinging for a straggler child. Metztli scooped up the girl and sprinted down the road. Black Bear reared around to face me. Gray Wolf shook his fur free of water and prowled forward. Rattlesnake slithered back into place, and Iguana's claws scratched the mud as he finished the semicircle. Above them, their brujas grinned in unison, gripping the criaturas' souls.

I stood alone in the town square, facing down a small army.

I shuddered in my wet clothes but spread my feet into the stance Metztli taught me, readying myself for a fight I hadn't known was coming so soon.

"This is Tierra del Sol, the birthplace of the people of the Sun!" I shouted to the brujas, where they stood as haughty spectators. "You won't harm anyone else while I'm here!"

The bruja I'd seen earlier laughed. "You still don't get it, do you Cece?" She grinned, and her fangs lit up like knife blades in the dark. "We didn't come here to hurt your people." She gestured to herself and the other brujas along the rooftops. "We're here for *you*."

Me? But why, after all this time? Why now?

There wasn't time to question more. In seconds, all four

criaturas dove for my throat.

I slid my feet through the mud and rain, stretching my arms up. The water moved with me, a wall sending two criaturas skating backward. Two more broke through the water wall, and I crossed my arms in a sharp, hasty X. The mud erupted on either side of me, slapping both back and sending them crashing into the city hall.

I grinned. "I'm not a new curandera anymore—"

A growl streaked past me and ripped through my ear.

I screamed and clasped my hand over the bleeding skin as the blur landed in front of me. Gray Wolf's yellow eyes glowed in the growing darkness, his white teeth decorated in red streaks from my throbbing, wet ear.

I wiped my tears and straightened up. Gray Wolf turned, tail slashing, and licked his chops. I pulled the water up from the ground again. His hackles rose, his teeth gritted, and he pounced, slicing through the air. I barely managed to sidestep him. His claws caught nothing, and I pieced my wave back together, pulling it high above my head.

The wolf swung around again, but this time, I was ready.

I moved to send it crashing down.

"I said stop!"

I recognized the voice—it was Santos, the chief of police, calling out somewhere behind me, probably from just behind the barricade on the north road. I looked over my shoulder, just for a quick, spare second, to see if he was calling to me or if someone else was in danger—

When a rock hurtled into my knee.

Sharp, cutting pain splintered up my leg. I screamed and tipped sideways when the joint refused to hold. As I fell, all I caught was an angry old man standing in the partially cleared wreckage of the barricade, another rock already in his hand and pointed at me. Santos grasped his arm to pull it down.

"You brought the brujas down on us!" the old man yelled at me. "I knew it was only a matter of time before you cursed us all too!"

I hit the ground at the same time as my upset water. I spluttered as the wave splattered against my face and flooded the square. The old man glared. Above my head, the brujas' grins widened. Tears burned my eyes as a few angry voices rose with the old man's.

How—

How could they do this?

I was trying to *protect* them. They'd just seen me, hadn't they? And they were fighting me too? I tried to regain my feet, but Gray Wolf was over me before I could even try to get my swelling knee to cooperate. My hair sank into the mud. I gasped as his jaws opened wide. I raised my hands to block his teeth, to try to protect myself, as he came down for blood.

The chief of police leaped between us.

The criatura's teeth sank straight through the man's shoulder. Santos cried out as the teeth pierced deep, and the impact brought him to his knees before me. Gray Wolf's claws held him captive, even as he tried to shake the beast off. I stared, frozen, horrified, as Santos's dark eyes screwed shut and blood bloomed across his shirt. He didn't run. Didn't scream. Just shouted for me and the others to flee to the haciendas at the edge of Tierra del Sol.

"Go!" he cried, and gestured me away. "¡Escapa!"

The people around us froze too, silent in horror and awe. Even the brujas looked surprised. The chief of police— he'd—actually saved *me*?

It was the first time someone in Tierra del Sol had ever chosen to help me. Tears filled my eyes, and the sky surged with a deepening storm. The crowd began to run up the northern road, as Santos had instructed, leaving him and I stranded. But Don Santos had come to help me. I wouldn't abandon him to Gray Wolf's attack, even if we were both wounded.

I gripped my hands into fists and punched Gray Wolf in the eye.

I wasn't really that strong, but it must have been startling enough to make him release his powerful jaws. His bruja glared from above, and his clouded yellow eyes turned on me. I held my breath and pulled the water, trying to gather it before the oncoming blow, like Metztli had warned me. Gray Wolf's powerful body bent in preparation. Santos tried to grab him, but his arms were too weak and damaged—Gray Wolf lunged for me again.

Juana stepped between us and kicked him in the side.

The wolf yelped as he flipped and splattered into the mud. Juana's hair was wild and wet as she stood between us, her bright red dress covered in streaks of dirt. The belt around her waist clinked, and she ripped our familia's fire opal knives out of their sheaths.

"Juana!" I burst.

Hope fluttered back up between my ribs. She twisted to glance at me over her shoulder. For a second, her eyes seemed to glow. It must have been the opal knives. She flashed me a smile before her gaze cut back to the surrounding criaturas.

"You didn't think I'd let you fight on your own, did you?" she asked, over the rain.

Rattlesnake, Iguana, Gray Wolf, and Black Bear shook out the rain from their bodies and repositioned themselves around us. Juana's jaw tightened.

"Are you okay, Cece? You're bleeding."

I touched my raw ear. "It's not too bad. My knee's injured, but—"

I looked to Santos. He clutched his bloodstained sleeve, taking in our situation too. He kept shouting for the citizens on the north road to run. Many did, but many stayed.

"Don Santos is worse," I whispered to Juana.

Juana nodded her understanding and flipped the bright knives in her hands. "I'll hold them back."

Rattlesnake coiled and sprang. And my big sister stood between him and me like a wall of fire.

She moved with precision. Somehow even more beautiful than she'd been on the day of the Amenazante dance, and twice as powerful. Rattlesnake hit the flat of her blade, his skin searing. Before the burn could deepen, Juana grabbed him by the tail and threw him into Black Bear's face. Gray Wolf sprang, and she locked blade-to-jaw with him, pressing him back, sweating. The more she fought, the more her skin seemed to turn the rain to steam. She looked like a force of nature, a red tornado cutting through the storm, battering back attacks.

Above our heads, I caught one of the brujas laughing. It wasn't a mocking laugh. Not condescending, even. It was just entertained. Like she was watching a performance go exactly as planned.

"This is going even better than I'd thought!" The bruja

elbowed the green-eyed woman beside her, who just scowled. "Just wait. In a bit, all her criaturas will come in one by one to save her, and it'll be even more perfect. Ooh, I can't wait to get the Great Namer's soul and give it to Queen Catrina—"

"¡Estúpida!" the green-eyed bruja swatted her. "That's not what we're here for!"

"But his power to Name would be so helpful—"

"Except that it's *useless* in her state." She scoffed. "Remember what we're after? Did you even listen to Grimmer Mother?"

Grimmer Mother? I twisted around in the mud to face them. So they *were* here for something specific, not just terrorizing my town. What could be so important that they'd rather have it than something as powerful as Coyote's soul? Catrina had been desperate for it when we were leaving Devil's Alley months ago.

"¡Ey, idiotas!" the orange-eyed bruja yelled at them from another rooftop. "Keep her distracted!"

The others suddenly shook to attention, and with their returned focus, Rattlesnake and Gray Wolf swerved and charged me instead of my sister. Juana didn't miss a beat. The sound of sizzling lit the air as she streaked left and right with the knives, her eyes flashing almost gold in the light cast from them.

"I've got this, Cece!" she called. "Just get yourself and Santos out of here! Mamá, Metztli, and Damiana"—she barely dodged a bite from Rattlesnake, and I gasped—"will be back soon!"

I hoped she was right. I hoped my friends would sense something was wrong and arrive soon too. Because the brujas' words were replaying in my head, leaving deep imprints like lead: all of this was just a distraction. That's why they'd targeted the orphans. That's why they'd made the barricades to keep the rest of the town out. That's why they'd staged an open attack against me.

So what were they really after?

And how did I stop them from getting it?

4
Thieves of Fire

My mind surged with questions, but I couldn't stay still, not when the brujas' four criaturas kept lunging at us, barely giving us room to breathe. Rattlesnake nearly sank his teeth into Juana's arms again, but she dodged at the last second, so he went flying into Iguana. I dragged myself over to Don Santos. Juana was right—I had to get him somewhere safe. Beneath his deep color, his skin was growing clammy, pallid. Had he lost too much blood?

"We'll get you out of here," I said, panting. I pulled on the water, and the liquid spread across the town square began to gather in. I'd made a flood once—if I could do that again, but more controlled, then I should be able to float him off somewhere safe. Back where the rest of the citizens had run off to. Santos's dark eyes watched the water gather around his legs as he clutched his bleeding arm.

"Mi mamá used to tell me stories about this," he said.

He sounded sleepy. A knot formed in my throat. That wasn't a good sign.

"Stories about the gods' souls and how they'd touched each of ours before they'd gone. She said that had been the nature of the curanderas before they'd fallen." He lifted his gaze to mine. It was growing filmy. Weak. I pulled the water around him faster. "She told me stories are truth bundled up for safekeeping." His breathing was shallow. "She was right."

Tears burned in my eyes. I reached for him, and the water wrapped around his torso like a blanket. He winced. I pushed, sending him safely back toward the way he'd come, back where some citizens were still watching in mute horror. A few ran at the approach of my water. A few stayed and reached for Santos. He fell into their arms, and for a second, I could breathe again.

Then Gray Wolf finally slipped past Juana—and kicked me out of the square.

"Cece!" Juana's voice cut through the air behind me.

Gray Wolf's paws dug into my chest like punches. My scream tore the rest of my breath away as he sent me flying back across the square, toward the open doors of the Sun Sanctuary. The jolt rocked my bones, and pain swelled in my gut. But I took a deep, shaking breath and called out to the water. The heavy liquid in my clothes pulled free of the fibers and wrapped around me—softening my landing with a splatter as I skidded across the tiles inside the Sun Sanctuary.

For a second, there was only ringing in my ears. I clutched my head and struggled to inhale again. My whole chest ached like my lungs had turned inside out. Heat bruised my side, and the ringing in my head slowly settled. I peeled myself off the hard tile.

"Ay, those idiotas never listen," a voice said. "I specifically said to keep you *out* of here."

I lifted my head, blearily searching for who'd spoken through the dark and the dust. The faded quiet of the Sun Sanctuary's interior encircled me like a cotton nest. My blurred vision settled, and I found a dark silhouette standing on the other side of the room, looming in the silence of the sanctuary.

Grimmer Mother stood at the front of the pews, cloaked in the burnished afternoon sun.

My insides tightened. Her criatura, La Chupacabra, sat hunched beside her, a low growl moving her throat, head jerking occasionally like she was disturbed by invisible flies. Grimmer Mother herself stood unnaturally still, like a statue carved into the sanctuary. Only the black moth tattoos on the backs of her hands fluttered. The eyes on their wings rolled backward to stare at me through the streaks of sunlight.

Dread bloomed in my gut. What had she said a minute ago? That the brujas were meant to keep me out of here?

"What do you want?" I demanded. My voice came out weaker than I wanted, but pain bubbled up in my blood. "I know you came for something, and I'm not going to let you take it!"

Grimmer Mother just laughed. "Oh, Cecita. You don't even know what it is. Just like Catrina said."

My mind whirled. What could Catrina want from the Sun Sanctuary? There was nothing here for anyone like her, no kind of power that she could use against us, nothing—

Something caught my eye behind Grimmer Mother. My stomach turned to lead.

The mosaic.

Across the back wall of the Sun Sanctuary was our five-hundred-year-old mosaic depicting the four gods and their creation of animals, criaturas, stars, and Naked Man. Their special stones—fire opal for Sun, turquoise for Ocean, moonstone for Moon, and coyamito agate for Desert—had been originally placed in the mosaic by the curanderas of ancient times. It had given me one of the first clues that I was a curandera too. Metztli even said the mosaic had been an essential part of many curandera ceremonies, including the identification and induction of new curandera apprentices.

The mosaic had always been a beautiful, peaceful reminder of where we came from.

And now, there were giant cracks running through it. Fissures so deep and large that they split the Sun god's face in half and cut Mother Ocean through the heart. I covered my mouth. Horror rose up inside me.

I gripped the pew. "What have you *done*?"

Grimmer Mother smiled. "You're too late to stop me," she said, "so I suppose there's no harm in letting you know exactly what kind of power you've been wasting."

She snapped her fingers. La Chupacabra spun around, pulling her fist back, and plowed forward, directly at the center crack of the mosaic.

"No!" I cried out. I tried to run forward, but my knee gave out. I slapped onto the ground just as La Chupacabra delivered a last, devasting blow.

The mosaic *shattered*.

Light burst out from behind its confines like an explosion of fire. I covered my face with my hands as heat and smoke and dust ballooned in the air. The acrid smell burned my lungs, and I coughed and choked as the distant, garbled sound of someone hurting filled the air.

I'm dying, that young, weak voice rumbled through the ground again, *but not for much longer.*

The noise of the explosion echoed off the walls. Slowly, I lifted my head. The floor was now a graveyard of the gods' images, sprinkled pieces of the mosaic's precious stones scattered wayward. This had been the most ancient piece of the curanderas we had in Tierra del Sol, some of the last of their remaining history. My heart broke with the castaway pieces. A tiny chip of turquoise had skated near me. I pulled it to my chest, squeezing it in my scratched-up hands.

Grimmer Mother stepped through the clouds of dissipating smoke. La Chupacabra hobbled behind her, following foot for foot, nursing her hand. It was bleeding, the knuckles clearly broken, her fingers bent the wrong way. My heart yanked sideways as Grimmer Mother strode up to me, rolling something bright between her fingers.

"I thought the mosaic would just be stone, but it was strengthened with a spell somehow. Even my criatura's strength took your entire battle to finally pierce it." Grimmer Mother said, as she kicked the crumbled stones of the mosaic away like it was nothing. I gaped in horror. She clutched that glowing something in her hand and grinned. "Well worth the effort, though, to crown Catrina queen of both worlds."

I had to squint at the light between her fingers to look at it. What was that? It was a large stone, glowing from the inside out, like a miniature sun. Actually, it looked like a soul stone—but no, it was too big to be any living person's. I would think it was fire opal left over from the mosaic, but the stone glowed so much brighter than any fire opal I'd seen. And it was clearly not Grimmer Mother making it do that—brujas usually couldn't make fire opal glow. If I looked at it right, it even seemed like fire rolled off its edges.

"What . . . is that?" I rasped out through the smoke.

Grimmer Mother only smirked. She covered the stone with her fingers again and squeezed.

"You act as if you've never seen the Sun before, Cece," she said.

I squeezed my turquoise stone so hard it cut into my palm. *What?* Was she saying—she couldn't be saying what I thought she was.

Her smile widened, and my doubts shuddered inside me. "Say goodbye to the light, Cece," she said.

My legs were shaking, and I felt sick to my stomach. I couldn't wrap my mind around what she was saying, or why there had been a soul behind the mosaic, or why she wanted it. But I knew I couldn't let Catrina have her way.

I summoned all the strength inside me, raised my hands, and lifted water drops from the tiled floor. There were fewer in here than I'd like, but I'd have to make do. I swung the water her way in a long, ready rope. It rushed directly toward her, but she only chuckled.

She pocketed the soul stone, and instantly everything plunged into darkness.

My water splashed and fell sideways. Grimmer Mother's laughter echoed around the sanctuary. I stumbled, searching for the light of the late-afternoon sun. No matter where I turned, I couldn't see anything. It was like the sun had been blown out. I turned in a circle, heart hammering, panting and desperate and blind—until La Chupacabra's foot slammed into my chest.

I flew back across the tile and banged against the stone wall. My head spun in the darkness. I scrambled to recover, but my weak knee and throbbing skull cried out. I barely managed to lift my head. I blinked furiously. My eyes slowly adjusted to the unnatural, imposed nighttime, but it didn't help.

Grimmer Mother and La Chupacabra had already vanished.

5

The People of the Sunken Sun

I had never realized how much I relied on the sun until it was gone.

It hadn't completely disappeared like I'd originally thought. I stood just outside the Sun Sanctuary doors now, bruised and aching, staring up at the darkened sky. The sun had been a circle of warm orange just minutes ago. Now it was reduced to a burning pink line on the horizon, like it had been rewound to the moment before dawn, and there, held permanently captive.

Cold tingles rushed down my skin. I replayed Grimmer Mother's smile over and over again in my head, everything she'd said as she strangled that golden fire opal stone in her hand. I shook my head. Tears filled my eyes. I didn't want to believe it. I didn't understand it. But I knew.

Somehow, Grimmer Mother had stolen the Sun god's soul.

I hadn't even known it existed. And now it was gone.

Below the Sun Sanctuary's steps, the town square was

refilling with citizens. The brujas, just like Grimmer Mother, had vanished. And my people weren't reacting any better to the artificially setting sun than I was. Many of them had surrounded my sister and Don Santos, who was now back at the center of the square. Some demanded answers from Santos, but most of my people were staring, just like me, at the sunken sun. Murmurs and screams cracked the previous silence and lit the area with panic.

"What's happened?" someone asked desperately.

"The sun's down! It's hours until sunset, how can it be possible—?"

"The brujas have done this! They've taken our sun!"

"*No!*" someone shouted, above the rest.

I turned with everyone else to look. A young policeman stood up at the center of the square, behind Santos. His knees were stained with his chief's blood. He gritted his teeth, turned, and pointed his finger at me like a knife.

"It's *her* fault!" he bellowed.

I froze as the growing crowd's eyes all turned on me. I stood alone and injured, holding my breath. I'd been used to people's dismissive and disgusted stares before. But this? This was hatred.

"Wait, no!" I called out. I straighten up, but my knee gave out. I stumbled sideways, against the wall, and barely caught myself on it.

The young police officer marched toward me, and a

wave of people began to follow after him.

"You don't understand! I was trying to help!" I looked across their faces, searching for someone I'd gone to school with, my familia, anyone. Panic crushed my heart. "I fought the brujas for you! You all saw it! I know you did, you saw me protect the orphans—"

"Our mayor is dead!" the young officer yelled over me.

I nearly swallowed my tongue. He was?

"Santos is badly wounded, and all because the Rios girl has dabbled in brujería and drawn a raid!" He rushed the steps of the Sun Sanctuary.

I dug my fingers into the wall and glanced between the water streaking the steps and the man's face getting nastier with every step. I could use the water to protect myself. But if I hit him, it would make them all angrier. Metztli said we needed them, and I knew she was right. But I didn't think *they* understood just how desperately we had to band together now.

"You touch my sister and I'll fight you myself!" Juana's muffled cry came, buried beneath the storm of the surging crowd.

"Leave the girl alone!" said someone in a weak voice— probably Santos.

The young officer didn't seem to hear anyone else. I stared up at him as he loomed over me. His hands wrenched into my jacket and yanked me away from the wall. He shoved me forward, half dragging me as my knee refused to hold. He grabbed my clothes so tight they cut into my armpits and strangled my throat. I grabbed at my collar, yanking it back to breathe.

"We'll do what we always should have done!" he called down to the people, and shook me. "We'll exile her today and leave her for the wolves she brought down on us!"

A divided cry wrested the town square, half filled with cheers, half with protest.

"Take her away!" some said.

"She's still just a child!" said a few.

Juana pushed her way through the crowd, eyes bright and dangerous as she aimed for me, but my insides shook. Fear pulsed with something deeper, something colder, in my chest. It was a feeling I didn't know how to name. But it swelled up like darkness, and I almost choked on it.

The young man grabbed my hair and started to drag me down the steps. I yelped and scratched at his hands, squeezing my eyes closed in pain.

"Today we rid ourselves of our curse—" he began.

The young man's fingers suddenly released me. I stumbled, barely catching myself now that I was free. The crowd around me went dead quiet. For a whole heartbeat, no one spoke, nothing moved. I dared to peek an eye open.

Four bodies stood between me and the crowd. Coyote, Little Lion, Kit Fox, and Ocelot all blocked their path to me. I looked up, heart racing. Coyote glanced back at me.

"Lo siento," he said. "We ran as fast as we could when we saw the sun go down."

I'd always been grateful for my friends. But right then, my heart absolutely overflowed with it. I fell on Coyote and buried myself into his side. Coyote wrapped his arms around me, warm and strong, and I clung to him for relief.

"Gracias, amigos," I whispered.

"You did very well holding off the brujas," Ocelot said. She gently touched the top of my now sore head.

Lion bared his teeth, and the crowd rustled with fear and wrath. The young man still headed the throng, but he looked with wild, cutting flashes of fear from Ocelot, to Kit, to Lion, and landing on me and Coyote. He stared at Coyote's hair.

"The Great Namer," he mumbled numbly.

I squeezed Coyote's side. My heart beat hard against my ribs. Would this change his mind? Maybe he liked the stories of Coyote too?

The man's face curled the next second. My hope withered.

"Now she's brought criaturas into our town!" He turned and yelled to the others.

Outrage stormed through the people. Even some who'd been calling for mercy before turned against me.

"We cannot trust her! I wouldn't be surprised if it was her water's curse that drowned the sun!" someone yelled.

Coyote started to herd me behind him. "Stay back, Cece."

Lion's upper lip pulled back in a snarl. "I've seen humans like this before. It's never pretty."

Ocelot flexed her claws. "A pity to watch history repeat itself."

"If we fight them, won't we make it worse?" Kit's ears flattened against the back of his head.

"The whole world will be a lot worse if we die today and Catrina kills them all," Lion snapped.

The young officer surged forward and grabbed at Coyote's shirt, knife raised. Coyote bared his teeth and growled.

"You—will—*cease*!" A flash of blinding white light shocked the town square.

Everyone fell back from me and my friends. I stumbled, and Coyote caught me before my knee could buckle. A cry went up across the square—then, everything was silent. Slowly, as our vision recovered, we all looked to Metztli where she stood at the center of the square, by Juana and Santos, flanked by Mamá and Damiana, her voice still shaking the ground.

Her eyes were completely white, her nails glowing brilliant and clear, her hair whipping in a wind that no one else could feel. Her nostrils flared, but the rest of her face was terribly, firmly calm.

"Tierra del Sol, you have forgotten what fire is for," she called.

People flinched and cowered back from her voice, as if the Moon herself had come down to chastise them. She strode toward me, and the angry mob parted before her on either side, too afraid of her different, confusing power to fight.

"This child is not to blame for your own fears. She never was. It has come to this because you did not fight with us as you ought to have done two hundred years ago."

Her voice rang through the square like a hundred voices. The crowd could only stare.

"But if you, children of the Sun, do not rise up now, the Sun never will again." She threw her hand back to point at the wounded, burning ridge of the sun's light on the horizon. "The new queen of Devil's Alley has promised to take over your world."

She reached the last step of the Sun Sanctuary's stairs, face-to-face with the young man who'd incited the mob. He trembled before her. She would not look away, and her very presence carried the pressure of lightning.

"We must band together and fight this evil. We must be one, or we will be *none*."

Her words rolled through the square like electricity. The hairs on my arms stood up, and Coyote and I huddled closer. The man finally faltered. His knees quaked as he stepped down and ushered himself away. Metztli watched him go before striding up to us. Juana, Lion, and Kit were hot on her heels and surrounded us.

"Are you okay, Cece?" Kit asked. His ears were out, pressed nearly flat against his head as he kept checking over his shoulders. The way he looked at the people of Tierra del Sol, they might have been dark criaturas, not simple, frightened people.

I didn't blame him. My skin crawled as their eyes hung on me and Metztli.

Juana stepped up on my right, wiping a smear of blood off my face. Her jaw was gritted so tightly, I was surprised she was able to speak. "If they ever touch you like that again, I'm burning this town down myself."

The wind surrounding Metztli slowly lessened. Her nails continued to glow, but her eyes returned to their deep black with stars floating in the irises. She faced the people and created a wall between them and me, mi hermana, and mis amigos. She stopped her gaze on Santos.

Mamá was crouched beside him now, bandaging his wounds. It looked like she had just barely managed to stop the bleeding in his shoulder. He looked to her and nodded a silent thank-you before he met Metztli's powerful gaze. The rest of the crowd—those who'd charged at me, and those who hadn't—watched him carefully.

"What say you, Santos?" she asked. "Your mayor is dead. These people now look to you as their leader and their voice."

Santos's brow dropped heavily, the way Papá's used to. My heart beat in my ears. He'd saved me. Surely—surely he wouldn't exile us the way the mayor had once tried to. Coyote squeezed my hand tight to calm the wild colors of my soul.

"You are . . . the curanderas from legend. Is it so?" He lifted his head to Metztli.

She gestured to me and herself. "We are."

Santos turned his gaze on to my friends next. His dark eyes brushed all of them and landed on Coyote.

"You are the Great Namer," he said, almost fearfully, almost reverently.

Everyone stared at Coyote. Mumbles and whispers roamed around us. Coyote took a long, deep breath, like he was bringing himself to face an old wound. White fear and weak—but still brilliant—pink lifted out of his soul.

I squeezed his hand.

You can do this, I offered him through my soul.

He straightened up. Slowly, he nodded, never looking away from Santos.

"I am Coyote, the Great Namer, the Legend Brother," he said, loud enough for everyone to hear. "I have been cruel and I have been kind. All I want in this life"—he looked across the crowd—"is to stay by my best friend's side, and make up for my mistakes." He squeezed my hand, then let go as he strode forward.

I watched him go, my soul going with him, as he crossed the distance and stopped in front of Santos. "To do that, I have to stand with Naked Man against what's coming. Catrina, the Cager of Souls, is queen of Devil's Alley now." He reached out a hand to Santos. "And she will try to destroy all of us if we don't stand together."

No one dared to speak. The urge to vomit gurgled up my sternum—and a dark seam I'd felt earlier opened up in my heart. Santos watched Coyote's hand, evaluating the enemies and despised legends who now stood before him. All of Tierra del Sol hung on his next word.

Por favor, I reached for Santos's soul across the way. *Don't let them destroy us.*

I couldn't feel his colors or hear anything from his soul. I didn't know him well enough. But his eyes met mine around Coyote. And I hoped.

"Well," he said, and then nothing for a moment.

I could barely breathe.

He nodded. "If we are to defend our home together, we have plans to make. Humans, curanderas, and criaturas alike."

He took Coyote's hand.

Coyote's eyes widened. My mouth dropped open. For the first time in centuries, Coyote wasn't just reaching out to humans for peace.

Now, finally, humans were reaching back.

With Coyote and Santos leading the way, my friends, familia, and I headed to the Sun Sanctuary by the light of a distant, sunken sun.

But that's the thing about light, I guess. Even a little can be enough to guide your way.

6
Souls of the Gods

The Sun Sanctuary had always been such a beautiful place, filled with peace and warmth. But as we all gathered together at the front of the room, the low light of candles the Sun Priestesses had just lit revealed the broken mosaic before us. Dominga del Sol waited with us, as the other priestesses retreated to tend to any wounded citizens outside. We stared at the leftovers of the mosaic, where gods' faces, and their creations, lay scattered on the floor.

"Destruction comes again, an endless tide, until we break the pattern forged by pride," Metztli said, as she stopped beside us, eyeing Moon's broken visage.

I'd never heard that saying before, but it touched something deep in my aching soul. I pictured the cycle I'd once thought of, with criaturas and humans all hurting each other because they'd been hurt. I nodded to myself. It wouldn't stop—until we stopped turning it ourselves. But—how would we do it, if we didn't all agree to do so together?

Santos winced as he sat down beside me on the front-most pew. His side and arm were bandaged up, thanks to Mamá, but he still looked like he was in a lot of pain. My stomach clenched. He'd gotten that wound for me, and he couldn't heal quickly like my friends could.

"Por favor," he said, "I must understand why the brujas came today and why the sun has gone down before its time. You said there is now a queen of Devil's Alley?" He looked to Metztli.

But Metztli, for some reason, looked at me. My cheeks flushed immediately with panic.

"Go on, Cece," Metztli said. "Tell Don Santos the full story. He needs to know you, to know where we stand now."

"B-but I'm still just in training," I stumbled out.

Metztli said curanderas used to be leaders in their communities. But she wasn't really trying to get me to do that now, right? I'd barely made it out of the square alive today.

"It's your story, Cece," Juana added. She smiled at me from where she stood by the mosaic. "Own it."

I couldn't argue with that. So I took a long, deep breath—and stumbled and tripped over myself as I tried to explain. No matter how many times I stuttered or got nervous, though, Santos listened intently. That made it a bit easier. And Coyote and Lion and Kit nodded to encourage me as I went, until my voice grew stronger, and I was able to tell Don Santos everything.

He asked questions now and then, especially about how the terrible El Cucuy had become Quetzalcoatl. "What is his purpose now, then?" he'd asked. "Coyote is the Great Namer. Tzitzimitl, the Protector of Progeny and Stars. What is his title?" That stumped me for a moment, because I wasn't sure. I knew his true Name, but not what his title, his role, his place was now that he wasn't the cruel ruler of Devil's Alley. When I couldn't find an answer, Santos simply waived me on. "Never mind for now," he said. "Continue, Cece." And then, he just waited and listened.

By the end of the explanation, his gaze changed as he took me in. There may have even been—I barely dared to believe it—respect in his eyes.

"This thing Grimmer Mother stole, then," he said, at the end, "you truly believe it is the Sun god's soul?"

My stomach cramped with the question. I looked to Metztli, hoping she'd say of course it wasn't possible. Maybe she'd even laugh at the thought. But instead, Metztli's face was grave. She looked to the broken mosaic and the tiny pieces left of Sun. She laid a hand to her chest, like she could feel the damage in her own skin.

"We are made from the gods," she said. "Our souls are touched with their power. We were woven from their bodies and from their souls. It is not beyond the realm of possibility . . . that when the gods sacrificed themselves, their souls remained. Perhaps this is why the sanctuaries were built in such specific places." She squeezed her fingers into a fist. "Cece, you said you have heard their voices, have you not?"

"Sí," I said.

Everyone looked to me for more. For confirmation of the unthinkable, the horrifying. But I didn't want it to be real either. Coyote's soul swirled with tangles of bruised purple hurt and sharp, bleached fear.

I clutched my hands together. "What would happen if brujas really did, um, steal the Sun's soul, Metztli? They couldn't . . . you know . . . manipulate the gods the way they do criaturas. Right?"

Metztli pushed her hand back through her hair as brown distress poured out from her soul.

"It wouldn't be the same," she started hesitantly. "The gods are far greater beings than we are, even though they sacrificed their bodies. Their souls are pure power. A bruja can control the soul of a criatura, but could not *over*power a god."

"But they could feed off their power, couldn't they?" Juana interrupted. Danger lurked in her eyes as she straightened. "Catrina used Jaguar's strength to heal her wounds.

Rodrigo lived off Ocelot's soul."

Ice collected in my chest. Metztli closed her eyes.

"Sí," she whispered.

Juana's eyes flashed, and her nostrils flared. Coyote's face tensed, and dark colors crawled through his soul and into the air. Lion, rubbing his forehead, sat in the nearest windowsill. Kit's ears flattened against the back of his head. Ocelot simply closed her eyes.

"There is good news and bad news in this," Metztli went on. "The good news is that legend has always shown that the gods' powers work in unison. This means Catrina could not use any of the gods' powers without having all four of their souls." She rubbed her mouth with her thumb. "Of course, this also means we must stop her from obtaining the other three. This will not be easy, when it is clear total domination is her goal."

"But why?" I burst. The ice climbed higher in my chest, but beneath it was a powerful, boiling geyser. "If Grimmer Mother steals the gods' souls for Catrina, and Catrina does this"—I pointed out the window, at the sunken light—"to all of them, what will be left for her to rule? It doesn't make sense."

Juana's eyes softened on me in a sad, pitying sort of way. "Cece," she said, with a knowing, grave tone that made me shiver. "I know you look for the good in everyone. But the truth is, some people prefer the taste of poison, even if it kills them."

I'd always believed that people hurt others out of their own pain, and if they only realized that doing so wouldn't heal them—they would change. But Juana's assertion came with so much confidence, so much clarity, that my soul shook with it.

"Like Papá," she whispered. "Remember, Cece?"

I couldn't forget. Instead of choosing to change for us, Papá had left us months ago. He said it was the only gift he could give. I knew that came from the kernel of goodness left inside him. But it still left us poor and hurting.

"Catrina must be dying," Lion spoke up. "That's why she's doing this."

The statement jarred me out of the pain and confusion. He'd been silent since we'd come inside, but he turned his red eyes on us all with blunt confidence.

"What makes you say this, Lion?" Metztli asked. "I cannot see into the doings of Devil's Alley, hidden as they are from the Moon."

"Because I know her." He said it matter-of-factly, even though all his knowledge of her had been gained through suffering. "She wouldn't be risking something like this if she wasn't at the end of her rope. Think about it: she's been trying to control El Sombrerón, Jaguar, and

Quetzalcoatl—the most powerful criatura alive—for the past few months. Her soul has amazing capacity, but even she has to be at her limits. She needs another power source to repair her soul, or else Quetzalcoatl, who she needs to break out of Devil's Alley and conquer the surface, will be the same thing that kills her."

I gasped. "That's why the brujas said she didn't want Coyote's soul anymore."

Coyote straightened. "I'd be more soul weight than she can take. That means I should be safe from her now at least."

"Safe from *her*, maybe," Juana cut in, with a sharp brow raised. "But that doesn't mean Grimmer Mother or any of the other brujas wouldn't ditch their criaturas to control the Great Namer. Don't let your guard down, perro."

Coyote frowned.

"The point is, Catrina's desperate," Lion restated. "And that means she's more dangerous than ever."

The heaviness of the realization sat on all of us. Catrina always seemed to know more, have planned better, than I knew how to keep up with. Would I ever catch up? Would we ever be able to stop her?

Something warm touched my hand. I looked up and found Coyote's fingers wrapped around mine. He smiled at me, quietly. Heat from his touch came up my chest and buzzed in my soul.

We're stronger than we think, his soul reached for mine. *You taught me that.*

Juana glanced at our joined hands and pursed her lips. Then she folded her arms. "Well, we can't give up now. We've got to try!"

Their determination buoyed up my aching heart. I nodded.

"Yeah." I took a big breath and nodded again. "Yeah, we have to make a plan! Knowing what she's after levels the playing field at least."

Juana straightened up in front of the mosaic. "That's right! We're going to protect our home." She slapped her hand back against the mural's stone leftovers. "So let's—"

I didn't hear anything else she said. Because the moment Juana touched the broken pieces of the mosaic, the few remaining pieces of the Sun's fire opal glowed a brilliant, bright orange. The light beamed and reflected off the back of Juana's waving hair like a halo. I sucked in a sharp breath. Coyote's mouth dropped open. Lion straightened in his window seat, and Kit and Metztli craned their necks back to stare at the bright, passionate light.

Juana had always been able to make fire opal glow. But this was far beyond that. This was light itself.

"Hey. Is anyone listening?" Juana asked, staring across at us all in confusion.

"Juana!" I burst. Relieved heat rushed up my chest, and I ran toward her. "Juana, you're a sun curandera!"

Juana balked. Clearly baffled, she glanced back at the glowing mosaic, at the shimmering fire opal, the stones all shining a beautiful golden color. She dropped her hand down and away, like she'd just been stung.

"No," she said. "No way. I can't—"

"Holy sunset, this makes so much *sense*! I thought I saw your eyes glowing earlier!" I grabbed her shoulders and jumped up and down. "Juana, this is amazing news! That means we're both curanderas. We can protect our home together!"

But Juana scrunched into herself. Lion suddenly busted up laughing.

"I *thought* I saw your nails glowing when you attacked Catrina!" He pointed at her across the room. She sent him a wild snarl, like he'd just betrayed her. "Ha! You *would* be a sun curandera."

"What's that supposed to mean?" she snapped.

"The stones do not lie," Metztli said. She placed her palm flat to the mosaic, and the moonstone pieces lit up. "Juana Rios, you are a sun curandera. And with your very presence, you have now become one of our best chances of facing the bruja army as a united curandera front, just as in the days of old. In time, you will be able to create fire, and if you master your abilities, you could even channel and change magma. You are the brightness and hope of light and warmth. You will help us break through the coming darkness."

Juana didn't retreat under Metztli's expectant gaze, but she shrunk a bit, like her words were boulders loaded onto her back. My grin slowly dropped. She didn't look at me. Didn't look at anyone. What was wrong? I'd felt Juana's soul reaching out with a warm, gold sureness so many times before. Even now, I could feel it coursing through the air, carrying her own certainty. She knew she was a sun curandera. Maybe she'd known for a while. So why did she look so nervous, when she was usually the one who made other people nervous?

"What's wrong?" I whispered.

She tilted her head down toward me. After a moment's hesitation, she said, "You controlled water in your battle against El Sombrerón. After just a week." She shook her head. "I've never made fire. I'm not—not even sure I can. Since—you know." She placed a hand over her heart.

Oh. I glanced down at where her fingers pressed to her chest, as if I could see where her soul stone lay buried beneath her ribs and the scar that now ran through it. When El Sombrerón had taken her captive all those months ago, he'd split her soul stone in half. She'd gotten it back, and fused both parts together, but the scar, she'd told me, would never leave.

I looked up at her. She still didn't return my gaze.

"Juana, you're the strongest person I know," I said in a soft voice.

Her eyes slowly ticked up to meet mine.

I smiled. "You faced down criaturas and brujas for me today. You faced all of Devil's Alley to get your soul back. You've always been bright, Juana. That hasn't changed." I laid my hands over hers. "And with your sun powers, we're going to protect all the gods' souls. Together. As hermanas."

Juana's gaze softened, and the light emanating from her soul grew just a tiny bit brighter. I figured that was a good sign.

"Speaking of"—Metztli clapped her hands, so we all focused again—"Juana is right. We need to hurry and identify the brujas' next target. There are three more sanctuaries they will seek to attack." She closed her eyes and touched her forehead. Her nails glowed. "The Moon Sanctuary, perhaps, to cloud my sight? The Ocean Sanctuary, to stop Cece?"

"What about the Desert Sanctuary?" Damiana piped up.

She'd been silent since I'd had to tell her part of the story, about when she used to be a bruja. Santos hadn't said anything unkind about it, but he'd stared at her, watched her more carefully. When we all looked at her again, including Santos, she shrunk into her pew. Axolotl patted her arm.

Metztli opened her eyes again, and the light dwindled from her nails. "The Desert Sanctuary has been missing for many years. Far, far before my time."

My stomach tightened, and I squeezed Juana closer. "That means Catrina won't be able to get the Desert's soul at least, right?"

Metztli hesitated again. My stomach went right back to twisting.

"I would love to believe so myself—" she began.

Lion jumped off his windowsill. "Except that Catrina wouldn't do this if she hadn't already figured out how to get the Desert's soul. She has to have some plan."

"As Black Lion says." Metztli nodded. "I cannot imagine Catrina would announce herself so blatantly by attacking the Sun Sanctuary first if she did not already have plans to retrieve the Desert Sanctuary."

I swallowed hard.

"Wait—" Juana twisted out of my hold. "Without the gods' souls, will we even still have connection with our powers?"

Metztli's face grew grave and focused. "Sí, we will. The gods' souls are unending power, so the powers that come with our connection to them will not cease. But the repercussions to their physical manifestations will still be dire. We must move quickly, to avoid any more of them ending up in the bruja army's hands."

My heart dropped. I mean, I was glad I wouldn't completely lose my connection with Mother Ocean if we lost her soul, but how much pain would that put her in? Would it feel like she was being pulled away from me, like it did when I first lost my friends' souls? That pain had been excruciating. My stomach turned to ice just thinking about it.

So I lifted my head. Squared my shoulders as much as I could. Whatever it took, I had to protect our world somehow. I stepped forward, ready to plan, when the Sun Sanctuary's entrance doors burst open.

We all turned. Mamá stood framed by the night, her forehead dotted with sweat, worry etched in her face.

"The Court of Fears," Mamá said. "They're back."

7
The Choice of Souls

I was the first one out the Sun Sanctuary doors, diving into the falsely imposed night. Hours had passed, though the sun hadn't changed. My knee was moving easier, and I was sure it was bruised, but at least it had recovered a lot faster than I'd expected. The cold prickled through the holes in my jacket, and I stopped myself at the edge of the Sun Sanctuary's first step.

At the bottom of the stairs stood the Court of Fears.

The four of them were arranged in a line, looking even scarier in the meager pink light of the drowned sun than usual. Bird King stood as the tallest on the left, his powerful red wings stretched out behind him, his gold beak mask catching the low light so its edge looked like a knife. On the right waited La Lechuza, her uncanny widow's mask craned up toward us unnaturally, her black wings wide as the sky and nearly blotting out the view of the square. Alux, half my height and with twice the power to intimidate, stood at the end beside her, his arms folded, his green-and-brown-splattered irises zeroed in on us all.

Tzitzimitl as always stood at the center between Bird King and La Lechuza. She was a raw and pale skeleton from the waist up, her flesh legs nearly vanishing into the darkness. She lifted her hand gravely toward us. In it hung a torn piece of cloth shivering in the breeze, its edges touched with what looked like drying blood. A greeting died on my tongue.

"We come with ill tidings, Cecelia Rios," she said.

There was no warmth in her voice, even though she usually greeted me kindly whenever she'd been away this long. Gooseflesh covered my back. That was a bad sign.

Metztli exited the Sun Sanctuary and ran down the stairs to meet them. "What have you found, amigos?" she asked breathlessly.

"The disparate bruja groups have gathered into an army." Tzitzimitl placed the cloth in Metztli's hand. Metztli stretched it out into the beaten form of a flag. I'd seen it only once before, flying from the capital building on the highest hill of Costa de los Sueños. "Led by Grimmer Mother, they are taking the city."

"For the Ocean Sanctuary." Metztli's gaze immediately turned on me.

Cool fear swam up my insides. But I clung to the

determination I'd summoned a few moments ago and stepped forward.

"We have to go now, then," I said. "The Ocean needs us. And so do all the people of Costa de los Sueños."

Metztli nodded to me, and there was a flicker of pride in her eyes. "Sí, Cecelia. Exactamente." She gripped the flag of her ancestral home and strode forward, into the center of the town square, where a puddle was still left.

Juana, me, Coyote, Lion, Kit, Ocelot, and the Court of Fears were hot on her tail.

"Cecelia, you will create a portal to Costa de los Sueños. Juana, Court of Fears, Ocelot, Black Lion, we must go immediately to retrieve the Ocean's soul before the brujas can." Metztli stopped beside the puddle's rippling edge.

"It has been long since we've seen La Sirena," Bird King said, almost wistfully. "It will be good to have the Court of Fears reunited."

"We will be at full power then," La Lechuza agreed. "Add in the ocean curanderita, and this should not be too difficult."

"Do not underestimate the brujas. Their army was far larger than we'd assumed," Tzitzimitl reminded. "And their hatred yet greater."

Alux scoffed. "We will see how frightening they are when we sink them to the bottom of Mother Ocean."

We gathered around the puddle. Coyote shuffled into

place next to me, and even before I had to ask, his soul reached for me and his fingers threaded through mine. I squeezed his hand. My heart was already pounding.

"It'll be okay, Cece," Coyote whispered. "We'll do this together."

I looked up into his gold eyes. Coyote had always made me feel safe, but right then his steady gaze warmed me all the way to my toes.

Together. The word filled my chest, bright and strong. And it would have comforted the fear away completely, if Alux hadn't suddenly stepped between us and pushed us apart.

"Hey!" Coyote and I said at the same time.

Alux stuck a finger up at Coyote. "You, Great Namer, are *not* coming."

I spluttered. "W-what?"

Coyote and I had done all our hardest things together. He was my best friend! I trusted him in battle more than anyone.

Coyote bristled. "Why not?"

"You are more threat to us in the hands of a bruja than ally in battle," La Lechuza entered the conversation. Her wings flexed.

He clenched his jaw. "But—you can say the same for Lion and Ocelot—"

"We can't Name," Lion reminded.

Coyote shot him a look. "You're not helping!"

Lion shrugged.

Coyote turned to the court, which now surrounded us in a semicircle, their hollow eyes and masked gazes and mottled stares hard and unyielding.

"I—I know it's a risk," he started, biting his lip. He shook his head, and scowled with his canines exposed. "But this is all happening because—because I didn't help the curanderas two hundred years ago. Because I made Devil's Alley the way it was. You have to let me make up for my mistakes!"

"And you can do so," Alux interrupted again. "By first restoring what you destroyed." Juana came out the building, her bag heavy against her side. Alux's gaze rested on her pointedly. "Or, should I say, *who* you destroyed."

Bird King leveled a stare on Juana over his golden mask. She stiffened and clutched the bag tighter to her. I glanced at her up and down. She was holding her bag like it was precious. I'd noticed for a while now that her bag looked heavy, but it never seemed like it bothered her, so I hadn't questioned it.

"Juana Rios," Tzitzimitl said. "You cannot protect them like this forever."

Lion and Juana swapped a quick look. My stomach stumbled.

"Juana." I took a step toward her between Tzitzimitl

and the Bird King. "What's inside the bag?"

She noticed my stare and bit her bottom lip, just for a second. "Okay, listen," she burst. "When we broke out of El Cucuy's castle, I figured it was only right to break them out too." Carefully, she pulled a wrapped cloth bundle from inside her bag. She cradled it like it was precious and untied it with shivering hands.

Sitting inside was a pile of beautiful human soul stones, each with their own lonely, thin scar.

Nearly a thousand of them.

Coyote gaped. "Are those the *brides of El Sombrerón?*"

I spluttered. She'd just had a huge pile of human souls lying around? In her *work* bag? Tiny, distant whispers reverberated through them all, and my throat tightened.

"I know it looks bad!" Juana rushed to explain, as Kit, Coyote, and I gawked at her. "But I didn't tell you because I didn't want to bring them back until we finished off Catrina. I thought . . . they deserved to come back to a better world."

Oh. I hadn't thought of that. When I'd helped bring back Juana and Metztli from their soul stones, they had been desperate to be free. But these women—who knew if some even remembered what it was like to be alive. And all of them had gone through what Juana had. She'd understand more than I would what they might be afraid of, what they might be feeling.

Juana bowed her head to look at the bag, hugging them close. Her soul ached with a stitch of sharp blue pain. I approached her slowly. She kept her gaze low until I stopped in front of her. She bore the weight of the many stones in her arms. Gently, I offered my hands. Juana finally, reluctantly, looked up at me.

"After everything they've gone through, Cece," she said, shaking her head, "do they really have to be brought back to the world in chaos on top of it?"

I knew exactly why she asked. Juana had gone through so much pain retrieving her soul from Devil's Alley. Every bride would have the same kind of scar she did, and they wouldn't be returning to the homes and the families they remembered to help with the healing. They'd be coming back to war. To uncertainty. On top of everything else.

I slid my hands under the white cloth she'd used to keep them safe. The souls were warm, and now that I was this close I could feel the distant call of voices—fear; pain; wondering; and hope, a desperate, knife-sharp hope. Tears filled my eyes. I lifted my gaze to meet Juana's.

"If it was still you," I whispered, "would you want the choice?"

Juana's chin dimpled. A muscle in her jaw jumped.

"Coyote is the only one who can give that choice back to them, Juana," I said quietly.

She squeezed the bundle tight. Coyote came up beside

me, his bare footsteps scratching the drying edges of the desert. Juana wouldn't look at him. Quietly, reverently, he reached for the souls. She resisted for a moment. I held my breath, aching for the spots of wild, dark colors filling the air around Juana's soul. She wanted to protect them so badly. She wanted to shield them from every painful thing, to preserve an innocence in them she felt she'd lost.

I swallowed hard. No wonder she was afraid she couldn't make fire.

Coyote paused when Juana held the souls tighter to her.

"I'll take care of them, Juana." Coyote lowered his voice. She didn't look at him. "I know you don't trust me, and I get why. So let me prove myself to you—and to them. I think the brides have been imprisoned long enough."

Flickers of both light and moisture caught simultaneously on Juana's lashes. She squeezed her eyes shut tight. I held still. All of us waited, listening, watching. Ever so slowly, Juana's grip on the souls relaxed, and she relinquished the brides of El Sombrerón to Coyote.

Coyote received the bundle in his arms as if it were as precious as a newborn baby. He gazed down at the soul stones and skimmed his fingertips over them. Orange confidence and blue sorrow poured through his soul. He cleared his throat, sniffed, and looked back up at me. Juana finally lifted her head again.

"I'll bring them back," Coyote said. His forearms tensed,

and I thought I caught a flash of something white snaking across his skin before he adjusted the bundle, before I lost sight of it. Strange. Hadn't I seen something like that earlier too? Coyote looked to the Court of Fears to Metztli to Lion and Ocelot. "You go make sure the brides have a world to come back to."

Warm pinks and confident oranges surged out of the nervous yellows and hesitant grays of his soul. The bright colors reached for me, and my turquoise light brightened. I outstretched my hand to him—one last touch to help me feel brave before I left—but Juana caught me by the jacket. I yelped as she pulled me away.

"We don't have time for you to cuddle with your novio," she reminded me, as she wiped her eyes. "¡Vamos!"

"I'm not—h-he's not my boyfriend—" I gasped, and my cheeks burned red as nocheztli paint. "Juana!"

She marched me back to the group. But as I was complaining at her, I noticed the hand she had gripped on my clothes was shaking. Just slightly.

"Are you okay?" I whispered.

She didn't look at me. "I don't know," she said. "Just—stay close to me. Por favor."

I touched Juana's arm. She looked out the corner of her eye, just barely, to meet my gaze.

"Ocelot, Lion, we will need you both to be by Cece's and Juana's sides," Metztli said, as I reached the edge of the puddle. "You will act as partners for our curanderas while the Court of Fears is our first line of defense."

Kit trailed up behind Metztli. "What about me?"

Ocelot turned and looked down at him. "You are staying here as well," she said matter-of-factly.

Kit gaped. "That's not fair! I can help!" He looked to me for support. "I fought with El Sombrerón and in the battle against El Cucuy! Tell them, Cece!"

I winced. He was right, but unlike everyone else, Kit was also on his last life. He was the most vulnerable, and if anything happened to him, I didn't think I could take it. I struggled to speak, but when I didn't answer right away, his cheeks flushed with hurt, and gray-blue betrayal soaked through his soul. Ocelot pointed him back inside, and his ears wilted.

"I'm not useless," he mumbled.

"Of course you're not, Kit!" I rushed to console him. "It's not that! It's just—"

A hand came down on Kit's shoulder from behind. We all turned to look at Santos standing by him, his good arm extended to rest on my friend's shoulder.

"It's just that Tierra del Sol could do with a lookout right now," Santos said. He looked exhausted. Bruises-under-his-eyes tired, even. But he said it with so much confidence, Kit perked up a bit. "With so many of our allies about to leave, and our people wounded and in turmoil, we need someone to protect us. You will help us, won't you, mijo?"

I sighed in relief. Tierra del Sol probably really could do with as many of my friends as could be spared to protect them. One more attack from brujas and our home could truly fall while we were gone. I silently prayed that wouldn't happen. I couldn't bear to think about Kit battling for the safety of Tierra del Sol while I wasn't there to help protect him.

If he ever got hurt protecting Tierra del Sol, after all they'd done to criaturas like him, I'd never forgive them.

I stiffened. Wait, where had that thought come from? The seam I'd felt in my chest came back, tugging deep and dark and hard, and I tried to shrug the thought away, far, far away, where its bitter aftertaste couldn't get me.

"Cece," Metztli's voice summoned me from my dark thoughts. "Quickly. There is little time left."

"Right!" I stepped forward and placed my hands over the puddle. I'd done this only a couple of times since I'd transported us out of Devil's Alley. But it felt easier and more natural with each attempt.

Under my palms, a ripple moved through the puddle, though no one had touched it. I closed my eyes and felt the ghosts of distant bodies of water, undulating across the world from this single, small puddle. Slowly, I sensed them like raindrops frozen mid-fall, hanging in my chest. I focused, searching through the different cool landing places. The local current of the Río Fuerte. A lake hidden in a cave in the western cerros. The isolated cenote in Devil's Alley far, far below the desert's surface.

My heart stumbled away from that one, even as I felt the distant throb of El Silbón's soul wandering near it. I missed him.

I shook my head to focus and stretched my senses further, until the greatest body of water of all roared up inside me. The ocean, lapping against the beach of Costa de los Sueños.

I pulled my hands around in a circle, coaxing the puddle into a spinning whirlpool—and a glowing portal opened before us from the puddle, revealing the distant waters of the ocean.

The Court of Fears and Ocelot leaped in without a second thought. Metztli and Juana took my hands, and together, we jumped through as I focused, pulling the two bodies of water together—and disappearing into a town hundreds of miles away.

8
When the Ocean Meets the Sun

When we arrived in Costa de los Sueños, the air was electric, and the ocean looked lonely without the sun to dance across its surface.

I burst out of the waves with a gasp. The portal closed, swirling shut beneath my feet, and sand came up beneath my toes. All around me, the Court of Fears, Juana, Lion, Ocelot, and Metztli popped out of the water, spitting out brine. I stumbled in a choppy wave that hit me in the chest, and Lion reached out and steadied me.

"Gracias," I said, as the waves swirled about my waist.

He gripped my arm a bit too tight. "Cece," he said, eyes carving up toward Costa de los Sueños. "Look."

I pushed my wet bangs out of my eyes just in time to watch an army of silhouettes gather at the top of Costa de los Sueños. First, there were only five. Then ten. Then twenty. Then fifty. Then a hundred. Two hundred. They lined the rooftops of the desolate city, the hilltops that I had once run down with so much joy, the jagged cliffs where I'd once fought El Silbón looming to our right. All the brujas and enslaved criaturas Metztli had been trying to track down—they were here.

And they had us surrounded.

My mind went blank. My soul swam with fear, rising up higher and higher as I spotted Grimmer Mother standing at the front of the army, foremost at the top of the hill. Her long, iron-streaked hair was free now, flapping in the breeze like the torn flag of the city should have been. Her grin cut wide across her face when she spotted me.

My skin went cold. I squeezed Lion's arm.

"Don't be scared," he reminded me. "You've defeated far worse than her, Cece."

"That's right." Juana unsheathed her fire opal knives beside me and lifted them, glaring at the masses set before us. "And you're not alone."

A drumbeat echoed from the hilltop. I stiffened. Grimmer Mother lifted a hand. About a dozen brujas, all carrying upright tlalpanhuehuetl drums, beat down on the jaguar leather in rhythmic, challenging thumps. I'd never even seen ancient tlalpanhuehuetl in real life before. There'd never been a need.

They were used exclusively for war.

"Court of Fears," Metztli said, voice deep and hard, as

the drumming intensified. "Are you ready?"

Tzitzimitl cut through the waves toward the shore. "We have prepared to fight this battle again for the last two hundred years."

She stepped up onto the beach. Bird King and La Lechuza joined her on her left, shaking their feathers free of the water. Alux brushed back his headdress and stepped up on Tzitzimitl's right.

"We will handle the bruja army. The rest of you—retrieve the Ocean's soul and take it far away. We must not lose more ground to such as these."

Tzitzimitl paused. The drums rose to a fever pitch.

"And, Cece?" She looked back at me with her hollow eyes.

I barely tore my gaze from the drumming army. "¿Sí?"

She bowed her head slightly. "Por favor—do not watch us."

The hairs on my arms stood on end. She turned away, but I could still see the sadness in her eye sockets. An old, well-worn memory flooded back through my mind, of the night she'd brought me back home when I'd gotten lost. When our town attacked her. When she'd nearly attacked them back—then looked at me with those same sad eyeholes—and let herself be taken instead.

Tzitzimitl wouldn't stop herself today. None of the

Court of Fears would. A knot formed in my throat. Of course. Just as the brujas' drums declared, today was war. I'd known we'd be fighting one. But the sorrow in the air around Tzitzimitl still pierced my soul like a knife.

Far above, Grimmer Mother let out a cry. The drums went horribly, suddenly silent. I held my breath. Lion growled. Ocelot rolled her shoulders, ready. Metztli watched with only small dots of light in her eyes.

The brujas stampeded down from the hills of Costa de los Sueños.

"Lechuza, Alux, Bird King," Tzitzimitl said, "you know what to do."

They all nodded and took off into the fray.

Metztli waded deeper into the sea to reach me. "Cece, quickly, you must take us all to the Ocean Sanctuary."

I wasn't actually sure if I could move six people all the way down to the Ocean Sanctuary—I'd never tried—but I nodded anyway, determined to do my part too. The Ocean's soul was on the line, and my friends were all fighting. Metztli turned to the horizon as a silhouette cut through the water toward us.

Metztli reached out for the dark shape. "Ah, La Sirena! Amiga, we must be fast—"

The shape shot past Metztli's outstretched hand, directly toward me, swimming with a wild fury through the waves. I hesitated. The shape looked different from what I remembered. La Sirena's silhouette was thinner. Her fins, silver. This shape even had a glimmer of something . . . pink.

Alarm bells screamed through my skull. Besides Axolotl, there was only one criatura I knew that was pink. A rumble caught on the mist as the criatura sliced right up to me. A pink dolphin tore through the surface of the water, jaws wide. And I found myself face-to-face with Boto, the dark Criatura of Nightmares and Captivity.

Don't look in his eyes, Mother Ocean's voice rose in the waves.

Everything slowed as his teeth careened straight for my throat. His black eyes rolled forward to look at me, and I barely managed to clasp my hands over my eyes in time. One look in the dark river dolphin's eyes, and I would be cursed with nightmares for the rest of my life. But how could I fight him if I couldn't *see?*

Before Boto's blow could land, Ocelot's and Lion's hands gripped down on my arms and yanked me out of the way, into the air, so my stomach lurched wildly.

"Cece!" Juana's cry shook the air.

I peeked through my fingers. Juana now stood in front of Boto, her knife out, between him and Lion and Ocelot. She must have dived in front of me to protect me—but even she was slower than Ocelot and Lion. Lion's eyes widened.

"Juana, no!" he yelled.

The pink dolphin's teeth latched down on her ankle. Juana's eyes squeezed shut. A scream pulled from her lungs. Lion's soul exploded with fear, and his hand released me. I tumbled down into Ocelot's arms, twisting, reaching for Juana.

Juana's panicked cry was the last thing I heard before Boto dragged her bleeding body into the depths of the sea.

Not Juana. The two words wracked my whole frame, and I pushed, stumbling into the water, out of Ocelot's arms. I planted my feet into the sand. I closed my eyes and drove my hands into the water, reaching, stretching, searching through the water for her.

"Cecelia, the Ocean Sanctuary!" Metztli reminded me. "We must see to the god's soul first."

"But he has Juana!" I couldn't think, couldn't focus on anything, while he had my sister. "I have to save her!" I stretched my soul wide, in and through the water, to find her.

Metztli grabbed me and spoke, but I wasn't listening anymore. Because that's when I felt it. There it was, all the leagues down: Juana's heat. She was like a pot boiling over, heating up so Boto was almost burning himself to hold on to her. But he wouldn't let go, even if she scorched him. He wasn't wearing a soul stone. He didn't have a choice. He'd kill her, even if it killed him.

I wasn't going to let that happen. I wouldn't let a dark criatura take her from me again.

"¡Cecelia, escúchame!" Metztli pushed in front of me and grabbed me by the shoulders. "Everyone is relying on us reaching the Ocean Sanctuary! La Sirena is nowhere to be found—Boto must have already captured her—but we cannot sacrifice the world for Juana!"

I looked up at her, tears burning in my eyes. I could feel my sister struggling. She fought, kicking, heating up the water, swiping her knife blindly as she struggled to hold her breath. I shook my head. Metztli's face tightened.

"She is right," Ocelot said. "Cecelia, we must reach the sanctuary."

My insides tore. The seam at the center of my chest pulled wider, darker, sharper than it had been even in the square the day before. I shook my head harder. This was all wrong. I shouldn't have to choose. We shouldn't even be in this situation. This was Boto's fault. This was the brujas' fault. No.

This was *Catrina's* fault.

"Cecelia!" Metztli's commanding voice shook in my ribs. "You must bring us to the sanctuary now!"

"Fine!" I screamed. The wind snapped against my skin.

I wouldn't leave Juana alone. But I could save her and the Ocean's soul at the same time, if I was strong enough. I spread my legs wide, the way Metztli had taught me to do before moving a large amount of water. I closed my eyes. Breathed.

Help me, I called out with my soul.

And the Ocean knew me.

I struck my hands forward. Light shot from my soul, down my body, and flew through the water like a blue comet, straight down the middle of the bay. The water shuddered and, with a rumble, split in half from the surface down to the ocean's sand-streaked floor.

Wind rushed through the crack in the ocean, pressing the water apart, so there were two waves in crescendo on either side of a newly revealed pathway. They exposed Boto and Juana. Boto tried desperately to climb the water as it rose higher and higher into the liquid walls. Far beyond them, the Ocean Sanctuary's deep stone walls, golden dome, and silver doors waited for our protection.

"Cecelia, you've exposed the sanctuary to the brujas!" Metztli looked at me in panic, in wild confusion. "The water was also its protection!"

My stomach dropped. Lion grabbed me and threw me on his back. Ocelot grabbed Metztli.

"Lion, take Cece to Juana, then go find La Sirena. She can take care of Boto," Ocelot said. She looked down at Metztli. "Get on my back. I will race you to the sanctuary."

Metztli sent me a chastising look. I withered under it, but she turned away just as quickly and jumped up on Ocelot's back. The moment she was in place, Ocelot took off down the ramp of the ocean's floor, sprinting as a gold blur to the sanctuary. Lion gripped my legs and bolted down the causeway I'd created, heading straight for Juana. He skated to a stop halfway between the beach and the sanctuary, where Boto and Juana were both lying in the mud and broken seashells.

Lion let me off and faced Boto. The pink dolphin looked at him, and Lion covered his eyes. But he must have memorized where he was, because he grabbed at him with his free hand.

"Where's La Sirena? Where'd you trap her, dark criatura?" Lion demanded.

Boto tried to fight him. Lion held his own as I stumbled toward Juana, where she lay coughing up water on her side. I spread my arms over her.

"Juana," I gasped. "Are you okay?"

She peered over my shoulder as the sound of feet rose behind us. "Cece," she rasped out. "Get up!"

"Can you stand? You're wounded!" I bent over the bite wound in her leg. It was already oozing blood now that she was out of the water. How would she fight like that? She couldn't rely on the Amenazante dance when she couldn't even walk. I had to get her out of here as soon as Metztli came back with the Ocean's soul.

"No, Cece, *behind you!*" Juana shouted.

I turned.

Grimmer Mother strode toward us on the ocean floor, leading La Chupacabra with her. She must have just slipped through the Court of Fears' defense. From the sound of screams and cut-off cries across the beach, most of her army wasn't as lucky. Her smile sliced up on one side.

"I would have had a much harder time reaching the Ocean Sanctuary without you." Grimmer Mother struck out her hand. La Chupacabra leaped for me. "Muchas gracias, mija."

La Chupacabra sprang above my head, feet poised to crush. I swiveled, trying to pull water from the ocean's walls to protect me. It came out weak and thin, and even that much made my ribs ache with the weight. Holding up the ocean was hard. I was already sweating, my body squeezed under the weight.

La Chupacabra crushed the side of my face into the sand, and my jaw burned under the pressure. Juana called

CECE RIOS AND THE QUEEN OF BRUJAS

my name. I struggled, scratching at her feet, as the small trail of water splashed down on us instead.

"I see your powers have grown, Cecelia," Grimmer Mother said, as she sauntered up to me. "To think—you can hold the ocean's might back. And yet, what a waste." She stopped half a foot from my head, her dark eyes hovering over me. "You'll be dead by the end of all this. With the power of the gods' souls and Quetzalcoatl's, Queen Catrina will remake this world into everything she wants it to be. And she's already decided you won't be part of it."

"You can stop this," I squeezed out, through the weight on my cheek.

I made myself meet Grimmer Mother's dark gaze. I'd seen her sadism, her cruelty, her coldness. But surely that couldn't be all she was. Even Catrina, beneath it all, was hurt. If Grimmer Mother could just see, just understand, that this would only hurt her—couldn't she change? That's all my friends had needed to see. That's all Juana had needed to know when she'd been so lost.

Light changes us, if we let it. I had to believe that.

"I don't know why you're choosing this," I gasped out. La Chupcabra's pressure eased for a second, so I took the chance to flip onto my back. In the next second, she pinned her foot against my chest. I wheezed. "We all need this world. We all need each other. We can unravel your pain together if you'd just face it *with* us instead of turning it into a dagger *against* us."

Grimmer Mother only grinned. She drew her obsidian knife. It was darker than night, sharper than death. "You have so much power, but you're still as naive as the day you first came to me. You think everyone can be saved? Well guess what, mija?" She dove toward me. "I don't *want* to be!"

The blade scored the air, aimed directly for my eye. I reached for the water, heart pounding. Waves peeled off, crashing down to help me. But I was once again too slow. Too unfocused. I threw my arms up between my face and the blade, readying for the searing pain.

Nothing came.

I peeked open a single eye. Grimmer Mother had frozen, her knife poised midair, her muscles trembling with a confused scowl on her face. Because on her forehead, the mark of binding lit up, gleaming and clean and sharp. Holding her back.

What? The knife struggled down toward me but couldn't reach.

"No se," Grimmer Mother ground out through her clenched jaw. "What . . . do you want, then?"

She was talking to Tía Catrina. Catrina could speak to

her through the Mark of the Binding. Of course! That's how she'd been organizing the brujas from Devil's Alley all along. Grimmer Mother's eyebrows pulled together with new understanding.

"Sí," she answered something unspoken. Her eyes darkened with a wicked smile. "But she doesn't need her legs for that."

She turned the knife down and slashed for my knees. I tried to twist away, mind still reeling. Juana's voice called out. I braced myself for impact.

And then fire roared over my head like an explosion of sunlight.

The impact sent La Chupacabra crashing into Grimmer Mother. The two skated across the sand, the fire leaving behind a streak of glass. The obsidian knife shattered as it fell beside me. I gasped and sat up, shaking. Juana pulled herself, half sitting, half lying on her side, to me. She grabbed my hands. Steam erupted from our grip, and I watched flames flicker across her fingers. But there was no pain, only warmth, from her fire's glow.

"Are you okay, Cece?" Juana's eyes were like golden lamps as she searched my face. I squeezed her hands, heart swelling, and beamed.

"Juana!" I said. "You did it! You made fire!"

She looked at our hands, where flames still licked the

edges of her fingers and sparked off her glowing finger-nails.

"I . . . did it," she scraped out. Her grip on me tight-ened, and I helped her hobble upright. Her smile trembled, but it still spread, it still claimed space, as she lifted her head to look at me. "I . . . I didn't think it was possible anymore. Because . . ."

I shook my head. "You can't lose that fire, Juana," I said firmly. "You *are* fire. It will always be there. No scar can take that away, as long as you keep choosing light."

Her chest swelled with a brave breath. Her soul, deep inside her as it was, rang with bright, confident oranges. She lifted her head and glared down the causeway, where Grimmer Mother was just getting up. La Chupacabra winced as she stood with her, cradling her burned arm. Grimmer Mother glared our way.

"We have it!" Metztli called behind me.

Juana and I turned. My heart lifted, soul flashing bright, as she appeared in the Ocean Sanctuary's doorway with a large, perfectly smooth turquoise stone glowing from her hands. It was circular, with a dome-shaped top, just like the sanctuary itself.

Gracias, Mother Ocean's voice reached out.

We'd done it. I beamed. Tears filled my eyes. Juana was safe, and we'd gotten the Ocean's soul. Above Metztli's head, Ocelot stood on the Ocean Sanctuary's dome, claws flexed. Lion called out from behind the sanctuary. Suddenly, La Sirena flipped out of the ocean, whistling, before splashing back down and tackling Boto. They'd freed her! I turned back to Grimmer Mother, a challenging smile pulling my mouth. Her eyes narrowed to obsidian chips.

"Bird King!" Juana called out. Her eyes flashed with gold. "I think you missed a couple!"

A red streak in the sky turned from the beach. I jumped as he landed, like a hammer, down on the causeway between us and Grimmer Mother. His red wings spread. The edges of his sharp feathers were coated in blood. My stomach jerked. What—what had the battle on the beach been like?

"The mother of brujas," Bird King said, and his voice rumbled. "Your army dwindles. But I will be glad to add you to the fallen."

Grimmer Mother pushed her hair back. "A battle is not the war. And you will not always be here to defend Tierra del Sol, Court of Fears." She stepped back. Then twisted to shout back at the beach: "Retreat!"

Grimmer Mother scrambled onto La Chupacabra's back like a rat. La Chupacabra sprinted away, toward the beach, where silhouettes of brujas began to move away. Bird King let out a predatory shriek and flew after her.

Relief poured through my body. I leaned into Juana to offer her more support. She let out a long, aching sigh that she'd been holding.

"That," she said, as Metztli jogged up behind us, "was the most awesome, horrible thing ever." She looked down at her ankle.

Metztli stopped in front of us. "Quickly," she said, as the soul in her hands rang with the beautiful, strong clarity of Mother Ocean. "We must return and place this somewhere safe."

9
Cost of the Ocean's Soul

Releasing the ocean back into its proper form felt like letting down a huge burden. I sighed in relief as I stood on the beach, with everyone else, and let the sea fold over itself, the waves clapping against each other, and once again enveloping the Ocean Sanctuary safely back into its embrace.

I wiped sweat from my brow. My insides were already tired, my muscles tight and worn from the battle. Metztli stood beside me, carefully pressing the Ocean's soul to her chest. It glowed bright and clear from between her fingers, the way a drop of water shines in the sun. She didn't look at me. Slowly, watching her cold expression, I reopened a portal to the puddle back home in Tierra del Sol.

"I said I'm fine," Juana grumbled, as Lion helped her hobble back into the swirling water.

He rolled his eyes. "Just get in the water. You made fire today, remember; you don't have to prove yourself to me."

Juana frowned—then gently laughed and leaned her cheek on the top of his head. Lion balked a bit and stumbled. She snorted and made fun of him until they slipped away into the portal.

Ocelot and the Court of Fears (minus La Sirena) followed suit. La Sirena thanked me before diving and disappearing below the waves. Soon, it was just Metztli and me. She closed her hand gingerly around the Ocean's soul and headed for the portal. I held my breath. But she didn't look back at me. Finally, just before she could enter the portal, I couldn't take it any longer.

"I'm sorry!" I burst. She stopped with her back to me. "I know it was risky, but it—it just didn't seem right that Catrina could make me choose between Juana and the Ocean's soul. I didn't want to lose anyone. I was trying to keep them both safe . . ."

Metztli's head bowed. Slowly, she shook it, so the white ends of her black hair shivered.

"There is nothing wrong with trying to save all that you can, Cecelia," she said. She turned to look at me over her shoulder. Her face was grave, and she looked older, more tired, than I'd ever noticed before. "It is, in fact, noble. But there is also no way out of sacrifice, Cecelia. You should not risk a whole world just to keep the few you love. That is what you did today."

I gripped my damp jacket tight. "She's my sister" was all I could bring myself to say.

Metztli sighed out her nose. "I know," she said softly, but there was weariness in the phrase. "And *my* sisters died to give this world two hundred more years." She turned in the water, the blue light of the Ocean shining from her hold. "Our job now is to ensure we preserve this world and all it can be. I know you already bear far more than what one your age perhaps should. I know your love is wide and powerful, and you wish for a better world. But this lesson must not be forgotten: we cannot grow, we cannot gain, without sacrifice. Our choice is only what the sacrifice will be."

I squeezed my hands together. Metztli was being far kinder than I'd expected after I'd risked a god's soul, honestly. But her words still stung, and their heaviness bore down on me. She waded through the waves and placed a hand on my head.

"Do not fear," she said more softly. "You are young. Your wisdom will grow with your love."

The Ocean's soul swelled with light between us. I closed my eyes as its pure, clear blues felt like they wrapped around my matching turquoise stone and soothed away the fear. The dark seam in my chest ached as the light tried to pull it closed. What was this feeling? Why was it so hard to carry? Why didn't I have a name for it?

Metztli's hand slipped off my head, ruffling the chin-length locks. I opened my eyes and watched her descend, and disappear, into the portal.

Then it was only me, standing on the edge of the beach alone with the wind and the waves. I looked behind me. The Court of Fears had already left, but the evidence of the battle hadn't. Stone statues of brujas and criaturas, caught mid-scream, mid-bite, mid-fight, turned the beach and the hills of Costa de los Sueños into a graveyard. I shivered.

So many lives lost to Catrina's war.

Metztli was right. Even in our triumph here today, there had been a great sacrifice. The dark seam in my chest widened a crack, and I winced on my way to the portal.

I was ready to go home.

By the time I pushed open the Sun Sanctuary doors, I was totally and completely exhausted.

I wobbled in to find Mamá, Damiana, all my friends besides Coyote, and Metztli grouped around Santos and Dominga del Sol talking about something. Juana sat in a chair as Mamá cleaned and bandaged her wound. I wandered closer, yawning and uneasy. What time was it? It was so hard to tell with the sun forever frozen at the horizon. I counted on my fingers. It had to be the next day by now, right? So I'd been up all night. Yuck.

Mamá's face softened when she spotted me. I plunked down on the floor beside her and rested my head on Juana's good leg. Juana laid a hand on my head and stroked my hair, the way she used to when Mamá and Papá argued. I closed my eyes for a moment and nearly fell asleep there, with Mamá whispering about how proud she was of us.

"You must be so tired, mija," Mamá said, and I startled back awake. She clucked her tongue and brushed my bangs back. Her touch was tender and warm and every comfort I needed in that moment. "You should go into the back of the Sun Sanctuary and sleep. Santos has had the Sun Priestesses give us the sanctuary as our base of operations. We have cots set up."

Juana nodded. "I've got to say, I love the irony. They didn't like it when Cece visited, and now she'll be living here."

She snickered. Mamá laughed, and I cracked a wider smile.

"Are they okay with it?" I asked, and looked to Mamá. "How's Tierra del Sol doing? Are they . . . on our side?"

Mamá's lips pressed together. The humor washed away, and my stomach tightened. It was doing that so much lately I wouldn't be surprised if I got sick in the middle of the night. Or, uh, while sleeping. It was kind of always night now.

"That does not have an easy answer," Mamá said. "I have been both surprised and disappointed so far. Many people I had thought would be the most opposed have listened to Santos, have softened their hearts, have helped us all. Some I had hoped would help have turned away. Tierra del Sol is not united. The majority has come around, if only because they know we are in danger, but there is an angry minority that comes and threatens the sanctuary. Santos is looking for ways to quell the growing threats."

I squeezed my hands into frightened fists. So everyone in the Sun Sanctuary was at risk too, even if it wasn't from the remnants of the bruja army out looking to steal the gods' souls. Would they be okay when I had to leave next?

Why couldn't Tierra del Sol just—just help themselves? We were on their side; why weren't they?

"Lo siento, Cece," Mamá said, reached out, and hugged me close. "I wish . . . I had been able to stop all of this with Catrina, before it even began."

I looked up at her. And sorrow lived in her eyes as memories.

"And what does that mean for Tierra del Sol?" the chief of police interjected into the conversation going on behind us.

I glanced back at the Court of Fears, Ocelot, Metztli, and Don Santos.

"Where do you anticipate the brujas will strike next?" Santos asked.

"The bruja army is weaker now," Metztli said. "The Court of Fears took out the majority of their numbers, but those remaining are still dangerous, especially when led by Grimmer Mother. They will go either to the Moon Sanctuary or Desert Sanctuary next. We do not know the latter's location, but as Lion pointed out, Catrina must know it, or she would not have risked this."

"And this is a problem?" Santos asked. He clearly felt out of the loop with all the curanderismo and brujería, but he was doing his best to keep track. "Because . . . ?"

"The Desert Sanctuary is lost, and legend says only a desert curandera could open its doors," she said. "We do not have a desert curandera. I fear Catrina must have one captured and in her army's control, if she hopes to enter the sanctuary."

"So we need our own desert curandera, or to retrieve hers," Santos surmised.

She nodded. "Sí."

Damiana leaned in. "Do we know how to find a desert curandera?"

Metztli hesitated. "Consuelo said that with time, curanderas can recognize one another, even before their power has properly awoken. They sense the potential of the blessing. It is how she found me." She looked to Tzitzimitl. "But . . . I have not developed so far in my abilities yet."

"Recognizing another curandera takes a lifetime," Tzitzimitl said, her calm, steady voice echoing out her open jaw. "In her time, Consuelo was the only one left who could do so. There is no need for shame, Metztli."

Metztli nodded and shook herself, as if sloughing off the sadness she so often wore. "Sí. Without such intuition, we must rely on luck or persistence. Perhaps both." She looked to Santos. "We could attempt to test the citizens of Tierra del Sol. Most humans have the opportunity to be a curandera. We might find one touched of the Desert among your people."

"There will be resistance," Santos admitted. But he seemed on board. "Many would be horrified to find themselves a curandera. But we must do all we can."

"Imagine being annoyed that you have extra powers," Lion scoffed. "Humans."

"It is settled, then!" Santos stood. He looked sweaty and stressed—which wasn't really surprising, considering he'd been running everything while he was still injured. "Come, we must organize a search for our salvation."

Metztli pointed to Juana as she and Tzitzimitl followed him toward the doors. "Juana, you come as well. We do not have time to waste. I will teach you as we search for our desert curandera."

Juana didn't look happy about it, but Damiana gave her a thumbs-up as she walked past, and Juana's gruffness melted away a bit.

"You will light up our future, Juana Rios," Damiana said.

Juana snorted a little, but her smile was unmistakable. "Save all that gushy mom stuff for Axolotl."

"I can come too if you want," I called after them.

Metztli's tired gaze softened as she looked back at me. "You sleep, Cecita. Juana will follow soon."

Mamá kissed the top of my head. "Sí. Get some rest, mija. You need it."

"But I can still help . . . ," I mumbled. I'd nearly messed things up earlier. I wanted to feel useful right now, so the dark seam didn't catch up with me.

Mamá chuckled and held me close. Her warm colors seeped into me like the heat from the cozy fireplace at home. I nestled myself against her for a moment before she pulled back, plumped my cheeks, and gestured to the door that led to the rest of the Sun Sanctuary.

"Coyote is back there," she said, with an insinuating smile. My cheeks flushed. "He's been very busy too. Why don't you just keep him company for a minute, and if you get tired and nod off . . ." She shrugged.

I could barely wrangle an awkward smile. "Okay, fine. Buenas noches—er, buenos días?—Mamá."

We separated, and I held her love close as I slipped away to find my best friend, hoping it would be enough to sew closed the dark seam inside.

10
The Brides of El Sombrerón

I'd never gone into the parts of the Sun Sanctuary where the Sun Priestesses lived. I rubbed my arm a bit awkwardly as I wandered down narrow adobe corridors, peeking into different rooms, trying to find Coyote. Near the end of the first hallway, a door sat propped open. I edged forward and peered inside.

Coyote knelt in the middle of a tiled room, his hands cupped around a fire opal stone as round as a pearl. I held my breath as it began to glow.

Coyote's arms were covered in tattoos—white tattoos ringing his forearms in intricate, circular marks, like endless worlds and night skies stacked on each other and interlocked in intricate chains. Not chains that hold captive and restrict. Chains that hold people together. They moved, rotating around his arms, swimming across his skin, as he whispered in soft tones. I breathed in awe, the hairs on my arms rising to witness it.

The stone in Coyote's hand glowed brighter. Wind picked up from nowhere, stirring his multi-colored bangs. He stared intently, even as the stone grew so bright it was blinding. I peeked through my fingers as a light, melodic drumbeat circled the room from nowhere.

"Your Name," Coyote finished, "was, and is, and always will be, Lesvia Canul Gutierrez."

The stone erupted between his hands. Coyote tilted his head back as the stone rose in the air in sparks and flames, twisting around, until the glowing, brilliant material formed the silhouette of a woman.

A large flash sent Coyote sliding back across the floor. I fell into the doorframe and had to rub my eyes. When I lifted my head, the air was still again, and a young woman, wearing a bright red dress, stood in the center of the room.

Flesh and blood again . . . Her soul's orange and yellow feelings hummed in the air.

I covered my mouth. Her warm words soaked into my soul. And I knew, without anyone speaking aloud, that this bride of El Sombrerón was finally home.

"Hola, Lesvia," Coyote said, as he shifted his weight on the ground. He tried to get up, then winced and rested back on the floor. Was he okay? She looked down at him with sparkling eyes, and he smiled. "I'm Coyote. And this is Dominga del Sol—she can help you . . ." Coyote gestured my way, but his eyes widened in surprise when he saw me.

Oh! Of course, Dominga del Sol must have been the one helping the brides once they returned. My heart warmed at the thought. I'd relied so much on her guidance in the past. I had to think the brides would benefit from that kindness as well.

I definitely wasn't her, but she was busy, so I stepped forward anyway and outstretched my hands. The girl hesitated—not like she was scared, but like she was remembering how to walk again. She tottered for a second before placing her hands in mine.

"Actually, I'm Cece," I said. "An ocean curandera. We'll introduce you to everyone later. But for now, you just need to know that El Sombrerón isn't here. You're safe."

Tears filled her eyes. Her chin crumpled, but she lifted her head, eyes bright and burning, as she nodded. Her mouth quirked up into a fragile, brilliant smile.

"I'd always hoped the curanderas would rescue me," she said.

Wait—no one since the Battle of Tierra del Sol had a good opinion of curanderas. What time was she from? I glanced down her red dress, and my stomach flipped when I realized it was embroidered with intricate, ancient patterns even older than Metztli's. I squeezed her hands as my heart stretched wide and trembled. Horror and grief rose in my heart like crashing waves, tearing up through that dark seam inside me.

This was so wrong. So unfair.

I barely managed to keep the feelings from crashing out onto her. "Lo siento," I whispered, and tried to smile. "I wish we'd found you sooner."

She laughed, and the tears poured down her face in glittering streams. "Chiquita, I'm just happy to be home."

She threw her arms around me and squeezed. Her laugh sounded like a crackling, roaring fire. She released me and rushed for the door.

"Do you know where mi familia is?" she asked. "Do they still live in the center of town?"

Oh. I gripped my fingers as words swam down my throat, out of reach. She—she didn't know how much time had passed. There was no way her familia was still alive. Her happy movement slowed, and she looked between me and Coyote. Her forehead puckered.

"¿Qué pasa?" she asked. "What's wrong?"

I searched for words, heart aching. Then Dominga del Sol appeared just behind her in the doorway. Lesvia jumped. Dominga del Sol simply smiled, her eyes wrinkling.

"Mija," she said. "Here, follow me. We have much to tell you and many to help you adjust," she said, as she stepped back. Lesvia followed her into the hall. "There are other brides of El Sombrerón who have returned as well."

Lesvia's eyes sparkled. "¡Órale! We've all been saved?" She kissed her palms and raised them to the sky. "¡Muchas gracias!"

I blinked. I'd never seen anyone do that. It must have been an old-timey thing. I smiled, and the seam in my heart thawed slightly as I watched her turn out of sight with Dominga del Sol. She was so happy. So grateful. I had to hope it would stand against the oncoming pain.

I glanced back at Coyote. His mismatched eyebrows turned up, and light shadows creased under his eyes. He looked tired. He tried to stand up as he smiled, but he wobbled slightly and sighed. I ran over to him.

"Are you okay?" I asked. "You look like you need to rest."

"Naming is a lot more tiring to do the right way." The tattoos on his forearms slowly receded, like they were being washed away by an invisible tide. "Now I see why I Named criaturas one at a time. But sí—I'll be fine. I think."

His knees trembled again, and I hurried him over to sit down on the bench against the wall. "How many brides have you restored?" I sat beside him. "You need to take care of yourself, you know."

"It's only been ten," he said, and frowned. He shook his head. "It took me so long to figure out how to do the first one. Dominga del Sol has been helping them recuperate afterward, but if I can't do more than this in a day, it'll never work." He frowned harder.

"What will never work?" I asked.

He paused. "Um." He rubbed his forearm where the tattoos had been. "Nothing. Just an idea I've been considering, for the final battle." That set off alarm bells in my head, but he suddenly sat up straighter and said, "How'd it go in Costa de los Sueños? Did you get the Ocean's soul?"

I nodded. "Sí, we did."

He squinted. "Why don't you . . . smell happier?"

I laughed at the odd question, but it faded quickly. I shook my head. "No, I'm really happy we saved the Ocean's soul from the brujas. The Court of Fears took down so much of the army. Metztli thinks we stand a really good chance against Catrina if things keep going like this."

Coyote watched me. He watched me the way he always did, leaning in, gold eyes intense and searching. Looking into me more than at me. His soul reached out at the same time, warm colors and questions circling toward my soul through the air.

I normally loved the warm touch of his soul. But I

flinched back before the tendrils could reach my soul stone.

I didn't want him to feel the seam still open somewhere inside me.

His exhausted expression turned to concern. "What's wrong?"

I picked at a hole in my jacket and didn't look at him. "I mean, everything, sort of," I mumbled.

He leaned back so we could rest our heads together gently. "You smell . . . angry."

I gripped the front of my jacket with clenched fists. "I'm not mad," I whispered. The seam in my chest tugged against its stressed stitches, and I tried to reach for the warm, calm waters inside me. My soul tried to flicker and glow, but it was paler than usual. I swallowed.

"I'm just—frustrated, I think. I want to save everyone. I want to make that better world we talked about. But with Catrina and the brujas and all the ungrateful parts of Tierra del Sol and . . ." My throat tightened. Anger and aching mixed inside me and overflowed into tears. "The Court of Fears turned hundreds of people to stone today. And they had to, I know. But how are we supposed to make a better world when the *people* in it aren't better?"

The question came out earnest and icy. Because the seam wasn't going away, and I didn't know what to do with it if it wasn't frustration or pain.

Coyote paused for a long moment. Then he twisted to

fully face me. His soul was calm and steady, with ribbons of focused orange and calm pink circling around me.

"I know what feeling you're talking about, Cece," he said. "It's the same one I wrestled with in my last life."

I met his stare, and a dark, fearful feeling dropped through my bones.

"It's hate," he said. "It's called hate, Cece."

Hate? My chest squeezed. The sharp seam in my chest came back to mind. It wasn't large and burning right now, but I could feel it throb lightly, sourer than ever, as I thought of what Grimmer Mother had said. How she'd embraced the fact that she was hurting others, and the way she took pleasure from it.

I couldn't remember truly hating anyone. Except El Sombrerón, probably. I rubbed my chest. Now that I thought about it—maybe that was where I'd first felt this dark sting.

Hate is too new a power for you to wield . . . A voice crawled up my skin. *Isn't it, Cece?*

I stiffened and twisted around. The room was still empty, the doorway vacant. We were alone, but the young, quiet voice had found me. My heart picked up its pace. Why was I hearing it? Who was it?

Coyote searched the room. "Do you hear something? With soul language?"

I shook my head. Then paused. Then nodded. "It's a

young voice. The first time, it said it was dying . . . and now it's asking me about . . ." I didn't want to finish the sentence. Slowly, I turned back to Coyote, aching, afraid—angry.

"I don't want to hate anyone." I shook my head. I'd never felt this way before, and I didn't want to. Tears burned in my eyes, and Coyote's face softened. "I don't believe in hating people. I can't—don't—I'm scared—"

My throat strangled any more of my attempts. Coyote wrapped his arms around me and pulled me to him. I buried my face in his shoulder, and he rocked me back and forth. I slipped my hands beneath his arms, gripping his shirt.

"I remember," he said quietly. "I get it." He tucked his head toward me, so I felt his cheek against my ear. "Hate is infectious. It comes in disguise as different things—anger at injustice, or wanting to protect people—and then it spreads into the desire to punish. Just . . . try to remember that stopping evil and helping good aren't always the same thing." He squeezed me closer. I dug my fingers into his back. "Hatred is why I Renamed the dark criaturas. It's the pull I've fought to break all this time, so I can make up for what I did under its influence, and give dark criaturas back their true Names."

"Like Quetzalcoatl," I whispered, throat tight.

He nodded. "Like Quetzalcoatl. We have to save him,

so he can have a new role to match his new name. We can't go back to hate. That only made things worse, and gave him a part to play that never really belonged to him."

Santos had brought up that same concern yesterday. Quetzalcoatl was no longer the king of Devil's Alley, but he was still the strongest of the criaturas. We'd left him so new and so fresh with his name. What place would it give him in the world, once we stopped Catrina?

Could we even give him a world worth returning to?

The door creaked behind us. Coyote and I twisted, still gripping each other as my tears stained his shirt, to find Damiana.

"Ah." She stiffened when she saw our position. She grinned awkwardly and pointed down the hall. "Lo siento. I came to show Cece the cot I put up for her. But if you two . . . need a moment . . ." She started shifting away.

I wiped my tears and hiccupped. "N-no, it's okay, Damiana." I sniffed and pulled away reluctantly from Coyote. "I told Mamá I would sleep. I'll come."

She watched me like she thought I'd break as I separated from Coyote. While I approached, Axolotl poked her head out from behind Damiana. Her bulgy pink eyes widened.

"When are you two going to get married?" she asked, grinning.

I coughed and choked on my own mucus.

"Axolotl!" Damiana reprimanded. "Don't say things like that!"

"But you are, right?" She beamed.

Axolotl clearly expected an answer as she grinned from me to Coyote. Heat burned all the way across my face, and I looked to Coyote for help. His eyes traveled the room, his lips pursed innocently, shrugging. I pouted. Well, he wasn't any help right now.

"Coyote and I are just friends," I said, and shrugged into my jacket, pushing into the hallway with them. "What made you ask that?"

"Coyote said so earlier." She looked at him.

It was his turn to cough. I gaped at him, and he conveniently started looking in Juana's bag for the next bride's soul.

"Weird," Coyote said, rubbing the back of his neck. "I don't remember that."

"But you *said*—!" Axolotl began, pointing an accusing finger.

"That's enough, Axolotl."

The three of us turned and found Ocelot striding down the hallway toward us. Her soul swung on her neck with each step, bumping against the sling that currently restrained her bundled-up right arm.

I gaped. "You were wounded in the battle?" How had I not even noticed? Well, I guess Juana and I had been battling against Grimmer Mother. But still!

"Boto caught me as I walked by the water and broke my arm," she said, with a shrug that then made her wince. I cringed with her. "It is fine, Cece. La Sirena dragged him off me after Lion set her free. It should heal in a day and a half."

She stopped in front of us, eyed Axolotl, and crouched in front of her.

"Your honesty is admirable," Ocelot said. "Pero, it embarrasses people when you point things out too early. Wait a few more years to tease them."

Axolotl contemplated that as my face nearly exploded with heat. I covered my cheeks, and Ocelot sent me a tiny, but definitely pointed, smile. I stomped my foot and turned around, huffing. What was wrong with everyone lately? Just because Coyote and I hung out all the time didn't mean we were like *that*. He was my best friend! And sure, he was really cute, and made me feel safe, and was kind of my favorite person—

Wait, where was I going with that?

Ocelot's smile only widened at my behavior.

Axolotl poked the dimple on her right cheek. "Ocelot, you have the same smile wrinkle as my mamá," she said.

Damiana chuckled uncomfortably. Strange colors tangled around her soul as she picked up Axolotl and sat her on her hip, even though Axolotl was really too big for that now. Huh. Strange.

"Do you need help setting up a place for the returned brides to sleep?" Damiana asked.

Ocelot shook her head and straightened back up, holding her sling. "I came to let Coyote know they have a place to stay." She peeked into the room and narrowed her eyes. "And to remind you that you too need to sleep, Legend Brother."

Coyote nodded. "Right after this next one."

Ocelot's mouth puckered. But she allowed it, turned, and led Damiana down the hallway. "They are searching in earnest for the desert curandera." Her voice faded down the way. "Let us hope we find one to foil Catrina's plans soon. The Court of Fears is scouting for the brujas as we speak . . ."

I went to follow after them, but a quiet voice held me back.

"Hey, Cece?" Coyote called.

I caught myself on the doorjamb. He stood at the center of the room now, holding another fire opal soul, his gaze soft and steady. My soul fluttered, even around the seam, just for a moment.

"You're going to be okay," he said. "You already have the antidote you'll need."

I wiped my nose again. "I . . . do?"

He nodded, holding himself a bit straighter, as orange confidence poured out his soul. "If anyone in this world has the one skill that counters hate," he said, "it's you."

11
The Game of Power

I didn't usually remember my dreams, and the few that I did were stressful and vague. But after I finally lay down to rest, one found me that was as clear and strong as rain cutting through the desert's dust.

I sat at a table in the center of a white void. The whiteness was filled with quiet whispers and streaks of color passing by like lazy fish through a river's current. I reached out for a stray pink ribbon. When my finger touched its edge, it rippled, and a voice poured out: *I wish I could tell her we're familia.*

My brow furrowed. I knew that voice, didn't I? It sounded like Damiana's. But everything felt heavy, a bit distant, in this world. The pink strand swam away in the sea of colors. Another orange stretch whistled past my ear: *If I sacrifice myself, I could put everything right.*

I watched the color slip away. That was Coyote's voice I'd just heard, I was sure. These were strands of soul colors, weren't they? The language of souls, passing me by in their purest form.

Was this really a dream?

"You've played lotería, right, Cece?" a voice asked.

When I turned around, Tía Catrina was inexplicably sitting across the table from me, shuffling a stack of cards. Her long dark hair lay like a waterfall across her slender shoulder, and her burgundy lips looked perfect and serene. Some part of me knew I should be afraid. But it was far, far down, in the back of my head. The white void was gentle. The colors were so strong. And my soul was sparking with the light I was desperately trying to hold on to. So I nodded.

"We used to play when I was little," I answered her.

We hadn't played lotería as a familia since the incident with Tzitzimitl when I was seven years old. Juana and I had still played sometimes after that, but we didn't have a lot of time with all our schoolwork before Papá left, and Juana was so tired from working the fields afterward that I never brought it up.

Tía Catrina nodded. She laid the shuffled pile of cards to our left, halfway between us. I blinked, and suddenly, we each had a bingo card sitting in front of us, and a pile of dried pinto beans to mark them.

"Do you remember the rules?" she asked, as she began to draw a card from the pile.

"Sí," I said. It was a simple game. You drew cards from the center stack, calling out the names under the pictures—things like "La Sirena," "La Dama," "El Sol," et cetera—and placed a bean on your bingo tile if you had it. The goal was to get a full row before everyone else. It was a game of chance. Luck.

Or cheating.

Catrina flipped the first card up. "El Coyote," it read, with a picture of my best friend mid-transformation, half coyote, half human. I stiffened. Lotería card decks didn't have a Coyote card. What kind of dream was this? It felt just like real life, but if I'd been wrapped in cotton, with soul colors threading around me.

Catrina placed a bean on her bingo sheet's Coyote tile. I checked mine. But he wasn't there.

Catrina discarded the card easily. "That's one for me."

"Why are you doing this?" I asked.

"I like games," she said. "Axochitl and I used to play all the time. She let me win when I was younger. But as we got older, she got greedier and decided to take that from me too."

"No," I said, "I mean why are you doing *this*? This war. This—trying to take over everything? What could owning both worlds possibly give you that's worth what it'll take?"

"I thought for so long you'd understand, out of everyone," she mumbled. "I saw you as myself. So afraid and impotent. But when you became a curandera, you forgot how weak you'd been. You became just like them—so unaware of how painful it is to be powerless because you finally had your own."

She gripped the next card from the pile so tightly, the paper warped. When she turned it over, Kit Fox, with his ears perked and worried, shone above the title "El Zorro Kit." I bit my lip. Another card that shouldn't be in the deck. What was going on?

"But I know power now, Cece," she hissed.

She placed Kit's card down and scanned her bingo tiles. I quickly checked mine, but he was missing too. I felt a prickle of sweat, even under the muffled quality of the air here. She sighed and placed a bean over Kit's face on her card, where it sat next to Coyote.

"There are several kinds of power, and some are stronger than others." Catrina flipped over the next lotería card to reveal Little Lion's face, only older, titled "El León Negro." My body clenched. "For example, some are born with charisma and physical strength. Others knowledge." She fingered Lion's card as she lazily searched her bingo sheet for his face. She found it, on the other side of Coyote, and placed a bean.

My stomach dropped. I was falling behind.

"Then there's beauty," Catrina continued, "one of the weakest powers of all." Her face soured. Her eyes darkened. "That was the only one I was born with."

"Why do you think beauty's weaker?" I asked. I'd seen how much Juana could do with her beauty. Inspire, radiate, convince.

"Because beauty is only the power of being wanted." She drew another card from the face-down deck. "It's a power that is more wound than weapon, and more gamble than guarantee." She looked at the card. Her face hardened, and she laid it down on the table between us.

A portrait of Catrina and Mamá painted its front. I took a long, deep breath as I looked them over. They were both younger, around my age. Mamá stood proudly, smiling, so bright and warm I almost thought she was Juana for a moment, except for the wider set of her shoulders that I'd inherited. Catrina, on the other hand, looked slight and shy, hiding in Mamá's shadow, clinging on to her, like Mamá was the only reason she had the courage to exist at all.

The card, beneath their picture, was entitled, "Las Hermanas."

Catrina clucked her tongue once, with disdain. "Axochitl was born with every power I wasn't given. People listened to her. She was happy. She was brave. And she was strong, physically and—on the inside." She scanned her card, brow crumpling.

There was hate in her voice as she said it. But the sharpness didn't quite show up in her eyes. She scanned Mamá's image, and anger and admiration fought across her face. She looked at her the way someone might the sun, if they'd only ever lived in the cold touch of shadows.

Slowly, I turned to my own sheet and scanned its tiles. Mamá and Catrina weren't there.

But they weren't on Catrina's either.

"Why do you hate Mamá so much?" I asked. "What did she do to you?"

I knew what Catrina had done and why it haunted Mamá. But out of everything and everyone else, Catrina's hatred centered on her sister. I knew Mamá wasn't perfect. But she was willing to grow when she realized she was wrong. What had happened between them?

Catrina sighed and reached for another card. "It's simple, really. Tu mamá promised she'd always use that power she was given so effortlessly to protect me. She promised to keep me safe from Papá. From anything. From everything." She flipped her card up. "And then she abandoned me."

The next card read, "La Abuelita." It was a painting of Etapalli, my abuela, the grandmother I had never known.

She was beautiful, even with her eyes closed and tears running down her cheeks. I swallowed as matching tears ached in my soul. She had Catrina's long, wavy dark hair and Mamá's wide cheekbones. Both of her daughters were in her. But one of them was the reason she was gone.

"Tu mamá protested so much when I tried to tell her she was cruel for wanting to get married," Catrina said. She idly scanned her card, as if bored by her dead mother's portrait. "She said she and her husband would stay with us in the house, so I wouldn't be alone with Papá. She said she'd still take care of Mamá. She said she just wanted to love someone too." She scoffed. "I wasn't enough for her even then."

I blinked as my heart seized. Wait. *That* was why Catrina had felt like she wasn't enough? Because Mamá had wanted to get married? She thought—she thought Mamá wanting a life was the same as abandoning her?

Catrina looked to my side of the table. She huffed. "Of course she'd choose you."

I glanced down. Abuela's portrait lay on my sheet. I placed a pinto bean over her weeping expression. I was still no closer to finishing a row, and Catrina was far ahead.

But she hadn't won yet.

"It won't be long now, Cece," Catrina said, as if she'd heard me.

I looked up.

She crushed Abuela's card in her hand. Scars and rips opened up in Abuela's aching face, and I flinched for her. "I promise you that."

I woke with a painful jolt. Catrina's promise haunted the air, and I peeled my crocheted blanket back so I could sit up, rub my face, and wrap myself in a hug.

What was *wrong* with Catrina? It didn't make sense to me. I panted in the cold, open room of the Sun Sanctuary's attic. Sure, people hurt others when they were hurt. I understood that. But didn't everyone want to stop hurting at some point? Why didn't she want to heal more than she wanted to—to hate? Hate even when it didn't make sense? Hate even what wasn't really the problem?

But even drenched in sweat and shivering, I found myself still hoping, in some terrible, painful way, that Catrina had a good reason to hate the way she did. Because if she didn't—how could I not hate *her*?

I rubbed my arms and looked up. Above my head soared the gold dome of the Sun Sanctuary. It was painted even on the inside, and it caught the low light of the moon from the window, so it looked almost silver in the quiet space. It made me feel strange. Lonely. Except that Damiana stood by the window, staring out the glass with her face focused and hard. Like she was searching for something.

"Oh," I said. "Damiana?"

She flinched. "Cece! Lo siento, did I wake you up?"

I almost laughed, except that my dream still sat on me like stones. Damiana hadn't made any noise; how could she have woken me? I guess she still felt a bit insecure in her skin, even if she'd grown a bit more confident around mi familia.

"No. I was having a, um, bad dream." I crossed the room and stepped up to the window. The softened shades of the desert waited just outside. It was still so strange, to see it ensconced in a false and confused night. "What time is it?"

"You've been sleeping most of the day," Damiana said. "It probably is actually night now."

I nodded, scanning the area. "What was it you were looking for?"

"Oh, uh, not *looking*, exactly . . ." Damiana quirked her head, like she'd seen something out the corner of her eye. I tried to trace her gaze, but nothing in the landscape looked particularly noteworthy. "It's more like listening for . . . a sound. A voice?" her words grew quieter, so I barely caught the end.

"Did you say a voice?" I asked. Catrina's hissing tone from the dream reached up my ribs, and I shuddered. It made me miss Mother Ocean's all the more. Maybe I'd ask Metztli to show me where she'd hidden the Ocean's soul, so I could drive out the leftover feeling of Catrina's. "What kind of voice?"

"I'm probably overthinking it," Damiana mumbled. "It's more like . . . the sound of hail hitting the dust. Or the way wind whistles through Joshua trees."

Damiana searched the horizon. Something about her description felt familiar. Mother Ocean's voice had been almost as much brine and spray as words for me. I squinted up at her. Damiana couldn't be hearing . . . could she . . . ?

Then, I heard a clatter of hail hit the ground. We both jumped and looked down. Juana and Metztli were outside, and from Juana's twirl, a crescendo of fire sent stones and pebbles clattering against the glass windows. Oh, that's all it was.

Damiana relaxed. "Ah, so that was it."

"She's getting so good!" I plastered my hands against the window. "Can you believe she's only just started using fire? Look, she's blending the curandera moves with the Amenazante dance."

Juana tottered for a moment on her bad leg. Metztli helped right her and looked like she was instructing her to focus on her hands for now.

"When I first met Juana, she was terrifying," Damiana

said. "But I recognized the dark place she spoke from. I'd lived in it." Her eyes softened. "It is good to see her be bright and dazzling, even with her scars."

Her words pulsed around me. I looked up at Damiana and the quiet longing in her eyes. Like she, too, hoped she could one day be bright, even with her scars. Except, I had a feeling she felt her scars were her eyes and her fangs. The signs of having once been a bruja, even if she'd long given up the heart of one.

"I think you're pretty inspiring too, Damiana," I whispered. She looked down in surprise. I smiled. "It takes a lot of resilience and strength to change after everything you went through. Gracias, Damiana. For your determination."

We needed every little bit we could get right now, especially with Tierra del Sol turned against itself. With only three curanderas where the world needed four. Damiana's face softened.

"You are too kind to me, Cece. But thank you, all the same." She glanced back at my bed. "Are you sure you're done resting? You might want to stock up while you can. I doubt we will have time for siestas soon."

"No, I'm good," I said. The memory of the nightmare scuttled up my spine. "They didn't happen to find a desert curandera while I was sleeping, did they?" I looked up at her, hoping against hope.

Damiana pressed her lips together and shook her head. My shoulder slumped.

"I guess it was a lot to ask for in one day," I mumbled. But where did that leave us now? We were down a curandera.

"They're still looking," Damiana said, and crouched lower so we could look eye-to-eye. She must have mistaken my expression because she stroked my hair back, as if to comfort me. "Perhaps they will find someone before the Court of Fears spots more movement from the brujas—"

Something rumbled. A voice. A call. I lifted my head to the sky, and distant rain clouds. Damiana looked too. Not as if she were searching for what I looked for, but as if she'd felt something.

They're coming . . . The Ocean's voice rumbled all the way up the sanctuary's walls, its tile, and into my bones.

"Cecelia!" Metztli called from below a half a second later. "It is time!"

12
The Call of the Moon

Damiana and I ran outside to meet Metztli, Juana, Ocelot, and Tzitzimitl near the back stairs.

"The brujas have already made it to the base of the montaña where the Moon Sanctuary resides," Tzitzimitl said, her headdress shuddering as she scanned us. "Alux, Bird King, and La Lechuza have still not returned from their scouting across the country."

Juana steamed in the chilly night air. "Cece can portal us there in time, right?"

"Sí," Metztli said. "But the Court of Fears is scattered. How soon do you think they will return, Tzitzimitl?"

"It could be an hour," she said. "Or half a day. It depends on how soon they discover the brujas are not on their routes."

"We don't have time for that," I said, and bit my lip. "We need to leave now if the brujas are that close."

Metztli roused herself with a calming breath. "Sí, we

must. Pero Juana and Ocelot are wounded, and with the Court of Fears missing too, our chances no son buenos."

"I'm still coming!" Juana insisted. I looked up at her, and she lifted her chin. "My ankle's wounded, but I can make fire now. You're not leaving me behind."

"I will go as well," Ocelot said.

Damiana gaped. I winced. A broken bone was even worse than a bite wound.

"Coyote cannot replace me without risking all our lives," Ocelot said despite our reactions, "and Santos has called Little Lion away to quell an uprising in the eastern quarter. The people of Tierra del Sol are still angry, Santos is still wounded, and he needs support here. That leaves me."

She sat up straighter. I frowned. Tierra del Sol was fighting itself *again*. How long until they learned? Would they ever?

"I still have a free arm, and I am a trained fighter," Ocelot insisted. "I will still be formidable."

"But you could break your arm all over again. Or worse!" Damiana interjected, intensely. I glanced at her. Nervous coral reds sparked off her soul.

"I offer myself willingly, Damiana," Ocelot answered, cold and flat. "Who are you to challenge my will?"

Everyone went quiet. Ocelot was dangerously close

to accusing Damiana of acting like a real bruja. Damiana winced and bit her lip, like she was wrestling back an onslaught of words.

"I just . . ." Damiana hesitated. "If you don't heal well, you can't protect others either. ¿Sí?" She swallowed and placed a hand to her cheek, like she was comforting herself. She peered up. "None of us want to risk Kit, so how about this? *I'll* go instead of Ocelot! I once fought as a bruja. And Tzitzimitl will be strengthened by the Moon as well, so her extra power can make up for . . ."

Damiana continued making her argument, but I had stopped listening. I stared at the way Damiana pressed her hand to her cheek, so her dimple showed. Her dark cuts of black hair. The slight almond shape of her eye. It was familiar. Too familiar to be coincidence.

I gasped. Everyone looked at me.

Metztli blinked. "You do not want Damiana to come, Cece? She makes a good argument."

"No, that's fine," I said. Or, more like wheezed.

Everyone stared at me as I buttoned my lips and cleared my throat, trying desperately to control my face. Because I couldn't unsee it now: The dimple on Damiana's cheek that really did match Ocelot's, as Axolotl had pointed out. The way Damiana's eyebrows were straight as pins, just like Ocelot's. And then there was the memory I'd seen once through Ocelot's soul, of a little girl with a mark in the shape of an ocelot on her cheek that matched the exact description Damiana had once given of her mother, who'd been half criatura, who'd had a birthmark on her cheek.

Damiana was Ocelot's *granddaughter*.

It made so much sense. The soul in my dream, Damiana's alternating hesitance and then worry over Ocelot. The revelation exploded in my brain. Everyone kept talking—but my heart beat in my ears. Damiana was Ocelot's granddaughter, and she'd never said a word.

Was she ashamed? I watched her profile as Metztli agreed with her, and relief smoothed her features. Why wouldn't Damiana tell Ocelot? Why was she hiding it? How many things, exactly, was she hiding?

Something tugged at my soul. I looked over my shoulder, and Coyote sat on the gold dome of the Sun Sanctuary in animal form. His gold eyes met mine.

You figured it out too? he asked.

I gaped at him. *You* knew? *Why didn't you tell me?*

I had a hunch. He padded closer, shrugging his shoulder blades. *But I figured, if she wasn't ready to share, I shouldn't say.*

He was right. But my heart ached as I turned to face the group. Ocelot's ocher eyes were a flat, though subtly annoyed, neutral. Ocelot had loved her familia. She'd died for them.

How would she feel, knowing she had familia standing right in front of her?

"It is settled, then," Metztli said. "Damiana will go in Ocelot's stead. Let Ocelot heal up for the next battle."

"Wait!" someone called from behind me. "I want to come too!"

My stomach dropped the moment I turned to find Kit bounding toward us from the back door. He was panting, his cheeks flushed with readiness, his eyes alight.

"I'll help!" He grinned. "I can go too! I'm—fast. Ish. And small! I can be a lookout. I'll help make up for Ocelot—"

"No!" Ocelot yelled at the same time I said, "Kit, no!"

His ears twisted back at our volume.

I quickly softened my voice. "You're on your last life, Kit. You can't go!"

"Well—so are you! So is every human!" He looked from me to Metztli to Tzitzimitl to Juana and Damiana. "Why's it different for me?"

The question unsettled me. He had a point, but how did I explain to him how badly I wanted him to be safe, especially when I knew he couldn't come back this time?

"It just is . . ." I mumbled. I must not have been alone in the feeling because no one else spoke up in his defense either.

Kit straightened, gripping his hands into frustrated fists. "Maybe you don't get it because you're human. But being a criatura, having my soul outside my body means I keep coming back—" He clutched the stone, where it swung around his neck. The brownish-green stone sat calmly in his palm, even as I watched flickers of frustration, of longing, spiral off it in red and light blue ribbons. "Maybe that seems like a blessing to humans. But for me, it's like never getting to really live. Ever since the first time we died, we just kept coming back. Everything gets blurrier and messier and more confusing every time, until you're not even sure if anything you've done matters." His caramel eyes narrowed on me. "I want to live a *real* life this time. And if that means risking it, the way you do, to really help the world I'll one day leave behind—then that's what I want to do. I want my life to be worth it."

Everything about his speech crumpled my heart. My soul flickered behind my shirt as I took in the dedicated, courageous orange of his soul. I knew criaturas lost more and more of their memories the more times they died. But I hadn't realized it made him feel so—lost. My soul wrestled with grieving blues as I looked down at his stone. I wished . . . I wished there was a way to put his soul back inside. And give him that more permanent life he wanted.

"He is not wrong about the pain," Tzitzimitl said in a

low voice. "But still, we cannot risk you, Kit Fox. We do not take humans lightly into these situations, either."

Ocelot got up and placed her good hand on his shoulder. Kit's ears wilted as he looked up at her, like he knew he'd already lost the fight.

"Do not wish for war, Kit," she whispered. "You know better than any of us that sacrifice will always find you. Do not go looking for it before it is time."

"But . . . ," he started again.

Kit was ready to sacrifice himself. And it was touching. But it also made me want to weep that he was in that position in the first place. It felt—wrong. He was only twelve now. At least I was headed for fourteen. A dark seam crept open in my heart again. How could Catrina keep doing this? Why did so many brujas follow her? How could— how *dare* they make my friend even consider risking his life?

It should be their lives at risk. Not Kit's.

The dark seam in my chest widened until it was difficult to breathe.

Coyote dropped from the roof. He landed besides Kit, and in the same moment, transformed in wisps of charcoal to human form again. He put his hand on Kit's free shoulder.

"I'll fix it, Kit," he whispered. Kit gave him a confused

look. "Just be patient a little longer. I can't tell you more yet, but I will fix this."

"But I want to help *now*—" Kit started.

"No," Ocelot said, cutting him short yet again. "You are too young. You are too unwise. You are not going."

Kit's nostrils flared. But before I could intervene, he shook everyone off, sped away, and disappeared around the Sun Sanctuary.

"I'll go get him," Coyote said. He strolled off, in Kit's direction. "He's right. Things need to change. I never should have . . . but I'll fix it," I barely caught him saying as he went. "Cece's not going to like it though . . ."

I twisted to look after him in alarm, but he'd already turned the corner. What wouldn't I like? What was he planning?

Metztli stepped up before our small group, clapping our hands and drawing our focus back. I straightened and tried to refocus. We had a god's soul in danger, and I planned to be better about protecting it this time.

"The brujas will already be scaling the mountain. We must be ready." Metztli set off for the town square. "¡Vamos!"

13
The Moon Sanctuary

Water portals were the fastest form of travel ever. And thank the Ocean for that, or we never would have been able to make it to the Moon Sanctuary before the brujas.

"The Moon Sanctuary lies atop a montaña, past the nearest cerros, where it has a clear view of the Moon when she reaches the center sky," Metztli had said, as I'd shifted through the bodies of water stretched across el Antiguo Amanecer. "There is a cave through which a river used to run. It is only a small distance from the top of the montaña."

I'd reached for the water she'd described. The cenote in Devil's Alley pulled at me, and I quickly turned my attention away. Why did it seem louder, or heavier, or stronger in some way than the other bodies of water? Maybe because it was actually made by an ocean curandera? Either way, I'd pushed past it and grasped the cool river by the Moon Sanctuary. It had welcomed me—and the return of the curanderas.

Now we all stood on the freezing montaña, in our soaked shoes, beside the mountain river we'd just climbed out of. I tilted my head back to look at the unfamiliar white flakes. Just ahead of us, a tall building stretched out of the fog. Its gold dome faded into the white stretches of the sky, and its stone walls were pearlescent, so it glowed atop the mountain like a ghost of times past.

The Moon Sanctuary.

"It's beautiful," I whispered, but my teeth chattered.

The air bit at my skin with an intensity of cold I'd never experienced before, even in the depths of the desert's winter. This montaña was higher than the cerros around Tierra del Sol. I huddled into my jacket for warmth, but it was so full of holes it was practically useless. I should really get a new one. Juana noticed and wrapped her arms around me, and her warmth created a wall between me and the bitter wind. Metztli pressed forward, peering up the short slope separating us from the towering Moon Sanctuary.

"It has been so long since I have seen this place," Metztli said with longing.

Metztli, Tzitzimitl, Damiana, Juana, and I moved up the slope together. Juana leaned on my arm some of the way, but her ankle was healing better and faster than expected. Fortunately, Mama had told her the bite wasn't as bad as we'd originally feared. She'd just need to be more careful than usual and rest plenty between battles.

We had just about crowned the mountain when familiar streaks of nervous-yet-excited yellow filled the air. I twisted to check over my shoulder, barely catching the swish of a tail diving behind a snow drift. I stiffened.

"Kit!" I shouted. "That better not be you!"

Everyone stopped dead and turned. Slowly, Kit's furry head peeked over a mound of snow.

I pushed through the snow toward him. "Kit, you said you'd stay!"

He leaped forward and transformed in midair, landing as a human in the snow in front of me. "Technically," he said, hunching a bit, "I didn't say anything. I ran off to wait for you to open the portal." He grinned sheepishly.

Usually I loved Kit's silly side (except maybe his hiding-frogs-in-my-stuff stage), but this was different. We were in a war now.

"Kit, this is serious!" I grabbed his arm and tried marching him down the hill, but he was too strong for me to actually move him. "I'm—sending—you—home!"

"There isn't time," Metztli called out.

Kit and I both paused, and she gestured us up the slope. "We cannot risk our advantage. Kit, if you must be here, transform back into a fox. You are not as easily spotted in that form. Keep an eye out while we obtain the Moon's soul."

Kit beamed. I frowned.

Kit ran by my side in human form as we finished funneling up to the Moon Sanctuary together. Where the Sun Sanctuary had heavy wooden doors, and the Ocean Sanctuary had silver, the Moon Sanctuary's were glass. My anger and fear settled back for a moment as I took them in.

I pressed my hands to the intricately formed ridges. "These are so different from the others." I let my hand drop from the entrance. "I wonder what the Desert Sanctuary's are like . . ."

"I have wondered myself," Metztli admitted. She smiled down at me, with both sadness and warmth. "Even in my time, no one had seen the Desert Sanctuary in over five hundred years."

"Wait, really?" Juana asked. "What happened to it exactly?"

"Consuelo said it was destroyed when Devil's Alley was Named, swallowed in the earthquake that formed the city of El Cucuy." She sighed. My heart squeezed. "Since that time, desert curanderas were often trained in the Sun Sanctuary, where they would at least be surrounded by the desert." Her eyes dropped to the lines of her hands. "But Reina, the last desert curandera in my time, said she dreamed of finding its remains one day, so we could rebuild it—once we had won the war."

But that had never happened. I looked up at the glass

doors and felt an echo of past sorrow. I bet the Moon, and all the gods, grieved that we were in a war again. History was repeating itself.

Would we be able to end things differently this time? Chills ran down my back. The dark seam in my chest feared and fought.

Kit touched my shoulder. "Are you okay?"

"I'd be better if you were at home," I mumbled.

His ears wilted until they vanished back into his hair. "Lo siento, Cece . . ."

My insides ached at the effect of my words. I took his hands. "No, I'm sorry. I know you just want to help. It's just . . ." How could I tell him that I was more scared than ever that something would happen to my friends? And not just because it would shatter my heart if something happened to them?

But because, for the first time in my life, I was afraid of what *I* might do if it did.

Kit watched me. His caramel eyes caught the light and flashed that knowing, older green, like he was searching for the thing I couldn't say.

"Kit, what did I say about your form?" Metztli interrupted.

Kit hunched. In a few strokes of paint-like lines, he crouched as a fox on the front step. Metztli nodded and grabbed the doors' glass handles.

"I'm home," she whispered.

The doors flashed bright white and separated. Kit and I stepped back with the gust of wind that poured out from behind the opening doors. Metztli led us all inside.

The Moon Sanctuary was the barest one I'd seen so far. The pale marble tile floors were swept completely clean, so not even a speck of dust marred the surface. Above our heads, moonstone chandeliers hung from the tall ceiling. Star maps and old, rusted metal telescopes waited on forgotten podiums near the windows. The moonstones hummed to life above our heads as Metztli swept across the tile. She glanced around, and the building seemed to breathe again for the first time in centuries.

"I have missed you too," Metztli said, so quietly I almost didn't catch it.

Kit stayed at the entrance, pacing the outdoor stairs. Juana, Metztli, Tzitzimitl, Damiana, and I gathered in front of the mosaic on the farthest side of the room. It was identical to the ones in the other sanctuaries. Metztli placed her hand, at its center.

"I have come to make a request of my home as a moon curandera," she called.

The room echoed with the bold start. A shifting began at the center of the mosaic. The stones were separating, ticking back one at a time, sliding back into one another. I breathed in awe. Metztli looked to Juana and me and gestured for us to join her mosaic.

"Go ahead," she said. "It will open faster if you add your requests to it."

We ran over and pressed our hands to the stone. The moment Juana's skin connected with the mosaic, the fire opal brightened, gold and warm. The mosaic began to separate faster.

"A sun curandera adds her light to mine," Metztli said. "Her fire makes its request of this, the Moon Sanctuary."

I added my hand, and the turquoise stones lit up.

"An ocean curandera adds her strength to mine," Metztli said. Her voice grew robust, commanding, reaching. "Her water makes its request of this, the Moon Sanctuary, for the soul that lies within its protection."

The stones hummed and slotted back faster and faster. Damiana came up beside us to watch. She clutched her hands together in awe. The coyamito agate flickered.

Then the mosaic shuddered and separated completely. The ticking and clinking of the stones faded as they revealed the cement compartment they'd been protecting. My mouth dropped open.

The Moon's soul was a perfect sphere, pure and white like a pearl, glowing in peace and clarity.

Metztli took it reverently in her hands. Juana and I leaned in, staring into her light. It was beautiful. I sighed in relief. Good. Now we could just go home and get the

Moon's soul somewhere safe too.

I turned, ready to head for the door—when something stopped me.

My light will go out this day, a voice rose from the Moon's soul. I looked back, staring at the stone nestled in Metztli's hands. *As will hers.*

Chills washed down my insides. There was acceptance in her tone. Faith and peace. Despite the fear she'd just left me with. I looked to Metztli as I tried to process what the Moon meant, and what I was supposed to do about it.

When I am gone, remember who your true enemy is, the voice returned. *It will be the only way to bring the light back.*

Metztli's face tightened. Could she hear her now that she was holding her soul? Or was she just feeling the warning?

Behind you.

Moon's voice beat like a heart in my chest. Metztli froze. We both turned. Everything moved too slowly, like molasses, as I craned my neck inch by inch to peer out the eastern windows.

Outside, the moon still hung bright and clear far above us. The snow was pure. The mountain peaks in the distance were ghostly and sharp. But my blood turned to ice as I spotted Grimmer Mother standing just beyond the window.

She held up Kit Fox, still in his animal form, dangling limply by his neck. His soul sat in her free hand.

I opened my mouth and screamed.

14
Battle of the Beloved

I sprinted forward before I knew that my body was moving and threw myself through the glass window, reaching for my friend's sagging body.

The frame shattered around me. Shards nicked my cheeks and my ears as I stretched forward through the sea of colored knives, desperately grabbing for Kit's body.

Grimmer Mother's mouth sliced upward. As I slammed into the snow, she dropped him. Right into my arms. I folded myself around him, hugging him to me, and checked his face, his chest. He was still warm. My soul lifted. His heart was still beating. He was alive—

Suddenly, he twisted, yelped, and scratched my face.

I jumped back and slapped a hand over the cut. My eyes teared up with the sharp throbbing. Grimmer Mother's feet stopped beside me. But Kit's small, greenish stone flashed between her fingers.

"If you want your friend back," she said—and looked up

where Metztli, Juana, Damiana, and Tzitzimitl had gathered at the window. "You'll give me the Moon's soul."

Kit leaped out of my lap and jumped away on his four legs. He shook his head out and growled. Jaggedly, awkwardly, like he was fighting her control, he stumbled around her legs until he stood facing me. My insides hollowed out as I watched Kit assume a stance, ready to pounce at me on her command.

"Kit," I whispered.

"He's just a child, you sadistic hag!" Juana spat from behind me. She gripped the wooden windowsill, heat radiating off her body. "You'd really hold a little kid hostage?"

"I've done it before." She shrugged.

She didn't care about how much pain she inflicted on others. I stumbled to my feet, my body tight and cold, as Juana, Tzitzimitl, Damiana, and Metztli stepped through the window and gathered around me. That same sharp, dark anger from our last fight rose up inside me. Juana dug her feet into the snow, favoring the uninjured one. Her nostrils flared, and her nails flickered. But neither of us moved. Not yet. In case the next thing Grimmer Mother did was make Kit leap off a cliff, or stop breathing, or who knew what else.

"Ah, even the Sun-Heart doesn't dare fight, ¿sí?" Grimmer Mother grinned. "That's the problem with you curanderas. You close yourselves off to a whole world of power by being unwilling to control souls, unwilling to kill. You refuse to retaliate. And for what? Nothing at all."

I stared her dead in the eye. "It's not for nothing. It's because we don't want to be like you," I said. Anger and love roared up inside me, aching for my friend and his stolen soul. "I want a world where we treat each other right. And love, and kindness, and empathy is how we get it, and I'm *tired* of the *pain for pain* you create!" Tears burned up my throat.

She smirked. "Like I said. You fight for nothing worthwhile at all."

My stomach clenched into a rock. I buckled my hands into fists, and a furious, indignant geyser soared up inside me. She'd never be reasoned with. She willingly chose to use her powers this way. But I had to get Kit back. I *would* get him back. No matter what.

Grimmer Mother extended her free hand. "The Moon's soul, Metztli the Bright One."

Metztli folded her fingers tight over the glowing stone. I looked to her, desperate. She shot me an aching but determined expression of her own.

"I cannot sacrifice the world for a boy," she said.

My heart dropped. I knew she'd say it. It's what she'd been trying to tell me. But then I noticed the quickest, faintest blink in her right eye. Oh. I glanced at Grimmer Mother. At Kit. Metztli had a plan.

Grimmer Mother's gaze cut to me. "Isn't it painful, Cecelia Rios?" she asked. Pleasure pulled at her mouth. "To have someone stronger than you holding what you want just out of reach? That's how your tía first came to me. I taught her so much, but in the end, she surpassed her mentor. And then she taught me."

The snow beneath my feet began to melt. Juana's feet were bare against it, steaming, turning the snow into water. For me. I glanced, as briefly as I could, toward the puddle forming around her feet. Juana met my eyes. She nodded. Of course. My brilliant, fiery sister.

I clenched my hands carefully. The water crawled through the snow, its sound hidden by Grimmer Mother's laughter and Kit's growling. I pulled it closer, closer, until it gathered directly behind Grimmer Mother, where she couldn't see.

I shot my water at the back of her head. Grimmer Mother cried out and fell forward with the impact. Juana, Damiana, and Tzitzimitl instantly leaped for her. She stumbled and stretched her arm toward us. Kit launched forward, teeth out, for Juana's skin. She dodged him, but he kept coming.

"I'll get his soul!" Juana cried out. "Cece, get La Chupacabra!"

Wait—La Chupacabra? Where?

Snow dropped onto my shoulder. I turned just in time to see La Chupacabra drop down on me from the Moon Sanctuary's roof.

She slammed me into the ground, and my water splattered free of Grimmer Mother. La Chupacabra hissed over me. I threw my arms up to block her spit-lined fangs. Juana was busy with Kit Fox, so Damiana swerved in and shoved La Chupacabra off me. The two scrapped, Damiana barely evading La Chupacabra's worst blows. My legs shook, but I just managed to gain my feet a second before La Chupacabra escaped Damiana's grasp—and dove on me.

La Chupacabra grabbed me by the throat with one hand and lifted me into the air. I clutched La Chupacabra's hairless, pale arm, as her needly teeth gnashed in my face. Everything slowed. Juana's attempts to grab Kit. Tzitzimitl charging Grimmer Mother. Damiana swinging around to help me.

I squeezed La Chupacabra's arm. A distant heartbeat moved through the air between us, like a call for help. I looked to Grimmer Mother. La Chupacabra's soul hung around her neck, jostled by the wind.

I stretched for her soul through the air. Her buzzing energy reached back. And a thought blossomed in my mind, even as Grimmer Mother's control tightened La Chupacabra's fingers on my throat.

If Tía Catrina could use soul language to control criatu-ras from afar—couldn't I use it to try to pry La Chupacabra free?

I'd never tried it before. I wasn't even sure it was pos-sible. Could two souls fight over another? Would it hurt La Chupacabra, or me? I narrowed my eyes on Grimmer Mother, as she sent Kit diving on Tzitzimitl next.

I didn't have many options right now. I had to try.

I stretched my soul out for the weak pulses of La Chupacabra's. It was covered in what felt like tainted, acidic netting—Grimmer Mother's influence? I stretched even further, weaving my soul's light past the cobwebs. Finally, I touched something more. Something important.

Lo siento, chiquita, full words squeezed out from La Chupacabra's soul.

She was there! I could feel her! I reached deep into the stone from across the distance with a desperate hope. La Chupacabra's hand shook. The foggy edges of her eyes faded, just a bit, to a sharper silver. Her face brightened with realization.

"Please let me go," I barely managed to squeeze out.

Grimmer Mother's net of control finally broke. Grim-mer Mother jolted with the severing. She whirled around, distracted, eyes wide, panicked. But she was too late.

La Chupacabra released me—

And Kit leaped up and bit his soul off while the mother

of brujas was distracted.

"Kit!" Juana and Metztli gasped, beaming.

He twisted and landed, stumbling, in front of Juana. My heart raced, and warmth and pink filled my insides. He'd stolen back his own soul! Himself! One of the hardest things for a criatura to do. I nearly laughed—before falling face-first into the half-melted snow with a splash. Grimmer Mother rounded on Kit and Juana. Kit growled. Juana's fists steamed.

"You filthy criatura, you wretched little curanderas—" Grimmer Mother started.

Anger flooded my body as I climbed to my knees. I caught the water splatters in midair, swirled them around me—and lunged them at Grimmer Mother. They hit her straight in the chest. She fell back, crying out as she skated back in the snow.

"I have him, Cece!" Juana scooped Kit's trembling body into her warm arms. His caramel eyes swiveled my way as she tied his soul stone back around his neck.

"Now we must go!" Metztli called to me. "We have to take the moon's soul somewhere safe before the rest of the bruja army catches up!"

But Grimmer Mother started getting to her feet. And after everything she'd done—for the first time in my life—I wasn't ready to let her go. She'd just keep chasing us. She'd keep endangering my friends. She'd keep torturing La Chupacabra. I was tired, sick, disgusted with everything she did. I hated it.

I wanted to stop her. Forever.

I curled the water up around her, like veins, like rivers, traveling up her body. Grimmer Mother kept slapping her arms and hitting her chest, trying to disrupt the water. Droplets sprang off, but her blows weren't nearly enough to stand in the way of a river cutting its course. The water crawled up her throat, over her mouth, so it muffled her scream.

"Cece!" Metztli's warnings blurred away.

The water wobbled under my direction. As if it were confused. As if my motives were no longer pure enough to harness its strength. *I don't hate her*, I told myself and the water. *I just have to stop her. I have to take away her power once and for all.*

The water tightened hesitantly around her neck. On La Chupacabra's soul. It shone a weak, dull gray. Her voice called out to mine again, but I was too busy trying to rip the stone free. Her voice faded. Clouded over. Grimmer Mother's eyebrows cut downward in concentration.

I was so busy pressing the water against Grimmer Mother that I didn't notice La Chupacabra springing behind Metztli—and ripping the Moon's soul free.

I whirled around. Tzitzimitl reached for the stone flickering in La Chupacabra's grasp. Metztli screamed. Juana sprinted forward, but La Chupacabra chucked the stone, so the glowing sphere flipped in the air, over my head—

And landed in Grimmer Mother's hand.

Instantly, the nighttime shuddered with a cry from far, far above.

All around us, the light dimmed. I would've thought the sun was setting, the light shifted so much, but the sun hadn't ever risen. And this darkness felt cold. Heavy. Wrong. Metztli looked pale. My insides crumpled with guilt and fear.

Hanging over us, the moon's brilliant, pearlescent circle eclipsed into a sharp, crimson slice in the sky.

"The Moon," I whispered. "She's turned to blood."

"And your ally," Grimmer Mother said, rising again with La Chupacabra back at her side. "Will now draw yours."

A roar ripped open the reddened night sky. I turned, inch by horrified inch, to Tzitzimitl.

The dark criatura clutched her skull in her hands as a strange, terrible growl echoed through her bones. Her ribs clattered, shuddering, her shoulders twisting in their sockets. Terror swelled in my throat until I couldn't speak. The red light of the eclipse was summoning the side of her I never thought—always hoped—I'd never meet.

Gone was the Protector of Progeny. Now, she was the Devourer.

15

The Devourer

Tzitzimitl raised her head as the red light of the moon poured over her. Her skirt, usually made of bright blues and greens and reds, transformed before my eyes into bright emerald snakes. They slithered around her flesh legs and nested around her rib bones. Her black eye sockets burned with pin-thin drops of lava-bright fire. Slowly, she pried open her jaw of now razor-sharp teeth—and roared so loud my eardrums threatened to rupture.

Tzitzimitl had always looked frightening. The first night I'd met her, I'd been terrified she'd bite my heart out. But I'd met her as the Protector of Progeny. I'd learned to see the warmth in her eye sockets, and feel the kindness in the voice that impossibly filled her bones. But now?

My friend was gone.

I covered my ears and cringed as Tzitzimitl's roar shook my organs. Fear crystallized all along the inside of my ribs—I could barely breathe. Her skull swiveled around, all the way, to look at us.

"The Devourer is hungry." Grimmer Mother grinned and started backing away into the snow. "And as legend says, she will only be satiated by feasting on the children of the Sun."

Tzitzimitl leaped right for Juana.

I screamed and plowed into Juana's side, so we fell into Kit, and the three of us tumbled into the snow. Tzitzimitl landed right where Juana had been standing, her snakes biting at the air. Her neck bones creaked as she spun her head around to look at us.

Juana grabbed at me, fingers burning hot. "Get behind me!"

Metztli slid down the slope toward us. "No! Kit Fox, there—push!"

Tzitzimitl rose up, and streaks of crimson light cut through her ribs, falling over our faces. I trembled beneath my friend. How were we going to stop her? Tzitzimitl was so powerful. And now, perhaps even more so. She dove forward, her mouth gaping wide—

And Kit Fox jumped on us in human form.

His extra weight sent us tipping backward on the slope. I yelped. Juana cried out. He gripped both of us as we lurched and went skating backward down the hill.

Tzitzimitl flew after us.

The hill we'd climbed earlier felt twice as steep now that we were tumbling down it. We screamed the whole way, lurching and bumping until we skimmed in a long, sickening circle at the end of the slope—and tumbled sideways into the river.

The icy chill sank into the bruises collecting over my body. I coughed and ripped my head out of the water. Juana grabbed my hand, and I helped her find her footing. Kit popped out with us, shivering, and Juana tucked him closer to her warmth, so steam began to collect around us.

"Metztli?" I called desperately.

Metztli and Damiana fell into the snow in front of us. I gasped. Tzitzimitl must have thrown them all the way down. They managed to get to their feet, but Metztli was already limping.

Neither of them was strong enough to fight Tzitzimitl. She was a dark criatura, and she wouldn't stop now until either she'd finished off Juana and the rest of Naked Man, or the moon returned to normal. It was just like she'd told me the first time I met her.

But even without a criatura or a weapon, Damiana stood between us. Even without offensive powers, Metztli barred Tzitzimitl's path.

There was no way we could fight Tzitzimitl alone. And we couldn't outrun her. She was my friend, and I didn't know how to help her, but I couldn't let her take my sister and friends' lives. I planted my feet in the riverbed; the icy, numbing mud sank between the seams of my shoes. The water rushed around us in whirlpools.

A million bodies of water gathered inside me. I searched them desperately as Metztli and Damiana struggled to dodge and fend off Tzitzimitl's snakes. We needed someone. We needed help. We needed—the Court of Fears.

The only ones who could rival Tzitzimitl's strength.

Seven portals opened in the water, as I connected to all the bodies of water I could—just hoping the Court of Fears would be near.

Por favor. I poured my soul out to all of them. *Ayúdenme.*

The portal directly in front of me glowed, lighting up the lip of the cave. Alux's green-and-brown mottled eyes found mine through the rippling water.

"Curanderita?" he asked.

"Alux! It's Tzitzimitl!" I gasped. Tears filled my eyes as Tzitzimitl sprang for us. "The moon's eclipsed, and now she's the Devourer!"

Alux didn't need to know any more. He yelled to someone behind him, dashed toward me—and leaped through the portal, beads of water floating around his skin.

He landed in the snow between Metztli and Damiana, who were both panting and covered in scratches. He instructed them to stay back. They stepped into the river with us as Tzitzimitl shrieked—and the rest of the Court of Fears surged out of my portal in a rush of feathers and masks.

In a streak, La Lechuza and Bird King spread their wings—and plowed into Tzitzimitl.

"You are lucky we had just united, curandera," La Lechuza said to me from behind her carved mask. She panted as Tzitzimitl and her snakes fought back.

"Perhaps *lucky* is not the word, with the Devourer released." Bird King struggled to keep Tzitzimitl pinned as well.

How strong was Tzitzimitl now? Two of the Court of Fears were barely restraining her. Alux leaped forward and landed on Tzitzimitl's ribs. Snakes wrapped around him, and he grabbed them and kept ripping them out of her bones. More and more sprouted as he did.

Tzitzimitl's arm shot up and punched Bird King in the face. A terrible cracking sound resounded, and Alux and La Lechuza took several beatings as they barely restrained her. Horror flipped in my gut. Even all three of them together might not be enough. What were we going to do?

Tears filled my eyes. I got us into this mess. I should have listened to Metztli instead of staying longer, instead of trying to save La Chupacabra—no. Instead of trying to crush Grimmer Mother. Instead of giving in to the dark seam I barely understood. Into an anger I had trusted, even as I told myself and the water I wouldn't.

"Quickly, you must go!" Alux called to us. "Retreat, curanderas!"

"What about you—" Juana started.

Bird King and La Lechuza fought, limb by limb, to hold Tzitzimitl down. The snakes wrapped around Alux's chest and crawled higher, so in moments, we could see only his eyes. He shook his head. Just a little. And closed his eyes. So did Bird King. La Lechuza bowed her head.

"We will do . . . ," Alux said, as stone sprouted over him and the snakes, "what must be done."

"No!" I screamed.

Alux didn't listen to me. None of the Court of Fears did. They already understood the situation. They knew there was only one way out.

They used the last of their strength to hold down their friend—my friend, my rescuer, the criatura who had saved me as a child—and let Alux's stone crawl over every inch of their skin. It traveled all the way to the center of Tzitzimitl. She roared and gnashed her teeth. The stone seeped up her skull, to her burning eye sockets.

And then all of them were silent, frozen statues adrift in the snow.

16
The Lost One

We stumbled through a portal into the Sun Sanctuary, the image of the frozen Court of Fears still etched into my mind.

I hit the puddle on the tile with a gasp. The water soaked most of the front room of the Sun Sanctuary, where our friends must have poured it for easier reentry. Metztli groaned on her side, clutching her stomach. Had Tzitzimitl wounded her? She brushed Kit's hands away when he tried to check. I peeled my head up, panic and pain coursing through my blood. The Court of Fears. I looked down at the water, the panic rising higher, higher. They were gone. They couldn't be, really. Could they?

Several portals opened back up across the puddle. Juana dragged Metztli away before she fell into one.

"Cece, try to calm down!" Juana called. "You're opening portals. Just breathe."

I searched the room for help—Metztli was definitely in

pain—but the space felt darker than usual, with both the sun and moon gone. Only a single candle sat at the far side of the room, where Little Lion was just opening his eyes.

Lion rushed over in a streak of black and crouched over Metztli. "What happened?" he demanded. "She smells like blood—"

Kit rested Metztli gently on the floor.

"I will be all right," Metztli said, as she rolled onto her back.

I sat up shakily in the water. I could see a splotch of blood on Metztli's shirt, but Juana lifted it and found a single, long cut.

Juana sighed in relief. "It's not very deep." She pulled Metzli's shirt back down. "But you're going to have a pretty cool scar."

Metztli let out a shaky sigh and nodded appreciatively. "As I said—I will be all right." She looked to Lion on her other side. "Lion, go and wake everyone. We must inform them of what has transpired. We have lost the Moon's soul, and the Court of Fears has fallen."

Lion's eyes widened, and he shot off into the rest of the Sun Sanctuary so fast that his body blurred. His muffled voice echoed in the distance.

I turned back to Metztli. "Lo siento. I didn't listen when you told me—I should have just listened—" I choked on a knot of tears, and they poured down my face.

The portals cast eerie light across Metztli's skin. Her eyes saddened, and she reached for me. I slipped around my haphazard portals and squeezed her hand.

"Cecelia," she whispered. "I know this is all hard on you. I was hard on you. Pero, you must remember that even in such terrible times, the light has not gone out, and you are not alone." Her touch was kind as it brushed over the back of my hand. "The Court of Fears can be restored if we win this war, using Coyote's powers. For now, breathe, mija. Cálmate. Close the portals before . . ."

Her eyes moved to something behind me. People filtered into the room, so I thought it was that. But her gaze widened, and her hand grasped mine in a death grip. "Now, Cece! Close them!"

I twisted around. The portal at the center of the seven bubbled, so the reflection of the cenote in Devil's Alley jumped and bobbed. My breath withered in my gut. No. Not that body of water.

I swung my hands in a circle, and the portal shrank inward. Two silhouettes flashed on the other side. One— El Silbón. He reached a dark arm toward me in warning. But it was already too late.

Jaguar sprung up from the water of the cenote.

Everything seemed to hang weightless for a moment as

dread spread through my veins like dark, heavy ice. Jaguar's amber eyes flashed above me in the shadows. Her braids swung around to frame her focused expression, water droplets tracing her cheeks.

She plummeted toward me—claws first. I grabbed Metztli and rolled us out of her path.

Jaguar plowed into the wall instead.

The impact rang in my skull. I closed the rest of the portals in a hurry and stood, rounding up the leftover water into a rope, as Jaguar's arm dug into the wall, bricks crumbling around her. Metztli yelped.

"The Ocean's soul!" she cried. "Stop her!"

Juana and I jumped to our feet, Juana wobbling only slightly on her bad foot. Wait, Jaguar had hit the wall on purpose? That's where Metztli hid the soul? Jaguar rounded back on us with the turquoise stone gripped in her clawed hand. The blue light withered across her face, as if her touch—or perhaps the touch of the one controlling her—made the Ocean mourn.

"Let her go!" I slammed the water rope forward.

It faltered before I could hit Jaguar. I scrambled to move it right, but the weight in the water had changed, like something was off. Was it because she had the Ocean's soul? Or because the water couldn't hear my requests over the growing dark seam inside my chest? I recovered in a moment and swung it back against Jaguar. No matter what,

I had to protect the people I loved. She nearly dodged, but I caught her around the knee and sent her slamming into the broken remains of the mosaic.

She didn't stay down long. She pressed the Ocean's soul in the buttoned pocket of her dark pants, then leaped out of the jagged stones to dodge my next whip of water. I chased her with it across the room, aiming for her hand, or a way to take out her legs so she couldn't run. She moved just seconds faster than the water. She jumped up into the rafters above our heads. Kit growled and lunged up after her. I gasped as she turned and immediately dove for him. But he kicked out her feet, so she tumbled down to the floor with a crash. I swelled my water up, over her head, to unleash a crushing a wave.

"Wait!" Lion's voice roared.

I froze. Lion shot into place between the water and Jaguar. He held a hand out to me, silently demanding I hold back. I gaped.

"The Ocean's soul, Lion!" I whispered.

He nodded. He knew. I swallowed. But I could see it in his burning gaze, even with only one candle left in the room—tremendous and tremulous hope. This was his sister, after all. He'd do anything he could to save her.

I knew what that was like.

"Give me just a minute," he mouthed.

I hesitated. Metztli's eyes narrowed, but she didn't argue.

She probably saw the wisdom in it too. If Lion could get through to her, we could get the Ocean's soul back and take one of Catrina's criaturas from her at the same time. Slowly, I pulled my water back, wobbling as I went, and let it rest in the corner nearest me. I turned back to Lion and Jaguar, holding my breath.

"Jaguar, it's me." Lion crouched in front of her, where she lay curled in the dent she'd made in the tiled floor. His soul pulsed with colors of navy blue and spots of red.

Jaguar slowly rose to stand, and the two circled one another. Lion didn't blink once.

"It's me, tu hermano."

I squeezed my hands together, waiting, watching.

Lion's eyes flashed as he continued his circling. "I know this isn't you," he said. "This is the part of Catrina she left behind inside your soul. I remember how hard it is. But you have to fight it."

They moved around each other once, twice. Then gently, Lion lowered his battle posture, Jaguar across from him. He approached her. She stiffened, eyes flickering between the stone in her hand, him, and the door. My gut clenched.

Lion placed his hands on her strong, dark shoulders. Jaguar's dark eyes glistened.

"Come back," Lion whispered. "Come on. Come *back*, hermana."

Jaguar's hands shook. Slowly, they reached up to touch

Lion's face. Her head bowed to look down into his eyes. For the first time in a long time, Lion's soul flashed with brilliant beads of pink-tinged hope.

"Little Lion . . . ?" she whispered.

His lips wobbled up into a smile. "Sí. It's me. You're here. You're okay." He laughed. "We're going to be okay."

She stared at him, hands trembling. "I . . . feel lost."

"You don't have to be anymore," he whispered. Her hold tightened on his cheeks. He didn't seem to notice. "I'll rescue you this time, just like you did me—"

Behind them, the door that led into the rest of the Sun Sanctuary creaked open a few inches. Jaguar stiffened. Coyote's gold eyes glinted in the low candlelight. Whispers moved behind him, and he appeared to be herding people back, away from the fight, until it was safe. But Jaguar's eyes clouded again. Her claws flexed. Fear welled up in my throat, and I started pulling water back up from the floor.

Jaguar lurched forward and ripped her nails into both sides of Lion, gouging him from his face down to his shoulders and chest.

Lion let out a wild, pained roar.

I tore the water from the ground and slammed it into Jaguar's side. Heat and anger flooded up my throat. I poured the water against her, beating her with it, until she was trapped in a corner of the room. The water was difficult to control. Half ignoring my anger, half surging with my desire to protect. Coyote leaped out from the door and dove onto Jaguar's back. He fell into the water and put her into a headlock.

"Grab—Lion!" Coyote managed to yell over the water.

I pulled the deluge back, but Juana was already by Lion's side. He had collapsed on the ground, gasping, shuddering. She checked his wounds and came away with blood all over her hands.

"Everyone out of the sanctuary!" Metztli hollered for the people huddled behind the door. "¡Ahora, ahora!"

People stampeded out of the back of the building and rushed by the windows. On the ground, Coyote fought with Jaguar, trying to hold her still and captive. White tattoos glowed across his arm. Constellations began to wrap around them.

"Come on!" he yelled at her, as she elbowed him repeatedly in the ribs. Sweat covered his already exhausted face. "I'm—trying—to give you—your soul back!"

She twisted at the last second and caught his knee sideways with a kick. A horrible crack resounded through the sanctuary. My stomach lurched. Coyote's white tattoos winked out as he fell.

The moment she was free, Jaguar rounded on Lion, lying nearly unconscious, and Juana, who had her back to her. Jaguar patted the Ocean's soul, glowing only weakly now, in her pocket. I pulled all the water left in the Sanctuary up into a wave. Her eyes met mine. And then she raced for my friend and my sister.

I planted my feet and turned the water into a wall in front of them. It assembled, thick and sturdy, wide and strong. Jaguar's empty eyes barely seemed to notice it as it came up right in her path—

And then swerved at the last second for me.

Oh. Time slowed, and my heart beat in my ears. She'd been after me all along, hadn't she? Her claws extended toward my chest, reaching for the soul waiting beneath my shirt. I rushed to pull the water back, sweeping just a few droplets between me and her impending blow.

Metztli stepped between us, and Jaguar's claws found a new target.

Silence bloated in the room. I stood there, with a ringing in my brain instead of thoughts. Metztli's body swayed in front of me. A blossom of red soaked through the back of her clothes. Far deeper than the wound she'd had before.

I tried to say her name. But my lips wouldn't move.

Slowly, she slumped sideways, and crumpled, silent, to the floor.

Tears filled my eyes. Metztli's hair fell over her face in streaks and coils of black, all tipped with white. Her hands rested limp against the tiled floor. The glowing white in her nails shuddered—and then winked out completely. I reached down for her, wordless, weeping, hoping to comfort her, check on her.

Instead, Jaguar caught me by the throat. I gagged as she lifted me away, off the ground, so my feet dangled inches off the floor.

"You've been so proud of yourself for protecting everyone," she said in Catrina's voice. "Now that you can't, you're beginning to feel what I feel. Beginning to see the poison of helplessness. Aren't you?" she demanded.

Tears bulged in my eyes as I pried at Jaguar's hands. I couldn't speak. But I knew what Catrina meant. And the more she forced her voice through Jaguar, the bigger that feeling grew, a hailstorm where rain usually thrived.

"But guess what, Cece?" Jaguar pulled me so close I could feel her breath. Catrina's words came out hot and wrathful: "It's only going to get worse from here. Because I have a desert curandera. She'll find the Desert Sanctuary soon, and then you'll have lost all four gods' souls." In a high-pitched, singsong voice, she whispered, "I'm taking everything I deserve. Watch me. Take. It. All."

The Sun Sanctuary's entrance doors slammed open behind us. Jaguar's arm jogged, and I choked. I craned my neck as much as I could, which wasn't much, and spotted Mamá standing there, eyes on fire.

"Enough!" Mamá boomed, and sprinted forward. "This is between you and me, Catrina! Face me, you coward!"

Jaguar's face tightened with Catrina's exact scowl. "We'll see who's the coward when I leave you to mourn your chiquita, as I left you mourning our pathetic mamá."

I'd only seen Mamá truly afraid a few times in my life, when Juana or I were in danger. But the fear that stained her face now was completely different. It was an old fear. A fear so fermented and chilling that I could almost hear the distant screams of Abuela Etapalli, the night Mamá had watched her die.

And it drove her fist straight into Jaguar's face.

The blow turned Jaguar's head, but it didn't move the rest of her body. Fortunately, that's all we needed. Because now that she couldn't see Juana on her right, Juana lunged forward from Lion's side, fist covered in blinding fire.

"You mess with mi familia," Juana cried, "you mess with fire!"

Juana slammed her fist into the ground. Fire erupted toward us, and Jaguar released me to dodge back. Mamá dragged me away from the path of the flames, but they turned and followed Jaguar's movements instead. The fire caught her clothes, and she, looking at each of us, clutching the Ocean's soul through her pocket, growled.

She threw herself backward through the Sun Sanctuary's stained glass, fleeing into the desert.

17

Metztli's Goodbye

My friends hurried to take care of Lion's wounds. But I knelt at the center of the room, my breath hidden away deep in my lungs, as I stared down at Metztli's barely conscious body.

The leftover water on the Sun Sanctuary floor rippled with each of her shallow breaths. My hands shook as I reached out. Mamá placed a hand on my shoulder. Her warmth steadied me.

From Metztli's low and broken position, I felt the weak flickers of her soul.

Ah . . . it's time . . . , it whispered.

No! I gasped and brushed her hair back from her face. Metztli's eyelids peeled open. There was only a single dot of light left in each of her eyes.

I clutched her hand, and her skin grew cold against my fingertips. I tightened my hold, like that would keep her here. Despite everything, Metztli managed to smile at me.

I'd watched more people die than I'd wanted to by now. But this—seeing her smiling, wounded and tender—that somehow made it all the more painful.

"I wish I could have taught you more," she whispered. Her breath rattled slightly, the way Abuelo's had before he passed. "But you will do well without me. I know." She reached for me, and I leaned down so she could cup my cheek. Her hand was freezing cold.

"Teach Juana," she whispered. Her lips grew paler, ashy. "Find and encourage the desert curandera. You will need to lead them when I am gone, Cece."

I shook my head. Her smile didn't waver.

"You will have to lead them in the fight for that better world you ache for, Cecelia. Do not give up on that dream. It will come, but only if you do not forget what it will be made of." She stroked my bangs back. "Kindness. Joy. Love. All opposites, all antidotes, to the hate Catrina will try to deceive you into partaking of. Do not drink from that well, Cece. It will never fulfill its promises."

She clutched my shirt. My insides rang with panic, but I didn't dare speak, didn't dare miss any of the words she was so desperate to offer.

"Hold always to hope, Cece. If we give darkness for darkness, we sink into nothing. Remember that light creates light," she whispered, "and you will lead them into a future brighter . . . than the . . . moon."

Slowly, Metztli's hand slipped from my cheek and fell to her chest. I cupped both her hands gently between mine. They were soft. So heavy.

Metztli? I called out, hoping against truth, with my soul.

There was no response. Just the quiet, calm colors of her soul fading into the Great After.

My chest iced over into wintry silence. Everyone left in the Sun Sanctuary held their breaths as I folded her hands, like a prayer, over her heart. My vision smeared as tears filled my eyes.

Metztli had lived her whole life in a war.

And now, she'd died in it too.

Tears cracked through the ice. My soul flickered to life, first brighter, and then darker than ever as it strobed. A sob rocked my gut but wouldn't rise up my throat. I bent my forehead to Metztli's and clutched her shirt, weeping.

Juana, Kit, and Coyote all gathered around Metztli and me. I couldn't look at them. But their souls still reached for me. Worried yellow and aching purples from Kit. A red and sharp blue from Juana, the clash of anger and sorrow. And Coyote, with clashes of gray and pink in his soul again, fighting an age-old battle between hope—and pain. Beneath them all, Metztli stared sightlessly at the ceiling. I reached over and closed her eyes.

A clamor of voices grew beyond the entrance door. The

people of Tierra del Sol had gathered outside. So many were demanding answers. Asking about the attack. Their voices fluctuated with a torrent of feelings. Fear. Anger. Insecurity. Confusion.

"The queen of Devil's Alley sent her criatura to attack. She has killed the moon curandera," Santos was trying to explain, trying to gain control on the rising panic. "Metztli de la Luna sacrificed herself—"

"She's dead?"

"They've failed us *again*?"

The accusation rang in my ears, and I rose before I knew what I was doing. My jacket whipped behind me. I stomped across the tile floor, heart crystallizing.

"Cece," Juana called. "Cece, you don't have to see them. I'll talk to them for you—"

"Cece," Coyote's hand tried to touch mine, but I was moving too quick with my new icy edges. "I know what this feels like. But—"

Rage pounded in my head, and my body trembled with grief as I pushed through my friends to meet the faces of my ungrateful town. I thrust open the entrance doors, Metztli's touch fading from my palms.

The crowd hushed for a moment as I stepped out into the meager, red moonlight. A sea of my people looked up. The police stood toward the front, facing a sweaty, pained Santos, who waited at the end of the stairs. Neighbors and strangers raised their heads. People who'd shunned me all my life now looked to me, expecting *something* from me.

"You lost the Moon's soul?" a police officer demanded first. "Isn't that what you were supposed to be protecting?"

"Is the criatura that broke out of the Sun Sanctuary just free in our cerros? Will it come after my children? Weren't you curanderas supposed to protect us?"

"I knew this would never work!" someone spat. "Everything this girl touches is cursed!"

"Speak, chiquita!" yelled a woman who lived on my street.

"Say something!" someone screamed.

It was so *unfair.*

I hadn't been able to save Metztli, but she had sacrificed herself for me. She had been ready to sacrifice herself for these people. These ungrateful, ignorant, cruel people. Anger tore the dark seam in my chest wider. It was the kind of anger I'd felt toward El Sombrerón. The kind I now felt toward Jaguar. The crowd blurred into villains as panic swirled in my gut.

"You—" I started. "I—I—"

Don't say hate. I wrestled with the word in my mouth. The weight of their stares slammed me in the chest.

Expressions boiled from confusion into concern into anger and then fear and resentment. I didn't want to care about how they felt. I wanted them to have to carry it all themselves. But even as I fought, the colors of their souls—clashing yellows, whites, blues, reds—merged with Metztli's last words.

If we give darkness for darkness, we sink into nothing. Light creates light. And you will lead them into a future brighter than the moon.

My fists trembled. The dark seam in my chest shuddered with the pain and resentment, and I had no idea where to put it. Tears burned in the back of my eyes, but they wouldn't rise, not with so much ice inside. I wished I could have responded to Metztli. *It's not right!* I would have said. *They give darkness for light, and there's no way for me to stop them. How do I save the light, when they want to drown it?*

I wanted to turn away from the watching, yelling crowd. For the first time in my life, I didn't want to help them at all. They were the ones smothering the chance for a better future.

The curandera sacrificed herself? For us? That's so . . . sad.

A single, quiet soul voice floated through the air, all in blues and sorrows.

I raised my head. A woman with thick eyebrows and gentle eyes caught my gaze from the center of the masses.

She'd sold tortillas in the market since I was little: Rosa, la Señora Gutierrez's granddaughter. She bit her lip and clutched her son to her. He gripped her skirts in return. They both stared at me, silently, waiting for me to speak. Hoping. Despite everything.

There were no demands. There were no accusations. Rosa watched with fear, and love, and a feeble but brilliant hope for the future of her son, her home.

Cecelia Rios will help us, won't she? her soul asked.

My fist slowly unraveled.

The dark seam in my chest was still there. But the words coming from it began to wither. Tears finally flooded my vision, melting the ice. I lifted my head higher but fixed my gaze to Rosa and her son alone. For her, I found the words I truly wanted. The ones Metztli had left for me.

"Metztli the moon curandera sacrificed her life to save me. . . and all of us," I called out. "Catrina, the Cager of Souls, my tía, the new queen of Devil's Alley, has sent her willing bruja armies and their unwilling criaturas to come against us."

A hush spread across the crowd. For some, it was an angry one. Others, fearful. Rosa held her son closer, trepidation etched on her face.

"I know you're scared," I said. My voice cracked. The water in my chest bubbled over and swept across the dark seam, cleansing the wound. Tears fell down my face. "I am too. But I learned that courage means moving forward anyway. I learned I was strong. I learned I wasn't alone."

I reached out my hands. Coyote knew, like he always knew, and stepped forward to take it. Mamá took the one on my left. We stood before them, criatura and curandera and human.

"If we do as Metztli wanted and stand together, we can *stop* Queen Catrina. Today, we can stand together as Tierra del Sol was always meant to, to unite against true evil, not just those we've typically considered enemies. To stand for what's right against those who wish to crush us, not those who are also hurt and harmed. I—"

The word stuck in my throat. Mamá squeezed my hand. Coyote's soul twined around mine, warm and steady. Though it was hard, I lifted my head.

"I will lead you," I called. My voice echoed over the shattered square. Rosa's eyes lit up. "You are my people. This is our home. Por favor, help me save *us*."

Fear and anger battled across the faces of Tierra del Sol. One of the police officers turned to Santos. "You can't seriously expect us to put our lives in this chiquita's hands!"

"Why not?" Juana tore out from behind us and descended the stairs. Her nostrils flared, and the police officer flinched a little at her wild, burning stare. "Do you even know who you're talking about? When none of you could help me, when no one had ever rescued a bride of El Sombrerón before, my *little* sister, Cece—she saved me." She turned to me, and my reflection looked bigger in her eyes.

Below us, a red dress shifted to the front of the crowd. Lesvia stood below us, hand in hand with a couple of other brides I hadn't met yet.

"No one had ever rescued a bride of El Sombrerón," Lesvia repeated. She met Juana on the last stair and placed a hand on her shoulder. Her eyes were bright and determined as she faced Tierra del Sol. "And now we're *all* home. I, for one, believe in light when it shines. I believe in Cecelia Rios."

The words rippled through the masses, with a power and hope that stirred them. The agreement of the brides of El Sombrerón traveled with them. The speech tugged inside my soul. The colors of the people began to change. There were still red, angry threads, but Rosa smiled, and tenuous hope stretched across my people in brightening pinks and strengthening spots of orange.

Juana's eyes flickered with gold light. "So, Cece?" she asked for everyone. "What do we do next?"

I was still unsure if this was really possible, with such

a fractured group. But the brides believed. Rosa believed. And more and more souls were looking for that light Metztli had spoken of.

So it was worth trying for.

"We need to find the Desert Sanctuary," I said. "Before Catrina gets there first."

18
The Taken Things

I watched Santos, Ocelot, Coyote, and Mamá bury Metztli under the crimson moonlight.

Juana and I stood beside them, holding candles that she'd lit with her bare hands, to offer light in the falsely imposed darkness. The air was cold and numbed the tip of my nose. I watched my breath fade upward, into the sky, streaking across the lost, red moon. Metztli looked peaceful, as they laid her in the ground. I hoped she was.

She deserved peace, after living only in conflict.

"Come, Cece," Mamá was the first to whisper. She wrapped her arms around me. "You need to rest."

"But the vigil . . . ," I whispered. When Abuelo had died, we'd spent the night after his burial eating his favorite foods, reciting his favorite songs, praying that he would make it safely to the Great After. Metztli should have at least the same.

"I think the best vigil for Metztli would be completing

all she sacrificed for," Mamá said, as she guided me back inside. "And you cannot do that without sleep."

Mamá was right. I was exhausted, deep down to the bone, deep down to the heart. The dark seam in my chest was cold and sharp on its edges, gaping wide, even as I worked to pull it shut. Seeing Rosa and all those who had listened had helped give me the strength to fight it. But watching Metztli sleep in the earth? That pushed back, just as hard.

"I can't even give her a proper vigil . . . ," I mumbled, aching in purples and grays, as Mamá led me up to the attic of the Sun Sanctuary.

"We will give her the full celebration on the Day of the Great After, next year," Mamá said, and kissed my forehead. She pulled back the blanket on my cot, and I slid obediently inside. She placed the crochet cover over me and patted my shoulder.

"Catrina took her life, Mamá," I whispered.

She stared at me, and that old pain waited in her dark eyes as it always had. She nodded and stroked my hair.

"Just like she took Abuela's," I said, voice hushed and tight. "Just like she took Coyote's, and tried to take Lion's, and why? How can we fight against someone who's so . . ."

I didn't have words for it. But the dark seam in my chest cracked open a half inch wider. I winced. Mamá took my hand and sat down next to me on the cot. For a while, all she did was stare out the Sun Sanctuary windows, across the various beds that we'd set up across the room, and the few already-sleeping bodies lying there. Blue and red soaked the room from the outdoors, so we felt caught between times. Daybreak and sunset. Night and dawn. Hope and hopelessness.

"Sí," Mamá finally said, and deep, navy blue grief poured out of her soul. "Catrina has taken many lives now. She has taken much. I think it is because she always . . . needed something. She needed to feel bigger. She needed someone else's happiness. Is it all my fault? I wonder. Because I couldn't sing to her enough? I didn't let her win enough times in our games? I couldn't dedicate enough of myself to her? I couldn't stop the way Abuelo was, only placate him?" Mamá closed her eyes and squeezed my hand. "I do not know. I wish I had been able to give it to her. But then, I wonder: Would anything have been enough?"

Mamá had never talked so much about her relationship with Catrina before. But the echoes of their life together entwined with her questions, and the aching, the sorrow, the terrible fallout of Catrina's actions made the dark seam in my chest widen even further. Mamá kissed my forehead again.

"I used to sing a song to her," Mamá said. "She'd stay up so often at night crying, so scared, so angry. It grew worse every year. By the time she was fourteen, she couldn't sleep at all if I didn't sing it and rub her back."

I looked up at her. "What song was it?"

Mamá rubbed her thumb over my hand. "I haven't sung it since she left."

We looked at each other. I waited, watching her expression, wondering whether that meant she hated the memories the song carried—or loved them too much to bear. Mamá smiled, and it looked like it hurt her to do so, but she smiled for me all the same. I squeezed her hand.

Slowly, her mouth filled with music, and she sang what she'd hidden away long ago:

> *Between the cerros y montañas,*
> *there lies the town where I was born,*
> *with memories of the mornings*
> *that I so happily lived.*

> *Tierra del Sol, that's my homeland,*
> *little enchanting town,*
> *with your ruins and legends*
> *you tell me of your tradition.*

Mamá stroked my hair. The song was so filled with warmth, but so much loneliness, so much sorrow, all at the same time. My eyes fell closed. Exhaustion pulled at the dark seam in my chest, and I felt myself slipping away into sleep.

In your lovely climate
and eternal spring,
our happy little corner thrives
because someone loves you.

I fell asleep clinging to Mamá's hand and the notes of her old song. And despite the sadness, the grief, and all there was to do, dreams still found me.

I was back in the white void all strung with currents of souls passing Catrina and me on either side of the table. Catrina was shuffling the rest of the lotería deck. We weren't finished with our game.

Slowly, Catrina placed the stack between us again. She lifted her dark, empty eyes to me.

"Draw, Cece," she said.

The deck caught the passing colors with its glossy face. I glared at Catrina, barely looking away from her, as I snapped a card up from the pile. I flipped it over. Beneath the streaks of roaming light, I caught the title: "El Cenote." It wasn't on either of our bingo sheets. But I swallowed at the image of the cenote in the dungeon of Devil's Alley.

The one that had been our escape. And the one I hadn't been able to stop myself from connecting to. The one I hadn't closed in time.

The reason Jaguar had come through. The reason Metztli was gone.

That dark seam inside me ripped open. I clutched my chest and gasped in pain. The air felt clogged, suddenly, as I breathed in reds and navy blues and acidic purples. My hands shook over my lotería card. My gaze rose to meet Catrina. She smirked. She knew exactly what it meant, and she regretted nothing.

"I hate you," I said.

It came out a whisper. But it grew. It swelled into an explosion, a careening flood after the breaking of a dam. My body trembled. My soul hurt and bled around the dark seam. I couldn't even believe I'd said it, the word I'd been avoiding, the one I knew Catrina had been looking for, provoking me to say. But it was true. And I wished with every fiber that it wasn't.

"I hate you," I said again, on a sob. *"I—hate—you."*

"Good," Catrina hissed.

She slammed her hands on the table and rose, eyes like haunted nights. My soul jerked, hot and scared. Dark streaks of color began to surround her, gathering like feathers in her hair.

"I *want* you to hate me," she said, low and sizzling. "Feel how I feel, Cece. Come swim in the mud with me for the first time in your innocent little life." She lowered her chin and grinned wide, manic, intent. "Hate is the opposite of the Ocean's strength. It will degrade your power, but it gives me mine. So come for me, Cece." She stroked her hair back, so the dark colors rustled with her movement. "In this battle, I will defeat you."

I trembled before her. Streaks of pained and malicious purples surrounded her in the air, doubling, only growing the more they were fed. I dropped the bean I'd been holding. It spun in the air—before landing on the last picture's tile, perfectly situated in the middle of my card. Metztli's face lay underneath, "La Luna" scripted beneath her pale, peaceful expression. Catrina looked down at it. She didn't have it on her sheet. Niether did I.

"Unfortunate that you couldn't keep that one," she said. "Isn't it, Cece?"

Tears burned my eyes. She was right. A sick feeling, like the soul equivalent to vomit, rose up inside me. I lifted my head to meet Tía Catrina's expression.

And jumped when she stared back at me in the form of an eleven-year-old.

I gasped. She looked so much like herself, but with bigger eyes, a shorter physique, and—I swallowed—dark cracks opening up in her skin, like she was made of ceramic instead of flesh and skin. She glanced at her shattering hand as her surprise deepened to fear.

"Oh," she said. A crack broke open wider across her terrified face. "You weren't meant to see me like this."

19
The Long and Endless Hope

I woke with a gasp and shot upright in my bed.

I was covered in cold sweat. I pulled my blankets up to my chin and bundled myself tight in the colored stripes. What was that dream? It felt so real. I shook myself and shoved back my covers, ready to get up and tell Metztli about my dream, to ask her what she thought it meant—

I froze. Oh. I stared out the nearest window, where the moon hovered like a streak of blood in the endless night sky.

My throat tightened, and my ribs felt like they'd crack like hail against stone.

Metztli was gone. What was I supposed to do now?

I stared across the room, where all my criatura friends lay sleeping in the cots I'd noticed earlier. Little Lion lay resting on the far side, framed by the window. He was bandaged across his middle, and patched up across his neck and face. His chest shuddered every once in a while, distressed, even in sleep.

I padded over to where he lay. As I neared, I spotted a woman who was hunched against his bed. For a second, I thought it was Juana—but it was actually Mamá. She'd fallen asleep with one hand on the inside of his wrist— checking the steadiness of his pulse. She must have gone right from my bedside to his.

There was something deeply beautiful about watching Mamá sleep by Little Lion's side. The dark ache inside me subsided as I watched them. The boy who'd hated humans because of Catrina. And the woman who'd once been ferocious to criaturas because of her past with Catrina. Both of them, now together. Little Lion, trusting Mamá enough to let her tend to him. Mamá, now trying to preserve the criaturas she'd once feared.

Tears welled in my eyes. But I was too tired for them to fall. Slowly, I turned away.

Something caught my hand. I turned to find Little Lion's red eyes cracked open, glowing in the dark.

"I'm sorry," he whispered.

My heart squeezed. He didn't need to explain what he was apologizing for. The image of Metztli lying on the ground pulsed through the air between us, and I wasn't sure if it was from my soul or his.

"I thought—I thought I could get through to Jaguar . . ." He sucked in a hard breath and swallowed, like he was fighting back sobs.

I'd never seen Lion so overcome with pain. Internal and physical, all at the same time. But for the first time, I couldn't tell him I didn't mind, and it was fine. I couldn't comfort him.

Someone had died yesterday. And it had been someone I loved.

Lion nodded, like he knew. I squeezed his hand, so he'd know I wasn't angry—not with him—and nodded.

"It—it wasn't your fault" was the best I could bring myself to say.

Lion's eyes glazed with tired tears. "It's not Jaguar's either," he whispered. "It's not anyone *else*'s fault but Catrina's."

My chin clenched. I knew he was right. But that dark, icy seam in my chest was open too wide, and my soul dimmed.

"You know that," Lion said, with an edge of fear. "Right, Cece?"

I did know. I knew I couldn't judge Jaguar when her soul had been manipulated by soul language, and Catrina had left so many invisible scars there. But grief bloated in my chest. Hatred tried to pull at my skin. And the struggle to keep it far below my hope was the hardest I'd ever fought.

Lion's eyebrows shot up as I released his hand, unable to

answer, and turned to the door.

I'm going to take everything you love, Catrina's voice rippled through the air. My stomach turned as her voice crawled up the stone tiles. *I'll take your hopes and your friends. Your power and your familia.*

Her words haunted me as I moved through the building. I wished I couldn't hear her. Was this how Jaguar felt? With Catrina lingering in the back of her mind, soul language crossing worlds and crawling through stone to get to her? How was I supposed to combat that?

I'm getting close to the Desert Sanctuary, Cece, she taunted. *What will you do when I have everything you wanted?*

I couldn't tell if she was lying to scare me even more, or if she was telling the truth and I was going to lose everything in moments. I shuddered, breath cold and thin. My knees shook as I wandered through the silent halls of the sanctuary. Her voice shook my very soul stone, where it swung beneath my shirt, over my beating heart. I needed something stronger to hang on to. Something to drive Catrina back.

You don't have anything strong enough to drive me *back*, Catrina's thin voice crawled in the walls around me.

The tears dropped silently onto my cheeks and rolled down my chin. I rubbed my eyes, and when I looked up, I found myself in the Sun Sanctuary's main room, standing before the shattered mosaic. The gathered, broken pieces glittered in the low, red moonlight. The stones of the four sibling gods stared back at me, surrounded by their creations—criaturas, animals, humans, stars.

I dropped into the front pew before the mosaic. Pain and grief pulled at the cynical seam in my chest. I fought to pull it back together, but tears just pooled back up into my eyes. I bowed my head and sobbed. Because I was more scared than ever. Not just of Catrina. Not just of what was out of my control, even though there was a lot.

For the first time in my life, I was scared of myself. How could I trust my heart, when, for the first time, it so badly wanted to hate evil more than it wanted to love what was good?

"Cecelia Rios. Why are you awake?"

I looked up, face dripping. Santos sat beside me on the pew, his arm bandaged and laced up against his chest in a sling. He still looked sweaty and stressed, but clearly concerned. I dropped my head to hide my tears. He clucked his tongue and put his good arm around me. I leaned into him, and he shushed me gently.

"Every good leader cries," he whispered. "You have earned your tears, Cece Rios. Go ahead and grieve."

Even though I was scared to, I buried my face into his side and cried.

"It's not fair!" My soul exploded with warring colors.

"This town—Catrina—all I want to do is try to help, and put things back together so we can all be happy, and all they do is make sure *none of us can be*! Why? And I'm trying so hard not to hate them, because I don't want to. I don't! Why is it so difficult?"

Feelings mixed together inside me, like a tornado crashing together in hot winds and cold surges.

"Sí," Santos said. "You have said it well, Cecelia."

I looked up, shaking, tears clogging my throat. He— wasn't mad at me? Santos was well loved in our community. He'd been known as a strong, powerful, and fair chief of police. And he—understood how I was feeling? Me, the outcast? The hated curandera?

His eyes were dark in the night, but his expression was soft. "It *is* hard for good people to hold on to hope. It is even harder for good leaders to do so. To hope that the sacrifices we make for the light will matter. That a better world *can* be made, even as others throw stones at the structures we build."

He released a long, deep sigh. It didn't sound the way Papá's had, like I was the one sucking the air and life out of him. Santos sighed like he'd breathed the same air as me before, and knew how hard it was to let it free.

"To try to lead people, you must see them in all their horror and their beauty—and fight for the beauty anyway." He gestured outside, where a mixture of police and volunteers were patrolling the building. They'd had so many cases of people trying to attack, they had regular watches now. "I know you know how to do this. It is why you were able to make friends with our ancient enemies, dark and animal criaturas. And it is why they chose the love you offered, after a thousand years of injustice." Santos reached out and rested his palm on my temple. "Do not let other people's hatred steal your love, Cecelia. It is too beautiful to be diminished."

I paused, under his warm, firm touch. When I was very little, Papá used to hold me just like this. Just sometimes. I used to love it. It was the most affectionate he ever got. Now, the chief of police, who I would have thought would have had cause to hate me more than anyone, was gentler and more encouraging than my papá had ever been.

He nodded with understanding eyes. They knew pain. His soul, the colors a bit more tangible now, flickered with fear, and strength, and hope.

"It is hard now for us," he said. "But we are Naked Man. We survived our first winter. We survived our first burning summer. The desert became our home. And now, we have you. We have Cecelia Rios, the curandera who can hear the gods. We will be all right, so long as we do not falter. It will simply take patience—and endurance. It will take surrendering to hope's promise."

My soul soaked in every single word. He stroked my

hair and nodded with a reassurance that I'd never been able to look to a father for. I gripped his jacket in my hands. He didn't seem to mind.

He was right. We had survived. And if we could do so a bit longer, we could thrive. I could hear the gods, and I would find the Desert Sanctuary before Catrina, and—

I gasped. Santos jumped.

"I can hear the gods," I whispered. My mind whirled, and I leaped up from the pew. "Damiana said she's been hearing something—a voice. I didn't realize before but—but there can be only one thing she's hearing!" I whirled around and faced Santos.

He looked confused but nodded like he hoped that would help.

"Damiana is the desert curandera!"

He blinked. "The bruja? Is that possible?"

I laughed. "I was a bruja once too. It's kind of how I discovered my powers. It's how I learned soul language!"

Hope started again like a dazzling waterfall inside me, and it scrubbed away the dark seam. The edges were still there, but buried beneath the mighty flow. I threw my arms up.

"Do you know what this means, Santos?"

He was clearly trying to catch up. "We . . . have three curanderas again?"

"¡Sí!" I cried, and started jumping on my toes. "And that

means we have a chance of finding the Desert Sanctuary!"

I charged into the rest of the Sun Sanctuary, flying through the hall, and ripped open the door to Damiana's room.

"Damiana!" I burst.

She leaped out of bed, hair askew, and checked on where Axolotl was sleeping. Then she stumbled around to look at me.

"Cece?" she blinked, dazed and befuddled. "What's wrong? Is there a fight?"

"Damiana! The voice you said you've been hearing— can you still hear it?"

Her cheeks flushed. "Ah, Cece. It's probably nothing."

"No, Damiana!" I bounced on my toes. "It's something inside of you that needs to connect with you. Can you still hear it?"

She hesitated. Then nodded. "Sí," she whispered.

I beamed. "Damiana, you're going to save us all!"

Damiana stood out in the desert, traced in the red light of the moon. It caught on the snake and rose embroidery down her lapels and highlighted the edges of her spiky black hair, before hitting her hot-pink irises and sharp white fangs.

All in all, she looked every inch a bruja. Every bit the image of destruction.

But I knew her. Her choices weren't destruction. Her future wasn't destruction. I smiled up at her. Even faced with the insecurity etched into her expression, I was confident, standing side by side with Axolotl, Juana, and Coyote. I'd woken them up in a rush, but they'd come all the same.

Axolotl was rubbing her eyes. "Why are we up again? Mamá said if I don't sleep all night I'll never get taller."

"We should put her back in bed," Damiana said, hunching. "We don't want to get her hopes up . . ."

Axolotl's bulgy, pink eyes opened wide. "What am I

getting my hopes up about?" she bobbed on her toes so her finlike hair bounced. "They're already up! What is it? Do I get to stop reading?"

Damiana cracked a smile. I muffled a chuckle.

"It's not that," I said.

Axolotl deflated a bit, but I stepped forward, facing Damiana. I cupped my palms together, holding the left-over pieces of stone that had fallen off Mother Desert's mosaic.

Slowly, I extended the agate toward her. "It's about how tu mamá is a desert curandera. She can hear Mother Desert and lead us to the lost Desert Sanctuary."

Coyote's eyes brightened. "You can?" His lips quirked up, so his fangs glinted too. "Damiana, that's great!"

She shifted uncomfortably and very obviously avoided looking at the outstretched coyamito agate. "Can't Coyote find it? I'm sure he has a far greater connection to Mother Desert."

"But I didn't make the Desert Sanctuary," he said. His mismatched brows tugged together. "I helped design it with the desert curanderas, but I left before construction started. We planned it so desert curanderas were the only ones who could open its doors." He squinted, gaze far away. Distant, old memories wound around his soul. Both good and bad. Those forced back on him by Metztli—and those he pulled on with all his strength. "We wanted to keep it safe from brujas," he admitted.

Damiana scrunched into herself and stepped back from the agate.

"You're not a bruja anymore," I reminded her, reaching out for her with my soul. But where I hoped to feel the pink of love or the gold of hope, Damiana's soul had retreated from my calm touch into cold, blue corners. Familiar darkness.

"I'm grateful you've let me stay with you and that you trust I have turned my back on brujería. But that's not the same as being a *curandera*," Damiana whispered. Her hand shook as she reached up to her forehead, to the Mark of the Binding still carved into her skin. "I belong to El Cucuy. That means I am Quetzalcoatl's, and now Catrina's because she owns him." She lowered her hands to her sides. "Even if I wanted to be a desert curandera, young Cecelia, I am simply . . . unworthy."

A flash of pain roared up in my chest. I'd seen that face before, the one Damiana wore. I'd worn it myself. I knew its lies, and I knew the truth now.

"You are *not* unworthy!" I said—and Juana's voice merged with mine.

We looked at each other. Right. Damiana had been there in some of Juana's hardest, worst moments. Juana's soul swelled with orange ribbons of determination. She nodded, and together, we stepped up to Damiana, reaching for her retreating.

"Damiana," I started. "You changed your life around. You protected Axolotl. You've risked your life to help us stop Catrina's destruction and takeover. You are *worthy*." My eyes filled with tears. "I think the real problem is that you still feel like you're not worth*while*."

"And that can change too," Juana said. "I asked you once, before I went through the silver doors, to come with me. You weren't ready then, and that's okay. But you are now." She laid a hand on Damiana's shoulder. "Come with us. Help us find the Desert Sanctuary."

Damiana's eyes shone with moisture, even in the moon's crimson light. "The Desert goddess is commanding and unshakable," she whispered. "She was known for her voice, that by her simple command all things bended to her will. I didn't even have the strength to leave Devil's Alley on my own. I can't handle power like that."

"I don't think you understand, Damiana," Coyote spoke up.

Damiana didn't step away again. She met Coyote's burning golden eyes, and there was something new in her face now. Something like searching. Something like hope.

"Mother Desert is not dominion or cruelty. She's not

dryness or wrath or command. Mother Desert is creation and compassion. She's stability and reliability." His eyes met hers. "She's a *home*, Damiana. She's the home you've always wanted."

Damiana's lips separated in a long, awed breath.

Juana gently rocked her shoulder. "You sacrificed just about everything so you could make a better life for Axolotl. You even fought to protect her from me. *You* are a home too, Damiana," she said. "But you have to believe in that part of you to give it power. Trust me." She moved her hand to rest over her own heart. "I would know."

"The only thing standing between you and being a curandera," I jumped in, "is your choice. That's how it was for me. That's how it was for Juana. That's how it was . . . for Metztli." My voice softened with her name.

Axolotl nestled into Damiana's side, peering up at her with all the faith in the world. "Come on, Mamá," she said. "I know you can do it. You're the best person I ever met."

Damiana's entire frame trembled. The white and blue terror swam around her soul, but gold and pink began to rise. I lifted the agate again to her, reaching for her, hoping for her. She looked to the stones. Slowly, she placed her hand over them. I held my breath. But her hand froze, hovering, not approaching. Still struggling to believe.

"I agree with them," a voice said.

Footsteps sounded behind me. I looked over my shoulder just as Ocelot stopped a foot away. She gazed at Damiana and offered a single nod.

"You will be as strong a desert curandera," Ocelot said, "as any who came before you. You are no bruja, Damiana."

Damiana straightened to her full height, as tall as Ocelot. Her chin trembled, but the shiver in her hand slowly, quietly, disappeared. My soul buzzed, and hers rose with brighter and brighter colors. Finally, she lowered her hand and grabbed the coyamito agate in a firm, steadfast hold.

The shards glowed a bright, beautiful burgundy.

"Let's go," Damiana said, and flickers from the agate danced across her strengthening smile. "It's time to save the Desert."

"We need to pack our things for the journey," I said, rushing into the Sun Sanctuary. "Ocelot, can you come with us now that your arm is healed?"

"Sí," she answered simply.

"I'll grab my things," Damiana said in a flurry.

We all hurried to get our things together. Coyote helped me pack a bag up in the attic, but before we were about to leave, Juana called us from across the room.

"It's Lion," she said. "I think something's wrong."

We assembled by his bedside near the window. Lion was

shivering, covered in sweat under his bandages. I clasped my hands together, holding my breath. His soul was a blizzard of confusing colors. Coyote leaned over and checked his forehead.

"He's got a fever," he said as he straightened up. "I think the wound's infected."

I hadn't known criaturas could get sick like we did. There was still a lot about my friends I needed to learn. I scanned over Lion's damp, weak frame, heart aching as his eyes flickered beneath his eyelids. It was scary, watching someone as strong and commanding as Lion look so helpless.

"I wish I could heal him," I whispered. "The old texts said ocean curanderas could sometimes heal the body when they were strong enough. But—but I don't know how. And now that Metztli's . . ."

I finally understood why it had been so hard for Mamá to say Juana's name when she'd been taken. It was a reminder that someone you loved wasn't there anymore. And that knowledge ached like a welt on the inside of my chest, where my soul used to be.

"I thought criaturas were supposed to heal fast," Juana said.

Coyote shook his head. "Our bodies have to fight sickness just like a human body does, and that means we don't have the same energy dedicated to healing wounds."

Juana's hands bundled into fists as she looked down at Lion, where he dozed in a stormy-looking sleep. His soul was cluttered with a mishmash of brown and drippy colors. Not quite awake. Not quite asleep. He was in a limbo of pain, and my soul ached with him.

Lion suddenly gasped and gripped his side, and Juana dove to sit beside him.

"Hey, hey, gato." She pushed back his spiky hair. "Just rest." She looked up at me. Her eyes were bright, sharp. Just the hint of a glow. "I can't believe Jaguar did this to him. You know she's like his sister." She stroked his hair as he settled down.

"Jaguar didn't have a choice," I said. Because Lion had said so, and he was right, even if I still felt only that smaller, but still present, dark seam of resentment when I pictured her in my head.

"Doesn't she?" Juana asked. She didn't ask it the way I'd expected it—with an answer in mind. She asked it like she was afraid that she and Jaguar were the same. Like she was wondering how much room for forgiveness there was, when you've hurt others out of your own pain.

"I guess I can't know," Juana whispered.

I watched heat and light wrestle in her eyes. "But I know we have to find a way to stop Catrina, Cece. Before she does more of *this*." She rested her hand on Lion's cheek and looked up at me. "Whatever it takes."

Whatever it takes, her soul echoed. Gooseflesh rose across my arms at Juana's declaration, at the unmoving decision filling her soul across the space between us. And I had the sudden, terrible feeling that she meant it.

"Cece," Coyote's voice called.

I turned. He stood a few feet away now, by the stained glass window. There were a couple of low stubs of candles nearby, their gold light flickering off the ends of his multi-colored hair. He looked so serious that my knees locked. I wasn't sure I wanted to hear whatever it was he had to say.

It's important, his soul beckoned.

I forced my feet forward, leaving Lion and Juana together, my bag abandoned at the foot of the bed. Coyote offered his hands. I hesitated to take them but slowly placed mine in his.

"Is this about whatever it is you've been keeping from me?" I couldn't bear to wait any longer, so I had to ask.

He smiled lopsidedly. "Sí."

"Is it about fighting Catrina?" Anxiety curled in my stomach.

He nodded, and the smile waned. "Sí."

He didn't speak for another moment, as the distant sounds of Damiana packing downstairs roamed up the hall and through the room. I swallowed. Grief rose in my soul, and it tangled in the ribbons of Coyote's determination.

"If anything goes wrong today," he began, voice soft, eyes low, "and Catrina gets her hands on all four gods' souls, we could be facing her entire army in a matter of hours."

I shook my head. "It won't come to that! We have Damiana now and everything!"

"But if it does," Coyote said, cutting through my desperation, "you know we need a plan B, right?" He looked for my confirmation.

I pressed my lips together. This felt a lot like what Juana was just saying, and I didn't like it. But I nodded. He was right, and I couldn't deny that, even if anxiety was already crawling up my veins.

Coyote's thumbs brushed over the back of my knuckles. "I have an idea. I've been working on it as I've been bringing the brides of El Sombrerón back one by one. The thing is—Kit was right. What he said, yesterday?"

He looked at me. I nodded; I remembered the impassioned speech well.

"Because we have souls on the outside of our bodies, we can keep coming back when we die, but we come back as a thinner, weaker, waned version of ourselves. It's exhausting." He bit his lip. "And the bruja army—they use that to their advantage. They use criaturas' souls to their advantage. So . . . what if they couldn't use any criatura souls anymore?" He finally lifted his gaze to mine, and his eyes flashed like a burning forge.

I stiffened. I could see exactly where this was going, and even though part of it was genius, I shook my head.

He pushed forward anyway. "If I could Name their souls back into their bodies, where they should have been all along, then Catrina wouldn't have an army anymore. It wouldn't even matter that *we* barely have one." I shook my head harder. He nodded faster. "And El Sombrerón and Quetzalcoatl's souls would be back inside them too—don't you see, Cece?"

I did see. It was fantastic. Brilliant. But I also couldn't help seeing the downside, the problem, the unthinkable consequence: "What would happen to *you*?" I asked, voice thin and tight.

Coyote had been restoring more brides every day, and he looked *exhausted*. Every single one he pushed himself to do seemed to add years, and he now had almost permanent-looking bruises beneath his eyes, weariness hanging in his gold orbs, weak and wavery hands, even as he gripped mine. Coyote looked away for a second. My heart raced.

"It could kill you, couldn't it?" I asked. "Naming is

draining you, and you'd be doing, like, thousands all at once, not just in a few days. That's what you're suggesting, isn't it?"

He nodded.

I gripped his hands in an anaconda-tight squeeze. "And you're completely vulnerable while you're Naming! If you wanted to get all the criaturas, you'd have to wait until they were all in the same battlefield, wouldn't you? And they'd be targeting you. How'd we stop them from killing you?"

He smiled ruefully and met my gaze again. There was too much confidence there. No—too much determination. It swelled in oranges and burgundies and pinks up his soul and poured around me in waves. My hands shook as I tightened my grip on him.

"You'd have to protect me," he said. His voice grew low and scratchy. "And sí, I may die. But it could win us the entire war. Save tu familia, mi familia. Cece, this might be the only way for us to win now."

My breath caught. I wanted to save everyone. But Metztli had told me, in the sea, under the storm, that sacrifice couldn't be outrun. And she'd proven it, with her own. Tears burned my eyes, and my chin crumpled. Did that mean I'd have to lose everyone now? Be willing to?

Could I still believe in a better world if it was paved on the graves of the people I loved?

I shook my head again and again, grappling with the question, but Coyote just leaned forward until I stopped. He rested his forehead against mine.

"I'm always here for you," he said. "I always will be, even if I can't be next to you."

My breathing quivered. It was a painful promise. "You said this idea was just plan B."

"Sí," he agreed, his bangs tangling with mine.

"Then we have to keep it plan B," I said, voice nearly dissolving into tears. "Promise?"

He nodded. "Sí. Okay, it'll stay plan B."

"I'll get the Desert's soul," I said.

He nodded.

"I will."

He pulled me into a hug, and I gripped his red, worn shirt in my hands. He smelled like sweat and cold and clear rain. I squeezed my eyes closed.

"You all don't have to be so sad," a voice piped up.

Coyote and I pulled apart and looked back at Juana and Lion. Axolotl had appeared beside them, carting a bunch of books in her arms. Lion peeked a tired eye open as she plopped on down beside him, pried open one of my old alphabet books, and shook out her fanned pink hair. She cleared her throat proudly.

"I'll keep Lion company while you're doing all your war stuff," she said, and gestured Juana, Coyote, and me away. She cleared her throat again and pointed to the first sentence on page one. "*A* is for *abeja*," she started.

Lion's brows tugged together. "I don't—"

"It's okay," she said, and patted his hand. "I'll teach you to read."

A laugh kicked against my throat. Coyote muffled a snort, and Juana hung her head to hide a grin. Lion sighed as Axolotl kept reading.

"See?" Coyote whispered to me, still hovering by my ear. "She's part of that better world we're fighting for. You've risked your life for it plenty of times." He moved back to look me in the eyes. "Now I'm willing to sacrifice to put back together things that I helped pull apart."

I wiped my eyes and let the tears fade away. I nodded and swallowed.

"Plan B," I reiterated, with emphasis.

Coyote nodded. "Plan B."

Then I heard something. A voice. No, two voices. They battled up through the foundation of the Sun Sanctuary, into the marrow of my bones, until they reached my soul.

No one rests until we find the doors! Catrina's distant voice reverberated through my soul stone. *Faster, faster! I want the Desert Sanctuary open!*

I'm dying, the other, younger voice said. *I'm dying, and I have to stop it.*

My skin tingled, and my soul trembled. Wait—I knew

this young voice. It was the same one that I'd heard during training, before the brujas attacked Tierra del Sol. Only, I recognized it from somewhere else now too. From my dreams. From the world of souls, where she'd sat across from me, eleven years old and shattering.

It was also Catrina. The young, fearful girl she was inside, clawing out in desperation. It had been Tía Catrina's voice calling out for help all along.

Coyote's brows scrunched. "What is it?"

"Catrina," I said. "She's looking for the Desert Sanctuary. Which means we need to hurry." I turned to everyone, head held high, trembling but determined. "It's time, everyone!" I called.

Juana stood up. Lion's eye opened a little as her hand began to slide away. He held on for just a second longer. Axolotl paused her reading.

"Don't get hurt," Lion said to Juana. "Don't be stupid. Okay?"

Juana actually smiled. "I won't. I'm leaving the stupid with you, gato."

Lion's mouth twitched upward. He released her, and Juana strode out the room, calling for Damiana, Mamá, and a bucket of water to make me a puddle.

"Lo siento, amigo," I whispered to Lion. "We'll be back."

Juana and I pushed together into the main sanctuary

room to rejoin our party. Ocelot nodded to us as we entered. Damiana stood with her back to us, surrounded by our packed things, her eyes closed. I felt the colors of her soul reaching as she stretched her newborn senses. They grabbed on to something distant.

"Have you found it?" I asked. We were running low on time.

"It's far away . . ." Her face scrunched. "North. Across—montañas? Beyond the cerros."

My heart pounded. I wasn't exactly great at geography, but there was only one area beyond the northern montañas. The great desert, the one even my people did not venture to live in.

Ocelot's eyes lit up. "Of course. El Abandonado."

El Abandonado was the most dangerous stretch of desert in el Antiguo Amanecer. It was farther north than Tierra del Sol, said to be hot as the surface of the sun, and nearly a hundred miles from the nearest hacienda or remnant of civilization. My heart sped up. Sí. Of course. El Abandonado would be at the very heart of the Desert Mother.

"Then let's go!" I shoved open the Sun Sanctuary doors. "Be ready, everyone! We're taking back the Desert Sanctuary!"

21
Into the Abandoned

Getting to El Abandonado wasn't easy. The closest body of water I could find was in the mountain range that created the desert's rain shadow.

Juana, Damiana, Ocelot, and I all stepped forward onto the unfamiliar mountain together. My breath turned to steam as I shuddered and rubbed my arms. We had trees in Tierra del Sol, but the ones here were thick and stretched far overhead, like a thousand arms trying to hide us from the sky. Scrubby branches and thick, dry leaves rustled over us, shielding us from the red moon's light. It made me instantly miss the more open cerros of home.

Find it! Catrina's voice shuddered through the ground, even here. I clenched, holding my breath. Her voice was losing its sweet, luring quality. Devolving into something frayed. Angry. Broken. *They're on the way, El Silbón! It has to be nearby!*

She was scared. Why was she talking to El Silbón? Was

he tasked with guarding the desert curandera she had captured? I lifted my head to the wind skating up through the trees. Once all of this was over, we could rescue both the desert curandera and El Silbón. I bet the desert curandera and Damiana would have a lot to talk about. And I still missed El Silbón—deeply.

We moved forward, down the slope of the northern montaña. Damiana led us, stopping every once in a while to listen.

"I'm not hearing words, Cece," she whispered at one point. "What if it's not even the Desert I'm following?"

"It's okay," I whispered back. "I didn't hear words for a long time either. Just direct us closer to the sounds of hail hitting stone, like you described to me before." I patted her hand, where it still clasped a piece of coyamito agate from the mosaic. It glowed steadily. "Trust yourself, Damiana. We do."

Eventually, we reached the wide and barren expanse of El Abandonado. By that point, we were all exhausted. I'd woken everyone out of their sleep, and I'd barely gotten any of my own with that nightmare. I dragged my feet through the rocks and dry, cracked sand. Hours passed as Damiana pulled closer and closer to the feelings of Mother Desert.

My eyelids began to droop. I tried to shake myself

awake, even as my limbs grew more and more sluggish. No, no, I could do this. We were on the right track. We could really do this. We could save the Desert's soul, and then we wouldn't have to resort to plan B. I just had to stay awake long enough for us to do it.

I repeated that to myself even as darkness tugged at my vision. And before my foot could take another step across the craggy, thirsty ground—

Everything around me dissolved.

Not into darkness, though. To white. To a void filled with colorful ribbons of souls flying through the air around me. I turned in a circle, struggling, confused. Wait. I knew this place. Had I passed out? I'd seen this only in dreams.

"Cece Rios."

I knew that voice. The same young, sharp voice that had shaken me during training. I finished turning and found myself sitting at the table again, directly across from child Catrina.

There were still cracks across her face. Not as many as last time, but still. She looked one bad fall from shattering completely.

She shuffled a pack of lotería cards and placed it again between us. Our tiled bingo sheets from last time still sat in front of us. Our beans were still where we'd left them, covering our different tiles. I was still behind by one.

"Why am I here?" I asked. I twisted around. I needed to get to the Desert Sanctuary! "Am I asleep? Are you?"

"So many questions." Catrina frowned at me. "We're both tired. We're going in and out of sleep, so crossing into the world of souls is to be expected. It used to be so much quieter without you here." She gestured to the cards. "But if you have to be, you had better keep playing."

I hesitated. So we were both half asleep. Would I wake up if I finally won? Slowly, I reached over and let my hand hover over the stack of lotería cards. She watched my hand but didn't say anything. Hesitantly, I pulled up its corner.

"Why do you want to keep playing this game?" I asked. "We could just stop. You could just—surrender." I stared at her ugly cracks. "Maybe you'd stop falling apart."

She just scoffed. "I *have* to play," she said petulantly. "Otherwise everything will be taken from me *again*."

"What was taken from *you*?" I asked. As far as I could see, she was the one who'd done all the taking. Lives, hopes, friends.

"Everything," she mumbled.

Young Catrina was even harder to talk to than older Catrina. "Okay, but what *specifically*?"

"Mi papá scares me. He's mean and yells," Catrina said. "Axochitl is the only one who can calm him down."

Ah. That story felt familiar. Except, my papá had never

yelled. He'd been as cold as frostbite. I pulled the lotería card up and revealed its face. The picture of an ancient woman I vaguely recognized stood with her long, wild hair dancing behind her. "La Curandera del Desierto" was inscribed beneath her. It must have been Reina, the last desert curandera from Metztli's age. I flipped it around to show Catrina. She started scanning her bingo sheet. But when I turned the card back around, it had a new face on it.

A teenage Tía Catrina stared back at me surrounded by cacti and the Ruins. "La Curandera del Desierto" still glowed in gold letters.

My brows furrowed, and my heart quickened.

"Axochitl kept me safe," young Catrina said. I couldn't look away from her teenage form on the card. "She didn't hear the voices I could, and she didn't like me talking about them. It worried her. But she kept me and Mamá safe from Papá. She knew how to calm him down. She kept our home safe," Catrina's voice tightened. "What was I supposed to do if she was gone?"

I looked up. Child Catrina was now a teenager as well, as old as Juana and just as beautiful. She searched for a "La Curandera del Desierto" tile on her sheet. It wasn't there. It was on mine. Slowly, I placed a bean down. Her face soured—but it couldn't hide the tears dripping through the cracks in her ceramic face.

"She was going to abandon me," Catrina whispered. "She promised she and her husband would stay and protect me, but I knew she would get tired of me needing her. Especially once Papá was trying to sell me off to a man who only wanted me because I was beautiful. Axochitl *had* to be tired of living for other people. No one understands that I was tired of living *through* other people. But I had no choice. I wasn't strong enough on my own, and whose fault was that? Not mine! It's not fair!" She shook her head. "The voices wanted to help me. But they were too *weak* for my needs," she snarled, and a fresh crack split her lips.

For someone so beautiful, her words and broken pieces were ugly. A war sprouted in my heart then, looking at Tía Catrina's fragile form.

I hadn't known what to do when I'd realized that Catrina not only did horrific things but also did them because she wanted to hide in darkness more than to heal in the light. I hadn't understood it. And it made me hate her. Because it was horrible. Despicable. Evil. Her pain was so stark, her desperation so self-centered. And yet all of it was also—understandable.

As I looked at her now, I saw true weakness. I scanned her broken, ceramic face, the disintegrating pieces falling from her fragile soul. She was breaking herself, again and again. The dark seam of hatred in my chest didn't want to feel sympathy. But sitting there across from the vulnerable image of my crumbling tía, I realized Metztli was right, and my heart couldn't help but soften.

Catrina glared at me when I didn't speak. "Are you pitying me, Cece? I thought you hated me."

"I did," I whispered. "It's hard not to, when you've become so cruel and selfish." I swallowed, and tears bubbled up inside me. Catrina's eyes narrowed further. "But I don't want to punish you for your darkness. What I really want is for you to embrace the light again."

Just like Coyote had said, they were different things, to want to punish evil or to build good. I reached out, slowly, for her hands. "What you're doing is killing you, Tía. I've heard the little girl in your soul cry out for help. Por favor, let me help you. Then we can both have that better world. You can finally have the strength you're looking for without taking it from someone else."

I nearly reached her fingers, coils of warm pink moving with me. She stared at my approach. For a moment, her eyes ached. Then she slapped my hand away, and I winced.

"Then I'll pity *you*, for being as big a fool as the rest of our familia." Catrina slammed a fist to the table, and a crack opened up through her right eye. Tears poured down her ceramic face. "Keep your self-important little *light*. There is no greater power than being able to take away that which belongs to others. *That* is the power I want, and I will crush you with it."

"You're wrong," I said. My throat was tight, my heart aching. But my voice was as steady as the ocean waves. "I'm sorry Abuelo was so unkind. I'm sorry that you were scared of the man he was trying to force you to marry. I'm sorry that life felt so big to you that you thought you had to pick between overpowering or being overpowered. But what you're describing isn't power. It's poison. And it will only end up devouring whatever power you did have."

Catrina glared at me with a disgust that made my skin crawl. "Do you think I care for your opinions, chiquita?" she spat. "I've asked you to play. Not to lecture."

She wasn't listening. She wasn't going to, was she? Anger and sorrow battled through my chest like hot and arctic winds. But slowly, the water rose inside my soul and swept them away. I had to accept that love was not the strength Catrina wanted. I had to make sure I didn't sacrifice my love, my healing, to hate her for it. But I also had to ensure she didn't destroy others along with herself. That was the true fight at the heart of this war.

"Very well," I said. "Draw, Catrina."

Catrina hesitated at the new, calm tone of my voice. But she reached out and grabbed the next card. When she flipped it over, a glowing square of coyamito agate filled its face. "The Desert's Voice" it was called.

Oh. I watched Catrina as she scanned her card for the

tile. But it wasn't on hers. Not anymore. She'd lost that gift a long time ago, hadn't she? That's what the cards were saying. She'd been someone blessed of the Desert goddess, capable of becoming a Desert curandera. And she'd traded it for brujería.

I placed a bean on mine, where the Desert's Voice tile sat at the center of my sheet. On it was a portrait of Damiana, holding the glowing agate in her hands.

Catrina and I were tied in this game now. One move away from victory or loss.

Catrina's eyes widened when she saw the stalemate. She rose, screaming in fury, and scattered the rest of the card deck with a swipe of her ceramic arms. I jumped as she slammed both hands on the table—breaking her brittle fingers—and loomed over me.

"So what if she's chosen the traitor Damiana?" Catrina screeched. "So what if Mother Desert has rejected me? I *will* find her silver doors before you. You think my power poison? I will make sure yours is the life it takes. Mark my words, Cecelia Rios!"

22
The Desert's Voice

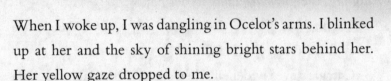

When I woke up, I was dangling in Ocelot's arms. I blinked up at her and the sky of shining bright stars behind her. Her yellow gaze dropped to me.

"She is awake," she announced.

My body was stiff, and my head hurt from Catrina's yelling. But relief washed over me as I turned and found Juana and Damiana standing around a particularly flat part of the desert, clear of all brush and sage and weeds. Between them, there was the slight imprint of a large diamond shape peeking out beneath the dust.

"Oh, thank the sun." Juana sighed in relief. Then her face instantly puckered. "Don't scare me like that again, Cece!"

I smiled awkwardly as Ocelot placed me back on the ground. "Lo siento. I didn't get much sleep."

"I told you she was just tired," Ocelot said.

Juana grabbed me and pulled me into her warm arms.

"Idiota, not taking care of yourself."

"I'm glad you're awake," Damiana said, and gestured to the ground. "I think we've arrived."

My skin buzzed with anticipation. Ocelot knelt at the very center of the cleared space and brushed sand away until a diamond-shaped tile appeared. It was a deep color, possibly made of jade—it was hard to tell by the light of a red moon. Juana grinned. Damiana's eyes widened, almost in disbelief, almost in joy.

I did it, Damiana's soul whispered into the air.

"The legend goes that this is the place the Desert goddess first touched, when she sacrificed herself to become the land we live on," Ocelot said. We all watched as she scooped the dirt into her hands. "This is for the children of the Desert what Tierra del Sol is for Naked Man." She pointed over the tile she'd exposed. "Listen, Damiana, and you will find her doors."

"Listen?" Damiana asked. She hesitated until she narrowed her eyes, and, hunching, she shuffled over to the tile. "For the noises I've been hearing?"

"For the voice that will teach you how to use yours again," Ocelot corrected.

That made sense to me. I'd started hearing Mother Ocean before I'd been able to properly master moving water. I smiled. Juana leaned on my shoulder.

CECE RIOS AND THE QUEEN OF BRUJAS

"She can do it," she said, with all the faith in the world. "A woman ready to give up everything to raise a criatura safely, to give her the home she'd lost—that's a woman with a voice that could shake the earth. Once she uses it."

I nodded—then winced as Catrina's voice climbed through the soil, faded by distance but still demanding, and rattled in my chest. *You had better find it*, she seemed to be chastising someone. The desert curandera she'd captured? *The Desert would not abandon me. Who does she think she is?*

Were they arguing now? I shuddered as I tried to press back her wrath. Her railings grew more desperate, more driven, more enraged. They rumbled through the ground, nearly shaking my bones with her resolve.

But then, as Catrina cried up from the ground, something interrupted her. Like a shield. A louder, stronger sound, drowning her out.

Please, Damiana's voice vibrated through the ground. It felt like a chasm, a mighty movement of the earth, pressing out and through the Desert, shoving Catrina's tirade back. *I know I've made mistakes, Mother Desert. Lo siento. But I want to set it right. And I want to help protect my Axolotl. My abuela. My new friends. My—familia.*

Where Catrina demanded, Damiana pleaded. Where Catrina felt cheated out of something never promised her,

Damiana took accountability for her past mistakes. Where Catrina threatened, Damiana reached out with humility.

And for the first time in months, I heard the quiet whisper of the goddess we lived on and with and through:

I hear, Mother Desert's voice poured out. *And I offer.*

The ground rumbled, and Damiana gasped. Juana and I grabbed each other as the stones around us shook. Ocelot grabbed Damiana by the coat and yanked her away from the jade tile she'd been sitting on. Because the jade diamond, the last remnant of the sanctuary, began to move.

The jade rotated, into a square, and then expanded into a silver-edged rectangle. Carved doors rose from the dust— and in the light of the crimson moon, I caught their silver faces. They locked into place before us, and from behind their cracks, strange colors glowed and sounds whispered. My mouth dropped.

"The silver doors!" I shook Juana's arm. "From Devil's Alley! Are they—part of the Desert Sanctuary? No way."

But I'd heard Mother Desert's voice a second ago, just like I had only once before, when I'd stood at the silver doors in the dungeon of El Cucuy. Juana looked just as dumbstruck, and we approached together, gathering behind Damiana and Ocelot as we drew awed breaths.

Ocelot's mouth softened into a real, relieved smile. "It makes sense now, doesn't it?" She looked at us.

CECE RIOS AND THE QUEEN OF BRUJAS

"The Court of Fears did tell me and Lion that the doors were part of Mother Desert, now that I think about it," Juana said. She pushed a hand back through her hair. "So, when Coyote made Devil's Alley—the Desert Sanctuary was folded into it?"

"But because Mother Desert's soul is inside, it couldn't come under El Cucuy's rule like the rest of Devil's Alley," I added, smile growing wider. I squeezed Juana's hand. "That must be why the doors take you wherever you need to be! Mother Desert can do just that! That's why she asked me to save Coyote when I was in front of the doors too!"

Tears filled Damiana's magenta eyes, and she covered her mouth with a shocked laugh. We all looked to her as the colors glowing from beneath the door played across her face. She wiped her reddening nose.

"You did it." I grinned up at her. "You did it, Damiana!"

She lowered her hand from her mouth and revealed her brimming smile. Ocelot's hand landed on her shoulder, and Damiana jumped. My soul filled as Ocelot's eyes warmed, and Damiana's eyebrows lifted with hope.

"See, Damiana," Ocelot said. "Your voice matters."

Damiana's chin dimpled. But she nodded, with a confidence that suited her well. Wearing it, she stepped forward, knelt to the ground where the doors lay flush against the soil, and lay her hands on its silver knobs.

"For most of my life, I have not done well with the potential you gave me," she said to the doors. "Yet you have still come to me. And I come to you now, heart changed, to ask you for a gift. Por favor—open the Desert Sanctuary you have kept safe all this time, so we can protect you too in return."

My soul warmed. Her voice had a quality that this world needed. I was so happy to hear her use it.

Damiana gripped the knobs tight, pulled, and the silver doors parted for us. With her leading the way, we stepped forward into the beautiful light shining out of Mother Desert's home.

23
The Desert Sanctuary

When we stepped through the veil of light, we entered a long hallway filled only with silence.

It was made entirely of stone, and it looked like it had been carved by hand. The place was dark and barren except for narrow windows lining the left wall. Light glowed meekly from beyond their glass. I glanced at them as we started moving into the long corridor. They resembled the windows in the Sun Sanctuary, except where it had pictures of the Sun god and humans, these depicted the Desert and animals. I stared at where a coyote curled up in the hair of the Desert goddess—before I noticed a shadow moving on the other side of the glass.

I gasped. Then slapped a hand over my mouth, to muffle the sound. But the shadow didn't seem to hear me. It simply paced in front of the glass, muttering to itself, as it shifted the shape of a bag on its shoulder.

"She can do it . . . ," the shadow muttered to itself.

"Have faith, Alejo. She promised."

My heart tightened. Was he talking about me? I pressed closer to the glass.

"Who's 'she,' El Silbón?"

I stiffened at the sound of Tía Catrina's voice. So did El Silbón's shadow. Ahead of me, Juana looked back at me in question. I couldn't speak. I gestured wildly for her and the others to come watch.

The slim shadow of Tía Catrina moved into the window's view. El Silbón's silhouette stopped. Hesitated.

"You, of course," El Silbón said. "Queen Catrina."

She tilted her head. Then she strode toward him, her footsteps clipped, sharp. He held terribly still. She flicked her hand, and before she even reached him, a small light lit up on El Silbón's head, and he cried out as he fell to the ground. I clutched Juana's hand. She squeezed it tight, hard. The clatter of his father's bones spilled across the ground. El Silbón clutched his head and cried, heaving gasps of pain into the air.

"If you have time to be praying for Cece," she bellowed, her sweet, honey voice abandoned, "then you aren't *searching hard enough*."

"You can hurt me all you want," El Silbón said, between gasps, "but the silver doors will not open for you. Mother Desert will not heed your call. You're not a desert curandera anymore. You can't control *everyone*. Quetzalcoatl is already too much for you. You—won't—last—long—"

He screamed, and suddenly, his body went limp. Catrina's shadow stood straight, seemingly unbothered, as she brushed down her dress. El Silbón's passed-out form lay splayed across the ground. I placed my hands against the glass, tears filling my eyes.

Catrina kicked his body to the side and strode out of view. My heart flinched like she'd kicked me instead. Only her voice remained, floating behind her: "Everyone, trying to make me look like the villain . . ."

I swallowed a sick turn in my stomach. With Catrina's shadow gone, I pushed my face against the stained glass window, peering through one of the clear pieces of glass. There, I could finally see clearly. El Silbón lay on the ground, his murderous father's bones spilled on the ground all around him, his face smudged away by his unfair Renaming.

"El Silbón," I whispered.

He had no escape, no way to resist Catrina's control, with his Mark of the Binding. But he'd still talked back to her. He'd still put his faith in me. My chin crumpled, and I sent my soul's light stretching for him.

I will get you out of this, I promised him across the distance.

Hands suddenly slammed down on the glass on the opposite side of the window. I cried out, and Juana wrenched me away from it. Ocelot stepped between us, her claws out. Damiana herded us behind her.

Catrina's eyes roamed the glass wildly, but she couldn't seem to see us. Maybe because we were in the Desert Sanctuary, beyond the silver doors? This interior world seemed to be housed somewhere in Devil's Alley, but with its strange magic, I couldn't be sure where or how it connected to the rest. Catrina pressed her ear to the glass, and her shaky, out-of-control breath rattled against the window, her hair spilling wildly over her shoulders.

"I know the sound of that soul," she seethed.

I hear you in the walls, Cece, her voice rumbled through the ground and up my spine.

My insides washed cold. "We should go," I whispered.

Juana grabbed my arm and, together with our friends, we took off down the corridor.

"So you found the silver doors?" Catrina boomed. "It won't stop me, Cece! I hold three of the four gods' souls now!"

Her hands slammed down on each window as we went, like she could feel my soul across the dimensional divide. I winced every time, heart thundering, soul flashing, as she tailed us down the corridor.

"*I know you're in here!*" Catrina's voice screeched through the hall.

I slapped my hands over my ears. We kept running, pushing toward the end of the empty corridor, where distant wooden doors embedded with coyamito agate waited.

Just give up! I called out, panting as I ran. *You can't stop us now, even if you want to!*

"Do you think you can hide from me just because you're in the Desert goddess's last realm? It's still in Devil's Alley! This is *my* world now! You can't hide when your soul's so loud!" Catrina's hands slapped on each window that I passed. "I can find you wherever you go, Cece! I'll break through these walls. I won't let you steal what belongs to *me!*"

We threw ourselves into the wooden doors at the end of the hall. Damiana plastered her hands to the agate. It glowed, bright and steady and with a sound like someone releasing a relieved breath. Wind burst from between its hinges—and the doors separated inward.

I yelped and we fell inside. Ocelot and Damiana whirled around, grabbed the doors, and thrust them shut. Catrina's screams vanished instantly, locked away like an animal shut in a box.

"Quick!" I turned in a panicked circle. "We have to be fast. You heard her, we have to—"

"Cece," Ocelot interrupted. I looked up. Her eyes were kind, and, placing a hand on my shoulder, she gently turned me around to face the mosaic. "Look."

It was beautiful. Covered in dust like it had been undisturbed for centuries, but just as filled with calm, caring beauty as the mosaics in the other sanctuaries.

Juana, Damiana, and I came to a stop in front of the mosaic. At our approach, the stones began to light up. Desert's agate glowed stronger than it used to. Sun's fire opals brightened like tiny fires. And the turquoise of Mother Ocean shone like the kind tide under the sun.

We were finally here. Our last stand for the gods' souls.

I took a low, steadying breath. Ocelot stood to the side, nodding her encouragement. We just had to do as Metztli had done. Juana and Damiana stepped up beside me, offering their power, their support. I swallowed and pressed my palm to the piece of jade at the center of the mosaic, cut into the shape of a diamond.

I felt something, even before speaking. A low, gentle drum, like a heartbeat waiting behind the stone. My heart swelled with hope, and my chin trembled. Was she already listening for us?

"Damiana." I gestured for her to join me. "Do you remember what Metztli said?"

Damiana nodded. With a meek smile, she placed her

hand beside mine. "I—I have come to make a request of my home, as a desert curandera," she said.

The heartbeat behind the stone grew stronger. I knew, more seamlessly than with words, that Mother Desert was listening. The tile stones beneath our hands hummed.

"An ocean curandera adds her strength to mine," Damiana said, and squinted, like she was trying to remember Metztli's words exactly. She nodded to Juana, and she placed her hand left of mine against the fire opal. "A sun curandera adds her light to mine," Damiana continued. "Her fire makes its request of this, the Desert Sanctuary. Together, we ask for the soul that lies within its protection."

The jade stone brightened. Juana gasped. Damiana's eyes widened, and she leaned in, as if she could hear the heartbeat beyond the stone calling her.

Suddenly, wind blasted against my fingers. The mosaic rolled back, the tiles folding away into the sides of the frame, just as they had in the Moon Sanctuary. An awed breath filled my lungs. Damiana laughed with joy. Juana squeezed my free hand. Ocelot moved up with us and stared at Mother Desert's brilliant, waiting soul.

Mother Desert's coyamito agate was shaped in a perfect pyramid, the angles too neatly executed to have been found in nature. Gently, I reached in. The stone pulsed with whispers. And as I cupped the soul in my hands, I heard her again.

Our children need you, she said. Her voice shuddered through my body, and even my soul shivered. I pulled her soul safely free of the confines.

"I know," I whispered. "And I—I'll do my best."

"What'd she say, Cece?" Damiana asked.

I smiled up at her. "You might hear her yourself, soon." Or at least I thought so. Maybe it wouldn't come in words for her, like it did for me, since she didn't speak soul language. "Or you'll feel her so well, you won't need words."

Damiana smiled. "Gracias for believing in me." She laughed, a little tightly and ruffled my hair. "You have a soul older than us all, ey, curanderita?"

I smiled. The colors between our souls warmed.

"Quickly, let's go," Ocelot spoke up. We all turned to her, where she stood near the exit doors. "If we keep this away from Catrina long enough, she may perish on her own, and we will win the war without another battle."

Plan A was working. My heart turned rosy, accompanied by the steady, warm sensation of the soul cupped between my palms. Juana and I strode forward together, to join Ocelot at the exit. Only Damiana didn't follow.

I stopped and turned back to look. "Damiana?" I asked.

She held stiff and still, straight upright. But she was

gagging, eyes squeezed closed as if in pain. Her soul spiraled with panic in sharp mustards and whites. Juana started toward her.

"What's wrong?" she demanded.

"I—can't—" Damiana squeezed out.

The inside of my stomach turned to ice. Juana closed the distance between them and reached for her face. Sweat dripped down Damiana's chin. My soul flickered in panic as Juana brushed her bangs back.

The Mark of the Binding burned bright on her forehead.

Did you think I wouldn't use every tool against you, Cece? Catrina's voice rumbled in the stone walls. A giant crack opened in the wall beside us, and I leaped back, heart pulsing with thunder and lightning and screams. *I've found you, and there is nothing you can do to stop me.*

Catrina's promise hung in the air as the wall of the Desert
Sanctuary exploded.

Steam and dust and water sprayed across the room. Ocelot crouched to protect my face, but tiny stones still shot
through the air like knives and battered my arms until they
left bruises. A wave of burning air followed, so hot I could
barely breathe, and sent us flying back into the far wall. We
hit with a crack, and I landed in Ocelot's arms, gasping.

Juana and Damiana had been thrown to the other side
of the room, just a few feet away from me, slumped on the
floor. My heart screamed. Were they okay? Across from us,
a giant hole punctured the stone. It glowed at the edges,
burning hot, chunks of the stone fallen. Debris filled the
air, disguising someone standing in the wreckage.

"Catrina?" I asked, breathless.

"That would be *Queen* Catrina," a velvet voice poured
in from the dark.

Out of the wound in Mother Desert, El Sombrerón appeared in a cloud of dust and ash.

My skin went numb as I watched him step into the room. He wasn't the little kid he'd been in Devil's Alley only three months ago. He had to bend his head to step up through the top of the large hole. Six feet tall, maybe even close to seven already. Face more shadow than expression, just the way I remembered. Except for two burning red eyes that sliced into view as he opened them beneath the brim of his sombrero.

A few feet away, Juana lifted her head—and froze. Her glare dropped into shock. Terror. I could feel the heat go out of her soul, and her breath audibly dried up.

I had asked Coyote about El Sombrerón, once he remembered his past life. How he'd found him. What he'd done. If his story was like El Silbón's.

Coyote's face had darkened. "He was nothing like El Silbón," he'd said. "Even as a man, he stole the daughters of his neighbors and trapped them away. He was the first monster I had ever met, far before I Renamed him."

El Sombrerón's voice shook the room like a low and beating heart. "You have something that doesn't belong to you." He stretched his hand out to me. "You will not defeat me again, curandera. *Hand it over before I crush you.*"

I swallowed as the command rocked through me. I'd

tasted his soul once, and it had felt like this then too. Acrid and burning and with so much pressure I feared it would somehow pulverize me just by being near it. But I clutched the Desert's stone to my chest. His red eyes sliced thin.

El Sombrerón leaped forward, quick as a vulture's wing, his gruesome hand outstretched for the Desert's soul. Ocelot slid around me and pounced on him. She hit with all her weight, her elbow jammed into his chest. El Sombrerón stumbled back. While he was off his guard, she launched herself up and around his neck, wrapping him in a headlock.

"¡Corre!" Ocelot commanded me. "Take the Desert's soul and run!"

My heart wrenched in two again. Damiana was still curled on the floor, rigid and unable to move, hands locked over her glowing Mark of the Binding. Ocelot strained as El Sombrerón began to pull at her arms. If I ran, I could take the Desert's soul far away. I could save everyone. After putting Metztli in danger in the first place, after losing the Ocean's and Moon's souls, I had to try.

I launched myself off the floor and ran for the doors. Juana rose up, eyes burning and ready. Together, we yanked at the doors, pulling them back. Juana took my hand, and we were about to spring forward—when something grabbed my hair and jacket from behind.

I yelped as it dragged me backward, tugging on my scalp. My jacket was sliced in two in El Sombrerón's grip, ripped to shreds and leaving my arms bare. My eyes burned. In one great slam, he threw Ocelot off his back, sending her crashing into the mosaic across the room. Ocelot flopped onto the ground, her back to us. I gasped. El Sombrerón wrenched me by my hair to face him. I gritted my teeth and yanked, pulled, fought. Strands of my completely tattered jacket fell between us. His free hand crunched down on my hands, where they gripped the Desert's soul tight.

"*Give it to me,*" his voice blasted over me.

I squeezed my eyes closed and stretched my senses. His hands were tightening on mine, and he'd break my knuckles if he had the chance. I needed water. I needed help. I stretched my soul, far and wide, desperate.

I didn't find water close enough. But buzzing out past the stone was the distant mark of El Sombrerón's soul, hanging around Catrina's neck. Hope jolted through me. I'd stopped El Sombrerón once using his soul. Maybe I could again.

My turquoise tendrils grabbed hold of the burning black stone, thrumming as dark and hot as I remembered. Only there was a new presence inside him this time too. Acidic and dark and hateful: Catrina.

Flashes of her breaking face moved through my soul.

My knees locked. Her scowl flickered through me. We met, in flashes, in confusion, screaming at the center of El Sombrerón's soul.

This soul belongs to me, Catrina hissed through him.

I tried to grip his soul at its edges, tried to wrench him free. She tugged, and her dark colors wrapped tighter around it.

I'm not going to let you stop us! I screamed into the clash of souls. *I'm going to save the Desert's soul. Without her, you won't survive. And when you're gone, I'm going to free El Silbón, the desert curandera you captured, and everyone else!*

Her laugh pealed through me. My insides trembled, from my soul stone to my bones. Her dark colors spread wide, burning and consuming El Sombrerón, adding to his destruction.

The desert curandera I captured? she asked, her laugh losing her calculated edge. *Cece, there was no desert curandera but me.* A grin flashed through the colors and rocked my ribs. *I'd thought the Desert would still let me in. But I knew she might betray me. And if she did, my last hope was that you'd rush to find the sanctuary for me. Why do you think I told Grimmer Mother to let you live when you fought her at the Ocean Sanctuary?* Catrina asked, and her snarl cut through my soul.

My heart dropped. No. That meant Catrina couldn't have even gotten inside here if we hadn't led her to it. I'd fallen right into her trap. Again.

The gut-wrenching reality hit like bricks, and Catrina took the moment to sideswipe me out of El Sombrerón's soul. I gasped as my eyes opened. I was now standing in front of El Sombrerón, both his hands paused around mine and the Desert's soul. No more than a second had passed. But his eyes lit up with renewed wrath. And his hands crunched down, ripping the Desert's soul from me so hard my fingers felt like they would break.

"No!" I scrambled at his sleeves, clawing up him as he lifted the flickering, triangular stone out of reach.

El Sombrerón narrowed his eyes, tilted his head—and punched me in the face.

His fist hit so hard my vision went black. I heard my head hit the nearest wall with a sharp crack, but by the time the pain swelled there, I was on my back. I coughed. Something coppery streaked my mouth. It stung bitter and hot.

He loomed over me with bloody knuckles, the Desert's soul in hand.

I shook my head, and everything swirled around me.

"Hey!" Juana's voice boomed.

Her red dress swished as she stepped between me and El Sombrerón. Her fists lifted, her eyes ablaze, steam rising from her skin.

"No one messes with mi familia," Juana's voice rumbled. "I let you live, after everything you did to me. But I'm not going to let you hurt anyone else, not again, El Sombrerón!"

"You," El Sombrerón said. He pocketed the Desert's soul, so it disappeared into his smoky coat, the same place he'd once kept Juana's soul. "I know you. You're the one who stole all my precious trophies." His red eyes narrowed, and the room shuddered as he charged.

Juana's hair nearly turned to fire. She screeched and grabbed him by his arm. He went to smash her, but she flipped herself up onto his arm, her hands sparking with flames now, and punched straight into El Sombrerón's throat. He choked and stumbled. While he shook, she grabbed him by the neck and tried to flip him in the Amenazante style. He was twice her size, and more than twice her weight. But Juana's eyes glowed. Smoke burned up from where she touched him. Flames shot out from her feet, making up for the weaker ankle. With their velocity, the two tipped, and Juana slammed him into the ground.

His arm caught her as he fell and smashed her head into the ground with him. She cried out. Kicked herself free and rolled away, clutching her skull. Huffed and panted. Our eyes met across the way. We were tired. We were wounded. How much longer could we last?

I tried to drag myself closer to El Sombrerón, where he lay, momentarily dizzied. We just had to grab the Desert's soul. Live long enough to take it back. My ribs ached. My head spun. Every inch felt like agony, and tears filled my eyes.

Blessedly, Ocelot appeared ahead of me. I blinked as she, hugging her side, knelt over him and started going through his cloak. She clutched something. Her eyes brightened. Hope flickered up inside me.

Until El Sombrerón grabbed her by the throat and rose to stand.

El Sombrerón lifted Ocelot over his head. "You think the Desert's soul belongs with you?" He laughed and pulled it out of his cloak. "With this, I finally have all I'm owed." His tone had changed, and it took me a moment to realize Catrina was speaking through him.

His red eyes slid over to me. "Now watch, Cece." He gripped the soul tight. I reached out. He pitched it back through the hole, where the flickering image of the Desert's soul vanished into Devil's Alley. "Watch as I show you all the other powers I spoke of."

Grief split my heart in two. No.

We'd lost the Desert's soul.

El Sombrerón threw Ocelot down to the ground. She nearly leaped away, but he slammed his foot down on her, crushing her into the stone before she could escape.

"All that's left," Catrina hissed through El Sombrerón's teeth, "is snuffing you all out. Then there will be no one to contest me."

"No!" a scream rocked the sanctuary.

I gasped and found Damiana fighting against her own body to stand.

She scratched at her forehead, at the Mark of the Binding that held her prisoner. "I will not bow, not anymore! I will not be cowed by your voice. I will not let you hurt my abuela!" she cried.

Ocelot's eyes widened.

"Not her, not my friends!" Her nails dragged across her forehead. "I have my own voice, and I *will use it!*"

The ground swelled with her words, sending everyone stumbling, falling, to the tile. Juana rolled into me and then yanked me close, turning herself into a wall between me and El Sombrerón. I pulled my arms around her, trying to shield her back.

When Damiana opened her eyes this time, they glowed a strong, resilient brown where they'd once been magenta. The Mark of the Binding brightened on her forehead, like it was fighting back, sharp and demanding, cutting through her skin. Damiana gritted her teeth—and a crack broke through the middle of the mark.

"This place is sacred!" she boomed. "It does not belong to you!"

Her voice shook through the ground, through the walls, and my skin was awash with goose bumps. There was a new sound in it. A firmness, an unyielding, fortified resolve that carried through the air like honey, as powerful as El Sombrerón's guitar used to be. Damiana straightened. El Sombrerón fell back at the power in her voice.

And Damiana's Mark of the Binding shattered off her skin.

Damiana moved her hands. As if it were one with her body, the floor lurched up between El Sombrerón and us, a tidal wave with angles instead of curves, and dust instead of dew. The very stones heeded her movements and sent El Sombrerón crashing back through the hole Catrina had ripped open. Damiana slammed her feet into the ground. Walls rose between us, one after the other, rebuilding the places Catrina had broken.

But Catrina's voice bled through the cracks, even as Damiana struggled to fill them. *You may have the Desert's pathetic replacement. But I have the goddess's soul, and I will rain my fury down on the world you love. Come meet me on the battlefield west of Tierra del Sol, where you curanderas failed once before.* Catrina's voice faded behind the wall as Damiana restored it. *We will end this where it began.*

The walls locked in place, blocking El Sombrerón completely from sight. Damiana gasped and stumbled. Juana rushed to steady her.

"Hey, hey, ¿cómo estás?" Juana said.

I stumbled over. "Damiana—you did it."

Her eyes batted open. The silence settled around us. Her gaze was still brown, even if her smile revealed her fangs. There was a hope there, a brightness, even an audaciousness I'd never seen in her before. Even if we'd lost the Desert's soul. Even if Catrina was about to raze whatever she could.

We were still alive. There was a chance to stop her. And that was only thanks to Damiana.

Juana grinned up at her. "Not bad for an ex-bruja, ey?"

Damiana laughed. Footsteps came up behind us. Slowly, we turned.

Ocelot stood there in the silence, her yellow eyes trained on Damiana. Oh. My gut flipped. That's right. Damiana—Damiana had said it. Out loud.

Ocelot's soul buzzed with old memories. Damiana's eyes widened, and panicked spots of color littered her soul.

"You called me your grandmother," Ocelot broke the silence, gaze pinned on Damiana.

Damiana paled. There was no question in it. And Ocelot's face offered no comfort, no support. Just the statement, brazen as the stones beneath our feet.

"Sí." Damiana's shoulders were stiff, up by her ears.

"You're my Linda's daughter," Ocelot said.

Damiana offered a floundering smile. "I don't really look like her, huh? I take after Papá . . ." Damiana laughed weakly and brushed her hands down the embroidery on her jacket lapels.

Ocelot didn't blink, didn't move, not even an inch. "Was your papá good to you both?"

Damiana's face melted. "Sí." She bit her lip. "He was the best. So was Abuelo."

Ocelot's face remained as stiff as her posture. But dots of light caught on the moisture growing in her eyes, the only indication besides the growing pinks and blues of her soul that this conversation meant the world to her.

"You knew Andres?" she asked.

"Sí." Damiana hesitated. "I was about ten when he went to the Great After."

"Was he happy?" Ocelot asked. Her voice quieted. "Did my husband live well?"

Damiana thought about it. The breeze from the cracked exit doors passed between them, blowing Ocelot's long braids and fluttering the edges of Damiana's coat. Her brown eyes warmed with memories, and the icy, scared tendrils of her soul bloomed with warmer colors—reds and burgundies, oranges and butter yellows.

"Sí," Damiana said, with a real smile this time. "We went through a lot. But I think that even through the pain, Abuelo was happy. I don't think he would have picked an easier way. I think he always would have picked you." She lifted her face, so her smile could shine. "I think he always would have picked you and Mamá, no matter what."

Ocelot stared and stared. Then suddenly, she crossed the distance between them, lifted her hands, and cupped Damiana's cheeks. My heart swelled, and Juana gripped my arm.

"I would too," she said. Tears shivered like glass droplets on her eyelashes. "I would always pick Andres, and I would always pick Linda." She brushed Damiana's tears away with her thumbs, and intently, pressed their foreheads together. "I would always pick you, Damiana. I wish I'd known you were right here all along. My own familia." She grinned. A true, wide, smile I'd never seen on her face before, lighting up her eyes and crinkling her face. "You were worth it all."

Damiana's face completely crumbled. The colors in her soul broke open—sorrow like hail, joy like sunrise over the cerros, and a resilience as strong as the montañas.

The world might be on its way to ending. We had a battle waiting for us on the outskirts of Tierra del Sol. But

I wasn't scared. Because in Damiana and Ocelot's embrace, I saw something. I saw the first signs of that better world I'd been hoping for. I found true, powerful proof that it could be real.

Damiana and Ocelot had found their home. And that testament was hope enough for me.

25
Nevertheless

The surface of El Abandonado was silent when we reached it, cloaked in the red light of the moon and the dusky streaks of the distant, unrisen sun. Even the stone was washed out, the cactuses gray, the stretches of dust and sand weak and thin where they'd been robust before. All signs that the Desert's soul had been taken. The last of the four gods' souls had been lost.

Now Catrina had the power to do all she wanted. Keep herself alive, yes. But what else would she do to us on her mission to conquer?

I shivered in the cold of the desert without my jacket. Its remnants still lay, irretrievably torn, in the Desert Sanctuary. Juana pulled me to her and shared her warmth.

"Do you think we have a chance?" Juana's voice lowered with the vulnerable question.

Behind us, Damiana was shutting the Desert Sanctuary, Ocelot helping her with the heavy silver doors. My sister and I stared out at the distant southern horizon. You couldn't see it past the montañas, but I could almost feel Tierra del Sol crying out across the far distance. The desert beneath my feet was quiet, serene. The calm before the coming storm.

"Honestly, I don't know," I said to Juana. "I started to hate Tía Catrina, Juana. I've never hated anyone before. That made me more afraid than ever to fight her. Because I was afraid I'd lose myself too, taking her down."

Juana looked over, and I could tell from the throbbing, familiar gray in her soul, that she knew well that kind of pain. She, with El Sombrerón. Me, with Catrina.

"But—" I looked up at her. "I've decided I won't fight her because I hate her. I'll fight for my home. My familia. A better world for both." I smiled, even though I was scared. My soul swelled with growing light that defied the darkness. "I'm willing to die trying to save whatever we can."

"Do you think that's what curanderas will always do?" she whispered. Her eyes lit up with fear and golden determination, all at once. "Will we always . . . die, trying to save people? The way Metztli and the others did? I think that's my greatest fear. That I won't actually be able to save anyone, no matter how hard I try." She squinted off at the sunken sun.

I'd been wrestling with that same fear. It should feel

even bigger, now that we'd lost the gods' souls. But some-how, it had less power. A sense of acceptance, of courage, of strength filled me up. Mother Ocean's soul may be in Catrina's hands now, but her power still flowed through me. And that was what I would cling to. Not the fear. Not the hate. Just the light.

"The curanderas of old had to face the battle of Tierra del Sol all on their own," I reminded Juana. I took her hand, and her warm fingers squeezed mine. "We're not alone this time. Our army isn't large, but we've come together as human and curandera, criatura and ex-bruja. We've never done that before. And the Great Namer hasn't left us alone—he's come with plan B."

I swallowed hard. The path ahead was still going to be so hard, but I knew now why Coyote had been so confi-dent before. It's because he knew what he was fighting for this time. He'd lost sight of it in his last life and regained clarity in this one. Just the same way I'd slipped away into hate, almost lost myself to it, before climbing back out.

I looked up at Juana. "Even if we're risking our lives, even if we might not make it—I don't think we've ever had a better chance. Even if we're few, we can fight for the light against the dark."

That was true strength, I thought. Being good, in the face of great adversity. Being loving, in the face of great hatred. Being willing to fight for what was right, even face-to-face with true injustice. This was the day the wheel of pain could finally stop turning. Even with all the risks that came with, I thought it was worth it.

Juana nodded. "If I'm going to die," she said, voice soft as feathers, "that's the way I want to go out."

We grasped each other's hands tighter.

"Let's go," she said.

I slipped from Juana's grip and knelt to the desert, placing my hand to the cracked, barren dust. "I'll tell them we're coming," I said. And I closed my eyes and breathed it in—the night air, the dying world, the life still waiting to be revived.

Coyote, I stretched my soul as far as I could. I sent it running through the desert's ground, spiraling outward in turquoise tattoos, shooting through the land and up the mountains like lightning. *Lo siento, mi amigo. It's time for plan B.*

I'd never used soul language at this kind of a distance, or not purposefully, anyway. Just accidentally, in my dreams, with Tía Catrina. But if Catrina could do it all the way from Devil's Alley, surely I could reach the person whose soul I knew best.

I'm ready, Coyote's voice suddenly reverberated through the dust.

Tears filled my eyes. I pushed my gratitude, my hope, my sorrow through the distance—and felt his in return.

He was determined, even if he was scared. I was going to move forward too, even if I feared what came next.

Slowly, I pushed off the ground. "Let's go defend our world," I said, "for the last time—together."

When we arrived on the outskirts of Tierra del Sol, there was no great army to greet us. Just a group of Santos's still-loyal police officers and a few Sun Priestesses behind Santos and Mamá, plus Coyote and the rest of my criatura friends—including a still struggling Little Lion. They stood a distance away, their backs to us as they discussed something together.

I approached with a cold fist squeezing my soul tight. *That's not enough*, I thought before I could stop myself. All of us together would be barely thirty people to Devil's Alley's thousands. Their eyes flickered toward us as we crossed the desert sand toward them. Faces lit up at our approach. I smiled a tired, aching smile. No, we were not nearly enough in numbers. But we'd come together, which was still better than we'd ever done before.

"¡Mis hijas!" Mamá cried, and widened her arms for us.

Juana and I sprinted forward and dove into her. She held us tight there, like she too knew how fearful our battle would be today. Like she'd known somehow that life would always bring us to this point. She'd been fighting to keep it at bay, all our lives, I realized. Keeping us from criaturas, from brujería, from anything that looked like it might take us down this path. I'd always thought my mamá was fearless. But she was braver now than she'd ever been when she'd refused to cry in the criatura months.

If I could die today, and keep you safe, her soul whispered, *I would. I wish it did not have to be you. But it is, and I will fight beside you until my last breath.*

Tears welled up in my eyes. I buried my face in her chest, so I'd always remember her strong embrace, the warmth and safety of her arms.

Mamá pulled back. "Before we begin this, mijita." Mamá reached into her bag and pulled out a streak of something wide and blue. She shook out the clothing and offered it to me. Her tired eyes smiled with new life. "This is a coat for the leader of the curanderas."

I took it carefully, in awe.

Mamá had made me my own jacket to replace the worn, hole-ridden one that had been torn up in all these battles. This one was a bright, vivid blue, and she'd stitched white and green circles and waves and swirls on the cuffs. I felt the tingle of her love left in the fabric. It was a sacred offering. A loving restoration for something broken.

Tears filled my eyes. "Gracias, Mamá," I said, and sniffled.

"Te quiero, Cece," she said.

Juana patted my hair back as I pulled the jacket on. She

nodded, and her smile widened. "It looks . . . curandera-ish," she said.

"You mean it?" I ran my hands across the embroidery. It fit just right.

"Sí," she answered.

"Cecelia Rios?"

I turned from Mamá and Juana, wiping my eyes on my new sleeve. The rest of the group who'd chosen to stand with us all looked to me.

Santos stood at the front. Even wounded, he was dressed for battle, his officers turned to soldiers. But there were only about twenty of them, instead of the fifty or so there had been before Metztli had died. And no one else from Tierra del Sol was there at all.

Beside them, Kit Fox and a still-bandaged Little Lion stood beside Coyote. To say I'd missed them was a huge understatement. My soul nearly wept again the moment I laid eyes on them, and I reached out, arms extended.

Coyote sprang forward and met me halfway. He threw his arms around me, and I squeezed myself as close to him as I could. I felt safe there, in our hug. Even though I knew in moments, we'd be in the most danger we'd ever been.

"I love you," I whispered to him.

"I love you too," he said back.

We separated slowly. My friends, the police officers, and mi familia all surrounded us, looking to us. I held on to

Coyote's hand and swallowed hard. It was time to truly face plan B.

"We have a plan," I called out to everyone. "And it might be the only way we can save our home. But it doesn't come without a cost."

I looked to Coyote. He still looked tired, with shadows under his eyes. I wished he could go into this at full strength, to have a better chance of surviving. But his soul was still filled with oranges and pinks. Even with so much sacrifice before him, he was ready.

Coyote told everyone the plan. I watched Kit's eyes widen, Lion's face fall, Ocelot stiffen, and Mamá cover her mouth. Santos's brows weighed heavy, mouth grim. No one liked it.

But it was everyone's best chance.

"That also means the curanderas' priority needs to be protecting Coyote until he's finished Naming," I said. "Juana, Damiana—I know we're all new to our powers, but we'll have to bring out everything we have for this." They nodded, and I looked to everyone else. "Try not to kill criaturas if you can. Free their souls until Coyote's done, and that can help us hold our own until it's finished."

Lion stopped near me. "I'll handle Jaguar," he said.

I hesitated, but he pinned me with his fiery gaze.

"I won't let her kill anyone else, Cece. I promise. But

you have to let me try." Lion's brow tightened. "She's—my Juana."

I squeezed my hands. Juana's face melted, just a tiny bit.

"Okay," I whispered. "Please be careful." I turned as Kit hesitantly came up to us. "And, Kit!"

He flinched. "Before you say anything, I know I got us in trouble back in the Moon Sanctuary. I know I'm not as fast as Lion or as strong as Coyote, but I want to fight for my world too. Por favor, let me help . . ."

Sweet, brave Kit Fox. I reached out my arms. His eyes widened and filled with tears. But he dove into me, and I wrapped him in an embrace.

"We can't do this without you." I rested my head against his temple. Slowly, his ears vanished back into his hair, and the warmth in his soul returned. "Fight with us, Kit."

He lifted out of my hold with a smile. He looked older than he ever had, as if the legacy of his old lives hung around him. Sí. This was the boy who had stolen his own soul back from Grimmer Mother. And it reached out to mine.

I searched over our few numbers, rousing all my bravery, all the water in my soul washing away the fear. Everyone looked to me for courage, as I had once looked to Metztli.

"I know we're few," I said. "But we're here. And as long

as we do our best, we have a chance, even if no one else comes—"

"What do you mean no one else, ey?"

We all turned. The sound of footsteps filled my ears even before I spotted the wave of red dresses and tattered clothing marching toward us, all led by Lesvia. My mouth dropped open as a hundred—no, maybe two hundred—people came pressing forward across the cerros, across the dust. They held pitchforks and shovels, knives and sabers, daggers and spears. All makeshift. All hopeful. Lesvia, at the front, led a wave of the restored brides of El Sombrerón. Behind her, in the mix of the people of Tierra del Sol, I spotted the young officer who'd harassed me so badly days ago, and Rosa, who'd spent her whole life selling tortillas, unprepared for war but still marching. Not a single face I looked over wavered.

Tears filled my eyes as the mixed little army met us on the battlefield. A sob of gratitude caught in my throat. If only Metztli could see this—

Tierra del Sol had finally come to fight by our side.

Lesvia stopped by us, holding a piece of her torn red dress aloft on a pole, a flag to rally under. Her eyes were bright. She looked to Juana. Juana's eyes glistened, and she nodded back. Bride to bride, they understood each other.

"We've come to fight for our futures!" Lesvia called.

"We've come to fight with the curanderas and criaturas!" She let out a cry. The crowd behind her echoed it—before everyone looked to me and fell quiet.

I gripped the embroidered edges of my new jacket. Their eyes fell on me, as they had so many times this week. But these people had come to join me, and they listened.

"¡Gracias!" I called out to them.

A few faces softened with a smile.

"Today, you've done what we as Naked Man have never been able to do before. Today, we've come together to fight. Muchas gracias for your bravery!" I said, and struggled not to cry in relief, in gratitude. "Now," I said, "let's save our world—and make a home for all of us."

The army let out a war cry, a cheer, a unified rally. Lion, Kit, Ocelot, and Coyote all looked across the group of Naked Man that had come to fight alongside them. Pink fluttered up their souls. My soul swelled with warmth—before the Desert's bones began to break.

All around us, the ground split. The cerros mourned and cried and ripped apart. The world rumbled and screamed.

Catrina was coming.

26
The Battle of Tierra del Sol

The land broke open in huge cracks like fallen pottery until a great, horrifying stretch of desert collapsed inward—into nothing. The echo blasted through the ground, shuddering in my stomach. And all that was left one hundred yards in front of us was a deep, dark hole.

Whispers cried up from its dark recesses. I could barely tell what I was hearing—until the peaks of a castle rose up from the center.

The castle rose from the ground as the rocks around it broke like cracking ribs. The tower jutted out, pushing aside and slaughtering plants, crumbling the foot of the mountain. Out rose the full length of El Cucuy's—no, Tía Catrina's—castle.

She stood on a balcony near the top, facing us as the queen of Devil's Alley.

Catrina wore the same long white dress embroidered with pink and red roses that I remembered, and a stare that barely seemed to see us at all, it was so flat and cold. Sand spilled off her silver-stitched sombrero on either side, leaving her dry and untouched by the earth she'd broken. In her cupped hands glowed the gods' four souls.

The castle reached full height, slicing the sky in half above our heads. We all stood shocked. Frozen, even as the earth quaked. The castle shuddered and locked into place above our heads. Tía Catrina smirked from her perch.

"Encantada de verlos a todos de nuevo," she greeted us. She lifted her hand to the sky, filled with the gods' stones. "Sí. Very nice to see you again." Her smirk widened.

The front doors of the castle boomed with a knock from the other side. Jaguar stood before them, facing us, as if she'd been summoned from the dust. The doors shuddered behind her with another thundering blow. Jaguar smirked. The heavy wooden entrance doors finally separated behind her. Beyond them waited Catrina's army. My breath locked away in my gut.

Jaguar now stood at the very front of the massive throng, framed by El Silbón and El Sombrerón on either side. Behind them, Gray Wolf, Black Bear, Criatura of the Pygmy Skunk, Scorpion, La Llorona—every possible animal criatura I could think of, and dark criaturas dotted around them—waited for Catrina's signal. My insides washed cold and tight. My soul dimmed.

Catrina tilted her head down to look at us with empty charcoal eyes. The wind blew her hair under her embroidered sombrero brim, and her burgundy lips slashed upward with a smile. But something about her looked different. Wrong. And it wasn't just the pain echoing through the ground, or the churning storm rising up behind her. The cracks I had seen in our shared dreams seemed sketched across her skin, like ceramic pieces of her were only temporarily glued back together.

"Can you smell that?" Coyote whispered. "Lion, Kit?"

Kit's ears popped out only to flatten back against his head. "Lion was right," he said. "She smells like . . . she's dying."

"Sí." Lion stepped up beside us, wincing only a little with his wounds. "Catrina's been dying for a long, long time."

The gods' souls shone in Catrina's hands. I watched their light sink into her veins, and pulses of their gold, blue, white, and red powers slip up her neck. The sketches of broken skin sealed up into smooth skin again. Their power was the only thing holding her together. But as she used them to sustain herself, I could hear the whispers from her soul, reaching out even now.

Breaking . . . a whisper floated through the air.

It was the voice of child Catrina I'd met in the world of

souls. And it was so quiet, I don't think even she could hear herself anymore. Maybe she'd taught herself not to. Maybe she'd buried that voice so far down to protect it that she hadn't realized she was the one who'd started hurting it in the first place.

"This was once my home!" Catrina's voice echoed over us, louder than it should have been, crowing as if she were part of the coming storm itself. "But now, I have power far beyond all of you who looked down on me"—she clutched the gods' souls, and her gaze cut toward Mamá—"and I will use it now, today, to be either your queen—or your end."

Her smile widened as her gaze switched to me. I met her stare across the desert, felt it burn against my skin.

"So, what will it be, leader of the dregs of Tierra del Sol?" she asked me, gesturing to my friends, my familia, the brave people of Tierra del Sol who had not abandoned us to fight alone. Dregs, she called them, when they were the bravest people I knew. "If you beg, Cece, I may even spare you."

Catrina waited for an answer. But I turned from her broken soul, pulled by a familiar ache, to meet El Silbón's empty, white holes over the distance. He stood weary and weak in his elongated, monstrous form, a lonely whistle reverberating across the way. I'd made him a promise months ago. And whether I was scared or not, today, Coyote and I would fulfill those promises.

We just had to get Catrina to bring out Quetzalcoatl. And survive him until Coyote could finish his work.

I stepped forward to face the queen of brujas. Juana and Damiana came up in line on either side of me. We formed a barricade between our criatura and human friends and Catrina's forces. From her place atop the castle, we must look so small. And sí, Juana, Damiana, and I were all inexperienced curanderas. But my new blue jacket flew out behind me like the waves of the sea, and my chest swelled with determination.

"Here's my answer. This land does not belong to you!" I called.

Catrina's mouth curled into a tight, angry frown.

"The gods' souls do not belong to you," I yelled.

Juana's fire stirred beside me, and Damiana's shoulders set, so the desert shivered with her movement.

"Criaturas' souls *do not belong to you!*"

Catrina lifted her chin and looked down her nose at us all. I squeezed my hand around my soul as its light brightened. My knees trembled. My gut clenched. I was scared. Terrified.

But I was also ready.

"We won't let you destroy our home!" I called. "Together—we will fight for what it can be! Even if we die trying!"

Her eyes turned to dark slashes. "So be it."

The army of Devil's Alley charged.

They moved like a landslide, their footsteps a cacophony of attack and stampede. I lifted my hands and began to pull water from the clouds, requesting the rain. Teeth and claws and unmerciful, clouded eyes raged toward us. My heart thundered, my skin covered in chills, as a wave of powerful, lurching enemies poured out toward us.

"We have to push Catrina to bring out Quetzalcoatl," Juana reminded. "The plan won't work otherwise. I'll take her left."

Damiana nodded. "And I, her right."

I looked back at Coyote. His eyes were sharp, focused. *You get her,* Coyote's soul said, as he charged forward to meet the oncoming army. *The moment she releases Quetzalcoatl, I'll begin.*

We nodded, our eyes meeting over the distance. Then I faced forward with my fellow curanderas.

"¡Vamos!" I cried.

We led the charge with Coyote, Santos, Kit, Ocelot, and Lion. The police did as requested, slicing soul stones free, battling the forces back. Cries and roars flew up on either side of the three of us as Juana, Damiana, and I made a beeline for the castle. Juana cleared our way with a torrent of fire, billowing out from her every step. Damiana sent mud sliding around our right, so the oncoming forces couldn't deter us. Catrina simply watched the chaos from her high place, chin lifted, eyes cold.

Rainwater followed us, gathering behind me as I whispered requests to the water. It gathered into a thick wave. Catrina's brows yanked together. We reached three quarters of the way to the castle, and I beckoned the water to rise above me in the shape of a snake.

"Give us back our home!" I yelled.

I sent the water roaring up the castle walls, the deluge aimed right for her chest. No criaturas could curb its speed; not even El Sombrerón—though Catrina tried to scramble for his interference—could stop its course. It shot toward her on target, and Catrina's eyes widened.

The Ocean's soul suddenly brightened in her hands, and the water wobbled in my grip. She sliced her arm through it as it closed in, and it lost all strength, all power, and cascaded down the tower. I locked my jaw. She whipped around to look at me, glaring.

A crack had opened in her face. She gasped and touched her skin. The Ocean's light dimmed and started traveling up her arms, up her throat, into her cheeks again, as it had before. The crack healed over.

"She can't rely on the gods' souls much longer," I said. "Every time she uses their powers to attack us, she can't use them to keep herself alive." I sprinted forward. "Juana, Damiana, all of us together now!"

Juana and Damiana both nodded. We charged together, Juana on my left, Damiana on my right, to the base of the castle.

"Damiana!" I pointed up, toward Catrina and the flashing of the gods' souls.

Damiana knew exactly what I meant. She leaped in front of us, and as she landed, the desert cracked open. Splinters of stone rose up the castle, layers and sheets lifting us higher. I climbed as their peaks rose up toward Catrina until we were still nearly ten feet high. I grabbed the water from the air, tugging it around me.

"Juana!" I called, as I tightened the water's hold on my waist.

Her eyes flashed. She took a deep breath. I slung myself into the air. Fire erupted from my sister's cry, exploding up behind me, so I rode the updraft when my water lost momentum.

I crowned the balcony, hovering, just for a moment in midair. My blue coat billowed out behind me. Catrina's cracked face met mine from under her shadowed brim. Fear flashed through her expression. I raised my arm. Damiana's and Juana's strength roared through me like electricity, like life itself.

And I struck lighting down between us.

The electricity burned the balcony. Catrina screamed.

The impact sent me flying backward. I collected the water mid fall, barely daring to take my eyes off what was happening above. Smoke and crackling filled the balcony. Catrina's enraged wail trailed behind my descent.

"Careful, Cece!" Juana grabbed my arm and caught me before I could fall.

My arm jogged in its socket, and I winced. Juana stumbled, clinging to a handhold in Damiana's rocks, and pulled me against the shelf. She tucked me into her side as we craned our necks back.

Catrina appeared at the edge of the balcony. The colors of the gods' souls throbbed in her skin as she used them to piece herself back together. But her hair was burning. Her eyes were wild. And panic rose in her soul with spots of red and white.

They're stronger together than I thought. They're going to hurt me! Catrina's soul cried out. It was the words of the desperate child. *They'll take everything I want!*

No, her older voice demanded, cold and sharp. *I have one last card to play. I will end this on my terms.*

"Fine!" she bellowed down at us, as she lifted the Desert's stone. Smoke still trailed from her clothes. "You think you can break me even now? I will break you first!" Dark veins crawled up her face. "I release you from the bowels of the earth, the cenote where I trapped you!" She lifted the Ocean's stone. "Be free from your prison and show them my wrath!"

The earth cracked open. Water rumbled far, far below, in the belly of the earth.

From the ground burst a flying, feathered serpent.

27
The Great Naming

Juana and I slammed into the stone with a powerful gust of wind from the rising serpent's wide, powerful wings. The wind hit like punches, and I tumbled off the rock shelf we were perched on. Juana snagged my hand, and water swept upward, surrounding us, and slid us down to the ground. Damiana skated down to meet us, and gasping, panting, we all lifted our heads to the skies.

Above us wound the beast, twisting in the air, fighting something no one could see. But I could feel it—Catrina's ribbons of dark purple, seething brown, wrathful red, all weaving through him. His wide, dark eyes swiveled down as he crowned the sky, piercing the thunderstorm. The low crest of the sunken sun shone like blood across his feathers. My heart filled with a painful, silent gasp as he shone despite his obvious pain.

"Quetzalcoatl," I breathed.

So that's how Catrina had managed him all this time.

She'd trapped him beneath the cenote because he was too powerful for her to survive. She may have carried his soul, but she hadn't actually been able to control him all this time. She'd reserved him for the last part of this battle, once she'd recharged her strength with the gods' souls, to turn the tide. Because he was the most powerful criatura of all.

My chest filled with heat and determination. He spread his wings, writhing in the thunder, and roared.

"He's here!" I cried out to our army. "Juana, Damiana, positions!"

Everyone knew what to do. Santos, the police, Kit, and Lion fought back against the waves of criaturas, bravely clearing a way. Coyote streaked across the field, and we sprinted for him. We met at the center, and he took his place in between us. We formed a triangle around him, and he took a deep breath as he shook out his arms. Above us, Quetzalcoatl's head shook left and right, like a horse struggling to free itself from reins. I could see Catrina's scowl from leagues away.

Obey me! I heard her command. The browns and toxic purples wrapped deeper into Quetzalcoatl, and the light of the gods' souls flooded up her skin, stronger than ever. She was struggling. I planted my feet.

I lifted my hands, breathing out, and collected a circle

of spinning water around me. The raindrops danced off the loop, like they were readying themselves as well. I looked to Damiana. She nodded.

"We're ready, Coyote!" Juana called, sweeping her red skirt back.

"No you're not!" an electric hiss swept up behind us.

I turned just in time to see El Silbón, his Mark of the Binding glowing, rip past us. My heart leaped up into my throat. Everything slowed. El Silbón surged for Coyote, where he stood with just the beginnings of white tattoos starting in his palms. Coyote lifted his head. His eyes widened. Fear knotted my tongue, but I threw my water after him, reaching, desperately, for his back.

El Silbón seized Coyote by the head. His needly fingers closed down on Coyote's face, covering his forehead, scratching into his curly hair. My water caught El Silbón just in time and tightened around his waist like a vise. He jerked forward to slash his needly claws, but the water anchored him in place, so he couldn't move.

"Now, Coyote!" I called.

Coyote grabbed the dark criatura's wrist. Pulled him free. Coyote's eyes glowed, bright and brilliant, gold and powerful as the Sun who loved him, the Desert who made him, the Ocean who comforted him, the Moon who discovered him.

"El Silbón!" He grabbed the dark criatura's other wrist. Coyote's chest and arms sprouted white tattoos as beautiful and intricate as the heavens. "I promised you your true Name. I promised you a life of your own again. Now I'll give it to you—and all other criaturas who want it."

El Silbón's white holes widened. The mark on his forehead burned, and he screeched in that tinny, electric tone. But Coyote didn't let go. His eyes narrowed, and he clung on to El Silbón as he now fought to escape. The tattoos on Coyote's body flowed down El Silbón's long, stretched limbs. They traced up his neck, outlining his head. An intricate circle, like a layered calendar, sprouted over the mark. It burned and rumbled—and the Mark of the Binding shattered.

"You weren't born from What Could Be to be a prisoner," Coyote said. "Not to be a dark criatura. You were, and are, and always will be . . ."

I swung water around us in a dizzying, stretching wall. It beat back enemies still trying to stop us before we could complete this all-important thing. But the hairs on my neck stood up. The follicles all across my body buzzed. Electric, ancient power hummed in the air like the moment before lightning strikes. White, glowing tattoos bonded Coyote and El Silbón in linking chains and embraced beauty.

"Alejo Guillermo Teutli," Coyote whispered.

The white tattoos wrapped El Silbón's body so completely in light that I couldn't see him and Coyote anymore. I squinted as my eyes watered. La Chupacabra tried to charge through at them, leaping high, high over the wall, probably launched by another criatura. Damiana side-stepped, breathed, and whispered a single word. A stone wall launched up from the ground and protected the vulnerable. La Chupacabra fell back into my water wall—and was swept away.

Drumbeats echoed from Coyote and El Silbón. Then, silence. I turned back to them as the light faded. I held my breath as Coyote stepped away, and together, we watched El Silbón's form settle into the man Alejo.

He looked like a happier Papá.

That was my first thought, as fire and earthquakes and raging beasts sped past us. Coyote stared up at him, and for a moment, that's all either of us could do. Alejo opened his eyes. He appeared just a bit older than Mamá and Santos, with laugh wrinkles around his mouth and twinkly brown eyes that were so warm they reminded me of cozy sunsets. He had a close-shaved beard with speckles of gray in it, long black lashes, and a head of thick, straight black hair. His hands slowly dropped from his cheeks, and he beamed down at both of us.

"Gracias," he whispered, and choked on a sob. "I—I so missed being me."

I couldn't help myself. Battle or no, chaos or no, I plowed forward, threw my arms around him, and hugged him tight. And I wept with him. He pulled his arms around me and stroked my hair tenderly. His chest jogged with muffled sobs, pain and rejoicing, grief and relief, all swirling through him. I held him tighter, like I could help him bear it all. After hundreds of years of being trapped, he was finally back. And if we could fight well enough, he might even get to stay and live his life again, the way he'd always wanted.

"I'm so glad you're back," I whispered.

Beside us, Coyote knelt to the ground. He was still covered in the tattoos, and they were growing across the ground, spreading in layers. I watched them lift into the air, like an invisible hand was painting the world around him in a perfect sphere. He panted. Shadows deepened beneath his eyes.

"Now . . . ," he whispered. "For everyone else."

Alejo squeezed my arm. "At last." He turned with us to the onslaught. Quetzalcoatl roared overhead, charging down. "Let us fight together, then, Cecelia Rios. Before it's too late."

I nodded. Alejo rushed to join Santos and Mamá, where

they called to him. He ran into the fray, unafraid, self-possessed once again. Hope surged through me like a rising tide, and I faced where Quetzalcoatl was quickly, violently, dropping down from the sky.

His dark eyes had clouded over completely. He rushed forward, his mouth wide with rows of carved, sharp teeth. I swallowed and sent wave after wave crashing into his sides, trying to throw him off course from Coyote. Catrina's soul language screeched and sent him piling through. Juana skated forward and slammed her foot into the ground at the same time as Damiana.

Their attacks accidentally combined. The desert broke apart—and fiery lava poured up from its confines. The heat glowed bright and painful as it splattered up onto Quetzalcoatl's belly. He roared and twisted higher into the sky, missing Coyote where he knelt, his sphere of Naming ever expanding.

The white tattoos began to crawl over criaturas. Kit gasped nearby as he looked down and watched them spiral up his chest, surrounding his soul even through his clothes. Sweat poured down Coyote's face as the cream patterns finally reached across the whole battlefield. His body shivered and shuddered, and pain creased his eyes shut.

You can do it, I told him, begged him. *Please be okay.*

Quetzalcoatl dove down from the sky again. He entered the sphere, and the tattoos wrapped around him, his soul fluttering around his neck in the wild wind. A coil bloomed over and around it. I bit my lip.

"No!" Catrina screamed from her castle.

I whirled around. She clung to her railing, eyes wide as she took in what was happening. She knew what our real plan was now. I spread my legs as Quetzalcoatl headed straight for me. I summoned all the rainwater in a meter radius, swelling it up, into a geyser, and slammed it all up into his feathered wings right as he opened his mouth.

The impact drowned his wings. The feathered serpent toppled over, skating through the ground, knocking humans and criaturas and brujas away with his mighty tail. I winced.

"Cece, behind you!" Juana yelled.

I turned. Juana was fighting back a crowd of dark criatura with constant barrages of flame. Damiana was pushing back wave after wave of criaturas and their masters. Just behind Coyote, in our blind spot, Jaguar loomed over my crouched, shaking friend.

"Don't touch him!" I barked.

Jaguar's claws came down for Coyote, to end him the way she had Metztli. I sent a thin sheet of water up, to cut her, to slice her, to stop her. A black streak moved between her and the water, and Lion plowed Jaguar sideways before I could land the blow.

They rolled to a stop just a few feet from me, punching

each other, grappling. Lion cried out as Jaguar landed a blow on the half-healed wounds she'd already inflicted. He managed to get a proper grip on her, and pinned her, barely, to the ground with her arms behind her back.

"Lion!" I sprinted toward him, pulling a river of water with me. "I'll protect you—"

"You made me a promise," I caught him saying to Jaguar as I neared. Jaguar tried to throw him off, but he pressed her harder to the ground. The white tattoos from the desert began to crawl up their bodies. "When I was just a cub, you told me that one day, things would get better." Lion sucked in a desperate breath.

Jaguar's face crumpled, and her hands twitched, like they were trying to stop fighting him and couldn't.

"You promised we'd enjoy it together. Today is that day!" Lion's eyes brightened. "Fight, Jaguar!"

She tried to twist around and bite his already wounded side. I lifted a torrent of water, gathering it high above my head. I knew how much he cared about her. But I wasn't about to lose another person I loved to Jaguar. My nostrils flared, and I lifted the wave behind me to ten feet, twenty, thirty—until it loomed over her.

Don't, Cece, Lion's soul language crashed into mine.

I froze, the tidal wave locked in place. I met Lion's eyes. His face was streaked with sweat, the corner of his mouth bloodied from their brawl. But his soul was adamant.

She needs help, he reminded me. The white tattoos crawled up his chest, wrapping around his quartz soul stone. *Please. Help her, so when her soul goes back, it's really hers.*

My body shook. I looked at Jaguar's foggy gold eyes, and the dark seam inside me peeked open again. The deep, ugly hate I'd felt for Catrina welled up my insides, burning my lungs the way acid consumes flesh and bone. The water started to trickle back, away from me, losing its trust. Every fiber of my body screamed to stop her before she hurt Lion the way she'd hurt Metztli. Jaguar's eyes alternated between clear and foggy. Her face crumpled as she looked at her brother. Tears even filled her eyes.

She was fighting Catrina. She'd been trying so hard—and for how long?—all on her own. Slowly, I stepped back and lowered the water. The water relinquished gratefully.

Lion was right.

She needed help.

I planted my feet, closed my eyes, and stretched out my soul. Coyote was sacrificing himself right now; I had to help in any way I could. Turquoise curls shot through the ground, sprouting out from me, and decorating the ground in glowing light. They swam up Jaguar and Lion, surrounding them in a circle of glowing blue patterns that blended with the white. I pushed and reached for that place inside her that Lion believed in.

You can do this, Jaguar, I whispered. *Let Catrina's voice go. You can stop this.*

Catrina's dark colors tightened in on her. Jaguar winced beneath Lion.

I'm not strong enough, Jaguar's soul mourned. *That's why she picked me as a child, out of all the criaturas offered her. She knew I was weak.*

My heart ached. Lion had felt the same. But I knew the truth.

She didn't pick you because you're weak, I told her. *She picked you because you're strong.*

Jaguar's sobs echoed as the white tattoos swept up her chest. Her andesite soul stone glowed. The tattoos drew her soul toward her chest, but Catrina's dark streaks fought them back.

Jaguar screamed. "No!" she roared. She shook her head; her braids flew and struck her back. The turquoise light began to bloom over her skin along with the white, brighter and brighter. "I won't let you hurt him—or me—anymore!"

There was a sound like shattering, but it wasn't part of the physical world. Catrina stumbled on her balcony, far above, clutching her chest. It rang through the world of souls: the ringing of Jaguar breaking Catrina's control.

Jaguar released her brother, crying, and pulled him into her arms instead. Lion coughed and gasped as he could breathe again. He sent me a quick, wide smile.

Gracias, Cece, I caught from his relieved soul.

Just before white exploded across the whole of the battlefield.

I fell back into the dust. Coyote's cry echoed through the air, and Jaguar and Lion collapsed beside each other, in the sand, facing each other. I coughed and wiped dust from my eyes.

Lion and Jaguar gripped each other's hands as their souls faded into their chests.

I let out a shaking breath. I watched their soul stones melt through their skin, glowing lightly as they slipped behind their ribs, and their skin sealed over. I covered my mouth with my hands. Tears filled my eyes.

Coyote had done it.

Lion's and Jaguar's eyes both opened. They stared at one another. Lion, even bleeding from the corner of his mouth, smiled.

"See?" he croaked. "She doesn't own us anymore."

Jaguar's chin crumpled. She nodded, hope rocking her soul where it now lay, hers again, completely and totally hers, inside her chest.

I twisted around. "Coyote! It worked, you did it—"

My voice died on my tongue. Coyote lay in the clearing we'd made around him, limp on his side. Motionless. My heart squeezed and withered in my chest. Lion and Jaguar were talking. I rose to my feet slowly, approaching Coyote's body. Criaturas all around us gasped when they realized what had just happened. They cheered. Turned on the brujas. Cries of victory, of disbelief, of gratitude roared up on either side. It was music, just like the kind Coyote had brought to Naked Man to save us in our first winter.

But Coyote was completely silent, his face turned into the dust.

No, please, I begged all the gods.

I fell to my knees at his side. His eyes were closed, sickly shadows smeared underneath. His chest wasn't moving. I shook my head and pulled his into my lap. It lolled to the side, dust shaking off his white, brown, and black curls. I brushed a hand over his face, but Coyote didn't even twitch.

"Coyote?" I whispered. Grief swelled up my soul, and it flashed wildly through my necklace. His was gone, his soul restored back into his chest as well. I reached my light out into him, searching for something, anything. *Please*, I begged and prayed again.

Juana and Damiana turned, laughing, rejoicing, as

criaturas fought back against their brujas. I looked up at them, tears pooling in my eyes. Juana's face fell. Damiana gasped and stiffened.

"He's not . . ." Juana approached gingerly. "No . . ."

Tears filled my eyes. I clutched his shirt in my hands, still searching with my soul. But I couldn't feel his colors. I bowed my head. Behind us, Lion and Jaguar quieted. I bowed my forehead to Coyote's, sniffing, aching.

His eyes batted open. I gasped as his gold gaze met mine. Colors suddenly surged back up his soul, as if it had been holding his breath, and his chest rose with a large, needed gasp. I straightened up. A single tear dripped off my cheek and onto his. I gripped his shoulders tight, my chin trembling. Was I seeing this right? It had to be true!

Coyote smiled, and his warm pinks flooded into the air and wrapped around my soul.

"See," he whispered. "I told you I'd do my best not to die."

28
Sacrifice

I sobbed and laughed after Coyote finally spoke. "You—scared—me!"

His grin widened. "'Cause you love me?"

"*Yeeees!*" I wailed, and then face-planted into his chest for a hug. He laughed and tried to hug me, but couldn't move his arms yet.

"He's okay!" Juana crowed to everyone. "Coyote, the Great Namer, finished Naming all the criaturas' souls back, and he's all right!"

"Kind of," Coyote mumbled by my ear.

"You did it, Legend Brother!" Kit, Lion, Ocelot, and so many other criaturas cheered.

I pulled back to look at him. He did still look exhausted, so tired he might really slip away into the Great After at any moment. But relief and tenderness flooded his soul and into mine. He nodded his head against the sand.

"It's done," he whispered. "I finally . . . set things right."

Tears burned my eyes. I smiled back. "You did, mi amigo."

He fingered my soul, where it dangled down onto his chest. "Well, almost. Here, I'll put this back too—"

"No!" I flattened his hand back down. "You look like you might really die if you even sit up. Stay there and get better—then we'll talk, okay?"

No brujas were going to be coming after my soul anyhow. They were too afraid.

Coyote, eyes already nearly glazing over with the need to sleep, nodded. The cheers of the criaturas swelled over the dismay, the horror, of the brujas. They were charging the brujas and driving them out of the land, chasing them down, attacking them, sending them off.

The army of Devil's Alley was done for.

I looked up to find Catrina and met dark eyes across the distance. The cracks in her skin once again sealed together with the gods' colors. She was helpless now. She was on the verge of death, and she no longer had power without the ability to control criaturas—

Catrina smiled. It was wide, and thin, and dark.

Did you forget something, Cece? Her soul hissed through the air.

The sounds of rejoicing around me muffled, fading under the power of her words. I stood up. Coyote said something, but I stepped away, searching for the source of the new dread crawling through the air. Something was missing. Something was wrong.

I looked to where I'd left Quetzalcoatl. He was gone.

Desperately, I searched the sky. Trepidation streaked down my insides like rain as I finally spotted him high in the clouds. He twisted around in the air, seizing and fighting, scrambling and biting at nothing.

His soul was back inside him. But he didn't look free.

Wait. My insides grew cold as he finally righted himself. Quetzalcoatl dropped his head, black eyes rolling to find me. No, it couldn't be. His body angled toward me. Catrina could use soul language, sure. But surely she wasn't strong enough to control him from a distance. Was she?

Suddenly, Quetzalcoatl's body dove down toward me like a bolt of lightning. My soul flickered, lighting up Quetzalcoatl's fang-lined mouth as he aimed directly for me. Water collected up my torso, ready to try to protect me, but it wasn't fast enough—

Quetzalcoatl ripped my soul stone from my throat and tore into the endless sky.

My body went cold. I watched the blue light flicker between his teeth, careening across the sky.

Catrina's laughter was faded, distant. But it gave me my answer.

Quetzalcoatl spasmed in the air above her, and Catrina winced. Dark veins crawled up her face, erased in moments by the light of the gods' souls. But as she straightened, she smirked with a confidence that didn't belong under bruised and shadowed eyes. She lifted her hand to the sky. Quetzalcoatl released my stone, and it fell down, down, down, like a raindrop—and landed directly in her hand.

My insides began to wither.

The moment her hands clasped my stone, a painful cold dragged down inside my body. I stumbled. I blinked. Everything I saw seemed to sway as the edges of my vision blurred. My blood felt too heavy to hold in my heart. I fell to my knees and winced as the pain echoed through me.

This didn't feel like it had the last time my soul had been in danger. Not like ash and pain and burning. It felt like someone was slowly pulling all the strength from my bones. Like—like slowly, stitch by stitch, *I* was being stolen right out from under me.

Catrina wasn't trying to destroy me like Rodrigo had. I raised my head, breath withering, vision darkening. Catrina's hair flapped in the storm like a flag. She wasn't trying to kill me like El Cucuy once had. I had been able to take that. As Tzitzimitl had told me, my water soul couldn't be burned to ash.

But it could be drained dry.

And that was something Catrina had practiced doing for years.

I told you, didn't I? Catrina's voice rang through my entire body. *The greatest power is to take.*

It echoed in my ribs, my skull. I clasped my hands over my ears and cringed with the invasion. Her grip tightened on my soul, and I felt it around my throat. All the feelings in my soul began to pull away. My strength, my power, my joy, my laughter, my hope, my grief—all of who I was leaked out from the center of my chest. And disappeared into Catrina's tight, razor-sharp grip.

"Cece!" Coyote called my name.

I peeled my eyes open. Things were fuzzy, but I could just see him on the ground, a distance away, hand trembling as he reached out to me. He looked so weak. So afraid. He'd seen what had happened. He knew what was coming.

And he couldn't stop it.

At his cry, Juana, Mamá, and my friends all turned to look at me. I just registered the fear growing in their faces—before a slam jolted through the land. Quetzalcoatl landed before the group surrounding Coyote. Juana lifted her flames. Damiana her stone. But Quetzalcoatl extinguished and crushed their attempts with one great roar. Cries and screams rang out across the desert.

Cracks opened like canyons through my soul.

I didn't have long.

Catrina still had control of Quetzalcoatl, and now I couldn't help my friends fight him. I had moments. Seconds. My friends would too, if I didn't do something.

I rolled my eyes back to look at the blurs of my familia, my community, my friends all fighting the power of Quetzalcoatl. Everyone faced it together. Together. They had sacrificed so much to get here. Their fear, their anger, their prejudices. Tierra del Sol, criaturas—we'd all changed to fight for a better world together.

Maybe with just one more sacrifice, this battle didn't have to end the same way it had two hundred years ago.

I lifted my head, slowly, to look Catrina in the eyes. My soul's light slunk into her veins. My knees felt like distant, breaking glass as I held myself upright, just barely. Catrina's dark eyes held mine, and a tiny smirk trembled in the exhausted corner of her mouth as she squeezed my breaking soul in her grip.

I closed my eyes, even as pain threatened to drag me down. My light, my water, my soul flowed like a struggling river in the heat of the desert. Thin. Weak. But the last of my strength was still there. I clenched my numb hands into fists. Reached, pressing forward, with that light—

Help me give Quetzalcoatl the last of it, I whispered to the Desert, to the storm clouds of Mother Ocean, to the Sun and Moon creaking over the edges of the horizon. Their souls vibrated, and I could feel the collective power reverberate through my soul, even trapped as it was in Catrina's hands. She glared down at where she'd foolishly gathered our souls together.

And then, I was ready.

With a stretching that felt almost like breaking, almost like flying, I sent the last of my strength careening out of my soul stone. I pushed it through Catrina's veins, climbing up her chest and throat as blue, curling tattoos, until it wrapped around her soul, where it lay buried and damaged beneath her skin.

I won't let you control him anymore, I whispered, as the last of it bled out my body. *Break free, Quetzalcoatl. Break free.*

Above her head, Quetzalcoatl's eyes began to glow blue, the way my friends' had during our first fight with El Sombrerón. Catrina cringed, gripping her chest. But I kept the last of my strength surging there, separating her power, wrestling her soul language back from Quetzalcoatl. Her eyes widened in understanding horror. The next roar of the mighty, flying serpent shook the clouds. They crackled with lightning and thunder that rocked the world. His wings glowed with might and power.

Por favor, I hoped against hope. Cracks broke through the center of my teardrop soul. I felt each one like a cut through my skin. I gasped through them, fighting to free every last ounce of his power, offering the last of what I had on the wind.

Across the distance, Quetzalcoatl turned his head to me. The glow in my nails flickered out. Dark cracks moved through my turquoise soul as its light finally extinguished. Only turquoise tattoos were still left, glowing around Catrina's buried soul. She screamed and clawed at herself. But her soul's words were trapped. Stifled.

She couldn't speak even a single word to Quetzalcoatl. Not anymore.

Quetzalcoatl's body suddenly changed in charcoal smears. His wings swept down, folding into a cloak. His fangs shrunk into a handsome human face. All the vestiges of the king of criaturas as I'd known him, returning to himself.

It was working.

It was worth it.

I smiled as Catrina's control over his soul shattered.

My body ran cold, and I tipped sideways. Catrina's cry and Quetzalcoatl's roar shook my eardrums. She squeezed my soul stone, cursing me aloud, railing against us all.

The last thing I saw was my soul stone crumbling into sand.

29
The Curandera of Paths Unknown

I lay on my back, staring up into the stormy sky as lightning roamed the thick, navy-blue clouds. Despite the flashing, everything was quiet. Wind blew, and the new blue jacket Mamá made me fluttered, but nothing made a sound. Like the entire world had fallen asleep.

My body should have hurt too, but there were no more cramps, bruises, cuts, or scars. I searched the skies, trying to process what was happening.

"This is far sooner than I'd hoped to see you, Cece," someone said.

A woman stepped close and looked down at me. She had a gentle, slightly sorrowful smile. She was older than Mamá, with eyes that reminded me of Juana's, and had long black hair separated into two braids, each resting over a shoulder. Her eyes crinkled as she smiled, and she reached out her hands. Something reverberated inside me.

I knew her, didn't I? Slowly, I took her hands, and she

pulled me up to stand. She smiled warmly, but tears welled in her eyes. My heart ached; her gentleness so familiar, but I was also completely sure I'd never met her. How was that possible? To know her, and yet never have met her?

Slowly, it dawned on me, as peace enveloped us amid the storm.

"Abuela Etapalli," I whispered.

She cupped my hands between hers. I couldn't quite feel the smooth look of her skin, yet the warmth bled into me. I laughed a watery, little laugh as I soaked her in. I'd *always* wanted to meet her, and now here she was. She laughed and squeezed my hands back, like she'd felt the same way all along.

"It's good to see you, Cece," she said. Sadness crinkled her mouth. "Even if you've arrived too early."

"Oh," I said. And for a second, that was all I could muster.

I was dead.

The realization hit me with a jolt. I mean, I shouldn't have been surprised. I'd known what I was doing, and yet, standing before my deceased abuela, my heart ached. It was over? I was done already? What about everyone who had to keep fighting without me?

"I'm already in the Great After," I whispered, as the weight of it sank in.

"Not quite, mija," she said, and stroked my hair. "Right now, you are in the waiting place."

I clutched her hands tighter. "But what about mi familia? Where are they?" I searched the area, but it was just us and the storm and the desert. "Are they okay? Did they defeat Catrina?"

"They are safe, thanks to you." Abuela brushed her hand over my forehead, like she could rub the fears away. "Cálmate, Cece. I know how hard it is to adjust to the peace here, but it is real. I had all the same fears when I was in the waiting place too. I understand how you feel."

My heart sobered. That's right. Catrina was also the reason Abuela died.

So many members of our familia had been lost to this same fight.

Abuela's brows pulled together in grief and sorrow so potent it bloomed in the air like blue dye. "I could feel my health and my mind starting to leave, even before Catrina tricked the criaturas into taking their revenge on us. Oh, but that night. I still remember looking up at her and tu mamá as I faded. How Axochitl wept. So hard I thought she would break. I wish I could have comforted her." Tears touched her eyelashes. "How I wish I had seen earlier that Catrina was choosing to nurture a darkness I should have fought against with her. But then . . ."

"You can't make decisions for other people," I whispered.

She nodded solemnly. I reached out to wipe her tears. But when I touched the drops, there was no wetness. Instead, the tear fell on my thumb as a drop of light: warm and tender and filled with her soul.

She smiled a bit, through her flushed cheeks and grief. Dominga del Sol had been right. Even now, Abuela Etapalli had a tender heart, full of tears. Just like me. I smiled a little and squeezed her hands. Or, maybe, I was just like her.

I guess I hadn't been as different from my familia as I'd thought. This water, too, was part of my heritage.

Abuela patted my cheeks. "But you have saved many today, Cecelia. Do you wish to see them?"

I nodded furiously. Abuela's face softened, and she turned with me to the east, gesturing to the wide desert. With the sweep of her arms, the silent thunderstorm and empty desert suddenly vanished—replaced with the battle I'd left behind.

Quetzalcoatl slammed into the ground in human form at the center of the battlefield. The earth rippled with his impact and sent everyone flying—except my people. As if he'd chosen to save them exclusively from the brunt of it. In the wave of stone, El Sombreron was crushed and buried in an instant. Distantly, Juana gasped. With only one move, Quetzalcoatl had destroyed the Bride Stealer.

Slowly, Quetzalcoatl rose from the ground and turned, his glowing cloak of feathers swishing across the dust, so he stood on the side of my people. His eyes were fierce. Where he had once looked new and fresh, back when he was first given his Name, he now was weathered, experienced, and focused. He lifted his head to meet Catrina's eyes beneath his snake crown.

Quetzalcoatl alone could win this battle. And Catrina knew it. Her eyes flickered with fear. Turquoise sand poured out of her hand. The leftovers of my soul.

"Quetzalcoatl!" I cupped my hands around my mouth. "Save them, Quetzalcoatl! Por favor!"

As if he'd heard, Quetzalcoatl nodded and took a long, deep breath. And as he let it out, the air rumbled. My spirit skin tingled. And far above the battle—the castle collapsed.

Abuela Etapalli covered her face with her shaking hand. "Mi chiquita . . ."

Catrina screamed as the stones fell down around her. I squeezed Abuela's hand as we watched Catrina scramble for escape. But there was no Jaguar to deliver her, no El Sombrerón left to fight for her, no Quetzalcoatl to command. The stone beneath her feet finally collapsed, and the queen of Devil's Alley fell with her shattered kingdom.

Catrina's white and bloodstained dress flapped in the

wind. Her embroidered hat flew from her head, ripped away by the storm. Her silhouette screamed and, finally, disappeared among the rubble.

"Retreat!" Santos cried, as the castle poured to the ground like a flood of brick and opal.

Quetzalcoatl didn't move, but my people and the freed criaturas surged backward. An avalanche of stone swept across the desert, somehow perfectly parting around Quetzalcoatl where he stood. Mamá called for Juana, and she and Damiana ran for her voice. She screamed my name, searching for me.

"Cece?" she begged. "Cece, where are you?"

The first flickers of fear filled Mamá's eyes, even though the battle was washing away. My heart ached and tore.

"I'm still here!" I called to her. "I promise, I'm still here, Mamá!"

The stones swallowed waves of Catrina's army, burying brujas and brujos. Criaturas were mostly spared. But even freed from their brujas, some still snapped and growled at my people. Not all were ready to forgive, to trust. They scattered into the cerros, leaving the devastation behind.

A silence swept over the broken land. Chunks of the castle began breaking and sinking away, into an endless hole. Quetzalcoatl stared. All my friends waited just behind his cloak. They waited, listening, for something. For signs that

Catrina would emerge? Or that she was finally—gone?

I clasped Abuela's hand, hoping, waiting for the victory bell.

But Quetzalcoatl didn't even check the wreckage or the rubble. Like he already knew, with perfect certainty, what the outcome was. Instead, he knelt down, in the place he'd stood all along, impossibly safe from the wreckage. He scooped something in his arms. And when he rose, I finally understood why.

He turned toward us, Coyote dangling in his right arm—and my limp, empty body in his left.

My body looked smaller than I'd felt inside it. I couldn't help but stare at it as it hung in the crook of Quetzalcoatl's strong arm. My round eyes stared up at the clouds, my gaze empty and motionless.

In Quetzalcoatl's other arm, Coyote's weak, fragile state was obvious. But he stared at me with hollow horror. He reached his trembling hand out with difficulty and touched my forehead.

"Cece?" he whispered.

Quetzalcoatl seemed to meet my eyes across the distance. Then he lowered his head to look at Coyote. "She is gone," he whispered.

I squeezed my hands to my chest as relief and grief battled in my soul. Abuela's hand touched my shoulder for comfort. Coyote shook his head.

"Not you, Cece . . ." His voice broke. Tears filled his eyes. "I should have made you promise me, too."

Quetzalcoatl turned with Coyote and me, slowly, to face the remaining army of Tierra del Sol. Juana, Kit Fox, and Ocelot's eyes widened. And breaths turned to gasps as the army realized what lay in his arms.

For a moment, all was quiet. Until Mamá's screams tore the sky.

Mamá pushed through the crowd to Quetzalcoatl. She pushed aside teeth and claws until she could stumble into place before Quetzalcoatl's silent posture. Her entire frame trembled. Quetzalcoatl offered me to her. She scooped me up in her arms and fell to her knees. She stroked my face. And wailed so loudly I could feel her pain shuddering through me, even separated by worlds as we were now.

All my friends, all my familia, even Santos and Dominga del Sol, all stopped to watch Mamá hold my empty body.

Juana came next, limping and sprinting across the field, tears already streaming down her face. In a wild flare of her red skirts, she skated into the dirt and dust by my feet. She buried her face in my chest, her fingers digging into my clothes as she sobbed. She loosened a single hand to slam the ground and cried out in a vicious, raging roar.

The sorrow pulled me toward them. I knelt beside them all, aching, wishing there was something I could do. Kit Fox cried as he ran for me. Little Lion tried to come, and he fell, bleeding, with his wounds.

"She can't really be . . . ," he started, wincing. "She can't . . ."

Jaguar helped him up so he could limp in our direction. All our army gathered around my body, and none of our enemies disturbed them now. Even when the last few left-over brujas and brujos tried, Quetzalcoatl reached out his hands, and the earth sent them flying back.

Santos knelt on Mamá's right side. She didn't look at him. But she looked so alone, so broken, with my dead body in her arms. He leaned gently over and closed my eyelids.

"She has given us a new world," he whispered, "with her own flesh and blood."

I looked from my grieving familia to Abuela. Her eyes were filled with tears too. She reached over to stroke Mamá's head, even though Mamá couldn't feel it.

"So much destruction . . ." Abuela whispered. She rose again and looked to me. My insides felt like an earthquake and a geyser all at once. I'd never realized how much they would weep, how much pain it would cause, to see me gone. Mamá looked the way Abuela had described her at her own death: as if she would break.

I shook my head. Abuela Etapalli's brows pulled together in pain and understanding.

"Do I have to leave them?" I asked, as my very being ached. All the colors inside me clamored. "Can't I do something? Anything!"

"Well that, mija," Etapalli whispered, "is a question for the curanderas."

My breath caught. Abuela gestured behind me, and I whirled around, hope spiraling through my being.

Four women stood together in a line, facing me, watching me, as if they had been here all along.

The first in line was the eldest of the four. Her hair was in a long black braid, except where strings of silver weaved through. She had warm brown eyes and smile lines. She was clearly old, older than Dominga del Sol even. And clearly loving. She wore ancient garb with deep blues and bright pinks. Oh, wait! I'd seen her before. It was the ocean curandera, Consuelo. Metztli's mentor.

"There is one way you can return to the living, Cece Rios," Consuelo said. She looked to her left. At the woman standing beside her, with long black hair stained white at the ends.

Metztli herself smiled at me. My heart leaped. I gasped. Here she beamed wide and brilliant, with a lightness and peace she'd always seemed unable to grasp onto in life.

"You stand at the threshold of the World of Souls, Cece," she said, with the whites of her hair fluttering in the sharp, thundering wind. She didn't even seem to notice the storm. "It is far sooner than I wanted to see you. But after all you have sacrificed, you are free to rest now, if you wish. And if you feel called to protect your familia still, it is also your choice to return."

The next woman in line stepped up. She had her hair in a tight ring of braids around the top of her head, decorated with a crown of flourishing roses and dahlias. Her eyes filled with golden light, just like Juana's, and her strong shoulders set as she smiled at me.

"We can help you," Yolotli, the sun curandera, said, "but only if you truly want to return to them. It is your choice, and your choice alone."

"These people do need a leader, Cecelia Rios," the last woman spoke. She had tattoos tracing down her cheekbones, of mountains and diamonds, so they outlined her smile as she looked down at me. It was Reina, the desert curandera. "Still, you have given even when faced with great pains, and that is counted to you by the gods. What will you decide?"

I looked at each of the curanderas' faces. There was no pressure either way. But when I met Metztli's eyes again, I knew my answer.

"I want to go back to them," I said. "Mi familia, and my people, and the criaturas who've been freed. I know I was angry at Tierra del Sol. But I love them too, and I want to spend my life fighting for them and building a better life with them."

Metztli's smile spread, warm and relieved. "There is a way to do this, and it is only because you have freed the Criatura of Death and Rebirth with your sacrifice." She gestured to Quetzalcoatl.

I stared at his strong profile, the long black sweeps of his hair, mouth dropping open. We'd never known what kind of criatura Quetzalcoatl was—there hadn't really been time to get to know him or his new title after he'd received his Name. I looked from him to the curanderas. Metztli nodded. I drew in an awed breath. So this is who Quetzalcoatl truly was. This was the title he bore.

"Many things are clearer here," Metztli said. "Quetzalcoatl's powers normally can only apply to himself. But with the gods' souls"—she reached her hand out to me—"and with us, today, a human can come back to her soul, even after it has been broken."

Hope billowed up inside me. Metztli took my right hand, Consuelo my left, and we walked hand in hand as curanderas. We lined up together behind Quetzalcoatl, where he stood behind my familia y amigos. He straightened as Consuelo stopped just a foot from him. He looked over his shoulder. His deep, dark eyes scanned the area we occupied.

"Consuelo?" he whispered.

My breath hitched. "He can see us?"

"No," Metztli whispered. Her face softened as she looked at him. "Quetzalcoatl has not had time with his new Name, and his new role, long enough to sense and see the dead—yet. But we have been here before, he and us. He can feel us."

Consuelo looked at me with a wizened smile. "Yolotli, Reina, and I have spent many centuries with our souls combined with his." She reached for him, and he looked to where she placed her hand against his cloak. "He knows our presence like his own."

I'd never thought about what that was like for them all. Two hundred years ago, they'd stood on this battlefield facing Quetzalcoatl, when he was El Cucuy, and died to keep him at bay. Now, they stood here again—but this time, all of them free.

"Perhaps it is fate that our souls know each other so well. Because it is that very connection that will help him realize how to use his new abilities." Consuelo said. She stepped closer to him. "Quetzalcoatl, we need your help."

He turned around, his cloak hiding my body and

grieving familia. He stared over our heads, searching without seeing, but listening.

"Anything, curanderas," he said. There was an ache in his voice. An acknowledgment of their complicated past.

"If you choose to," Metztli said, "You can bring back Cecelia Rios, the ocean curandera. You can be the means by which the next generation of curanderas survives. Request the help of the gods' souls, retrieve the leftover sand of Cecelia's soul, and we will guide you. For you are Quetzalcoatl, the Criatura of Death and Rebirth."

I didn't technically have skin anymore, but my transluscent spirit tingled all over. Quetzalcoatl's eyes widened. The curanderas looked completely sure, as if being on this side of life had given them a fuller, deeper knowledge of What Could Be. My heart warmed. He'd gone from King of Fears, the terrible ruler of Devil's Alley, the first Dark Saint—to a guardian over death and rebirth.

I waited with bated breath, watching Quetzalcoatl. The shock left his eyes, replaced by a spark of recognition. He knew his title—knew and embraced it. He turned to mi familia, gaze landing on my body. Without a word, he bowed his head, leaped into the air, and transformed into the flying serpent we'd fought earlier. I watched him soar into the rubble of the fallen castle. A terrifying, beautiful hope rose up inside me, brighter, so bright it was nearly blinding, when he emerged with a handful of my turquoise sand—and the gold, blue, white, and burgundy stones of the gods.

"Everyone," he called. "We are not done here."

Mamá lifted her head as he walked past me and the curanderas, to kneel next to her and my body. Her eyes were already swollen, cheeks stained with tears. He reached out and began to lay the gods' soul stones on my body's unmoving chest. He arranged them in the shape of a diamond, in the same order the curandera murals always had them.

My insides tingled. For a second, I even thought I could feel my fingers.

"When I was given my true Name, the gods gave me the role I would need in this age of the land," Quetzalcoatl said. Everyone watched him, barely daring to breathe. "Cecelia Rios died saving me." He nudged the Ocean's stone near my heart. "And in return for her sacrifice, the gods and I will bring her back to you."

Mamá's eyes shone with hope so great she looked barely able to contain it. She nodded. With her silent agreement, Quetzalcoatl poured my soul sand—the leftovers of the turquoise stone—into a pile over my heart, at the center of the diamond. Then he looked up, at Coyote, where he lay across from my body.

"I will need you too, Legend Brother," Quetzalcoatl said. "Only you can place the stone back inside her."

Coyote's tired eyes brightened. Without hesitation, he said, "I'm ready. Let's bring Cece back."

30
The Grave of the Queen

Quetzalcoatl's and Coyote's hands met over the turquoise sand splayed across my jacket, next to the Ocean's stone. They both closed their eyes. White sprouted from my chest, streams of tattoos spiraling, linking, until a circle melded the gods' souls together. More lines swept from them to mine. Coyote's face scrunched, sweat streaking his forehead. Mamá squeezed him, helping keep him upright. I squeezed my translucent hands together, hoping he'd be okay.

Wind whipped up from around my body. It stirred the sand of my soul, lifting it, until the grains began to assemble into a familiar teardrop shape. Tears filled my eyes. They were doing it! The gods' stones glowed bright and beautiful as their light began to wrap into Coyote's white patterns of Naming. Their colors blended together, and I saw that the white light from Coyote had been made from their combined strength all along.

Quetzalcoatl's cloak shone iridescent, reflections of the gods' light. I held my breath as my soul stone re-collected under his fingers, floating an inch over my ribs. Coyote gasped and panted. But when he opened his eyes and saw it, his gold eyes brightened. He caught the stone in his hands and, gently, pressed it to my chest.

A bright, glimmering seam opened in my body. He slipped my soul inside. Tingling rose all across my translucent skin, shimmering deep inside.

Consuelo crouched by Quetzalcoatl's side. "And now, you say these words, hermano . . ."

His eyes flickered, and he nodded. Metztli guided me back toward my body, where it still lay in Mamá's arms, beneath Quetzalcoatl's and Coyote's hands.

"Be ready," she said, with a smile.

I beamed.

Quetzalcoatl opened his eyes. They were deep, nighttime black, and brilliant, reflecting the light of the gods' souls.

"With the Ocean's might, I assist you as the Criatura of Death," Consuelo instructed.

"With the Moon's mind, and the Sun's soul, I lead you as the Criatura of Rebirth," Quetzalcoatl repeated her next refrain.

"With the gods' wills, I offer my turning of the wheel

between the Great After and the current age," Consuelo led.

"And return you to the Desert's dust," Quetzalcoatl finished.

Wind soared up my translucent body, and I began to feel the distant echo of a heartbeat in my chest. I stood over my body, over my friends and loved ones, and I looked to the four curanderas and Abuela Etapalli one last time.

"Te quiero, Abuela," I whispered. "Gracias for meeting me here. I would have felt so afraid without you."

She folded her hands over the place her soul floated in her semitransparent chest. "Te quiero, mija. Tell your mamá and Juana I love them too." Her smiled crinkled, tender and wide.

I looked to the curanderas next. "What about you?" I asked. "Is there anything I can do to show you my gratitude?" Tears burned, warm and strong, in my eyes. My body below me shuddered.

They'd done so much for me. They'd done so much for *all* of us, and they'd never been thanked for their sacrifices. The curanderas all looked at each other. Consuelo hummed a laugh and cocked her head at Yolotli and Reina. They turned wide smiles onto Metztli and nodded. Metztli's eyes crinkled with a brilliant smile as she met my gaze.

"*Live*," she whispered. "Live in the light, Cece."

I laughed. Nodded. Swallowed a knot of tears.

"I will," I promised.

Slowly, a sleepy, pink, warm cloud resonated through me. I closed my eyes. Breathed it in. It was gentle. Filled with kind and loving whispers, all moving through me like ribbons.

When I opened my eyes again, I was staring up at Coyote, Juana, Mamá, and Quetzalcoatl, gold shimmers settling over my eyelashes.

My breath came back with a jolt. My skin tingled, bright and sharp and beautifully powerful. I flexed my hands. Coyote removed his. The four looked down at me. Mamá's face morphed from stiff, painful hope to summer beaming. Juana gasped and slapped a hand over her mouth.

"Gracias," I whispered. My voice felt a bit rusty, new and awkward. All the pain of my battle wounds were coming back, and I winced. But I was grateful, even for the pain. I smiled up at teary Coyote, at grinning Lion, at sparkly-eyed Kit. "I'm—I'm back. I missed you—"

"Cece!" my friends cried, and dove on me.

Quetzalcoatl barely rescued the gods' souls from my chest before my criatura friends and familia squashed me into Mamá. I wheezed. But Mamá was laughing, and Juana let out a loud, celebratory grito. Lion squeezed me, Kit buried his face in my neck, and Coyote hugged us all in his strong arms. He pulled up his head, so his face and mine were just inches apart. He beamed.

"Bienvenido de nuevo," he whispered.

His breath smelled like the desert wind, and it stirred my bangs. I smiled, and warmth spread back through all my limbs. Coyote smiled wider, so his cheek dimpled, and his eyes brightened like gold coins. My heart beat hard and steady and joyfully in my chest.

"Glad to be back," I whispered.

"Mi hija is alive!" Mamá crowed above me.

She squeezed us all close. It wrung all the air out of me, so I struggled to breathe, but I'd never been so happy to be drowning in my friends and family. No, wait—drowning in mi familia. Because Coyote, Lion, Kit, Ocelot—they were my familia too. They were *our* familia.

Slowly, Juana stood and brushed all my friends off me. She pulled me up beside her and squeezed me into her side, rocking us back and forth, like she always used to, to comfort me.

"Don't ever do that again," she whispered. "Promise?"

"Promise." I laughed. I wasn't going to waste this gift. It was too big, too beautiful.

I stopped in Juana's hold and stared out at all the criaturas, the ones I didn't know, or didn't know well. A rainbow of different smiles turned back at me.

"Thank you," I said. I cleared my throat and straightened up, so my voice could reach more of them. "Muchas gracias for what you've done today. Because of all your sacrifices, we've won our right to a new world, and I even get to live in it with you all. Gracias."

We looked at each other, and all the adults began to chuckle and talk and chatter. Damiana pulled La Chupacabra into the group, and Axolotl jumped up and down with Kit as they gathered more criaturas in.

"There's so much to be done," someone said.

"I don't think we can go back to Tierra del Sol," another said. "The dissenters have taken control of it. Can we camp out here?

"There's so much rubble, and that hole in the desert . . ."

"There *is* much to be done," Santos called out to meet their concerns. His eyes crinkled, and they were warm, and comforting. "Tierra del Sol is in fragments. Those who did not stand with us run it now. But all of us here? We can make something new." He looked out to the wide desert cerros before us. "What will we call a new world such as this?"

Damiana smiled at him. "We must start smaller than that, ¿sí? Maybe a city first?"

"We will need somewhere we can all live," Santos agreed. "Somewhere we can build."

"A city of criaturas and humans—and curanderas," Juana said.

I beamed up at everyone, with Mamá squeezing my hand and tossing around ideas for where they would go, what they would make, what resources they'd use, how they'd plan it all. The chatter grew into warm clouds— until something whispered through the air.

It wasn't so much a sound as a pressure, but it mourned deep and wide and solemn. I turned amid the chatter, looking for the source of the soul language. Now that I was looking, I couldn't see Quetzalcoatl anywhere. He wasn't with the group. As everyone laughed and celebrated, embraced each other, and even patted me on the head, I searched until I found his unmistakable cloak of iridescent feathers.

Quetzalcoatl now stood in the rubble of his old castle, his back to us. The gods' souls were secured in his grasp, but he stared down at something hidden. My soul pulsed in my chest.

Is it . . . the end?

Catrina's soul, ripe with quiet mourning, spoke up from the rubble.

She was still alive. I slipped out from the group's celebration. My shoes kicked up dust as I ran across the battlefield and scattered stones, until I came to stop beside Quetzalcoatl.

Catrina lay on the desert ground, surrounded by bricks and broken stones. She looked wounded. She panted and struggled as her hair poured over her face, but she couldn't seem to get up. Her eyes rolled up to look at us. She stared at the light of the gods' souls, safe and out of her reach in Quetzalcoatl's hands.

Catrina was an adult, here and now. But all I could see was the little girl I'd sat across the table from, playing a game that had become sinister when it was meant to be fun. Dark veins crawled up her face the way the cracks had broken her in the world of souls. She shifted with difficulty to lie on her back, staring up at me.

"He saved you," she said. She laughed, just once, and then coughed. "Quetzalcoatl saved your soul. But he won't save mine, will he?"

The answer was obvious, but my heart couldn't help but ache for her. I looked up at Quetzalcoatl for confirmation of what I already knew.

"No," he answered her question, and slipped the gods' souls into his cloak. "I am now the guardian of death and life. From here on, I keep the balance, as the gods keep our world."

I looked back down at Catrina. She stared directly at me, meeting my gaze, expecting some answer, as if she hadn't heard him.

"She cannot see me," Quetzalcoatl said. "Now that I

have come into my powers, few will be able to. Until it is their time."

Oh. The wind stirred our coats, and I looked back to Catrina, where she lay alone, surely knowing what was coming. Even knowing everything she'd done, there was no joy in seeing her lie in the ruins of this castle, shaking with the damage she'd inflicted on her own soul by harming others'. My chin dimpled as I watched her shiver.

When I didn't speak—didn't comfort away her fears of death—the nasty, sinister edge evaporated from Catrina's expression into the trembling, fearful look of a little girl.

"Was it me, Cece?" Catrina whispered. Her eyes darted everywhere, filling with glistening, empty tears. "Was I really . . . ?"

She didn't finish the question. But I heard the more honest version, leaking out of her soul: *Was I really the villain after all? I was so sure I deserved to be queen of every world because my own hadn't let me be important. But . . . but was I wrong?*

I sniffed, struggling to breathe through mucus and streaks of dirt and tears. "It *was* you," I whispered, as gently but as truthfully as I could.

Catrina had done so much damage. Not only to others but also to herself. I listened as the soul inside her crumbled to dust. I listened as the Desert mourned. I watched as

Catrina took a shuddering, pained gasp. But she nodded. It was a tiny, small movement. And her eyes looked like a little girl's, not like the terrifying woman who had tortured my friends just moments ago. They were both her, I realized. It was the terrified, selfish, angry little girl inside her that the horrifying, cruel queen had been trying to protect. But doing so had only hurt them both.

It was me, the little girl inside her finally admitted.

I kneeled down beside her and cupped her hands in mine. They were cold and shuddered at my touch. I squeezed them tight, so she wouldn't be alone, as the sounds of her soul breaking continued.

I wished so hard, so painfully, that she'd faced this truth before being brought to her breaking point. If she'd let that little girl speak—if she'd been willing to see herself and others, if she'd wanted to find another way besides the breaking of other peoples' souls—things might not have ended this way.

She seemed to know that. She let her hands slide out of mine, and she closed her eyes. The ends of her hair began to turn to dust. So did her shoes, her fingertips. She curled into a ball and cried. I reached out for her again—until Mamá knelt between us.

Despite all the anger, all the fear, and all the pain that Catrina's very name had stirred up in her, Mamá scooped

Catrina up in her arms like she too saw the little girl Catrina had hurt everyone else to protect. Catrina's eyes opened to meet hers. Mamá's hand shook as she traced her little sister's cheek.

And for just a single moment, Tía Catrina's eyes shone. Her hands shook as she gripped Mamá's dress. She watched Mamá with a desperation that begged her older sister, the powerful person she'd both looked up to and hated, admired and despised, to save her.

But Mamá couldn't save her from this. So she held her with a conflicted, shaking grip, rubbing her back, brushing her hair as it turned to sand. Slowly, an old, aching song rose from Mamá's lips.

> Between the cerros y montañas,
> there lies the town where I was born,
> with memories of the mornings
> that I so happily lived.
>
> Tierra del Sol, that's my homeland,
> little enchanting town,
> with your ruins and legends
> you tell me of your tradition.

Catrina's eyes widened as she recognized the song. The same lullaby that Mamá had once used to sing Catrina asleep, she now sang to lay her to rest. Mamá's singing warbled and ached. And Catrina—Catrina surrendered. She closed her eyes as her fingers finished crumbling.

> *In your lovely climate*
> *and eternal spring,*
> *our happy little corner lives*
> *because someone loves you.*

In Mamá's warm shade, Catrina, for just a moment, looked at peace. She rested her head against Mama's shoulder—and the desert wind scattered the last of her body to dust.

Mamá held the sand of her sister in her palms. She stared down at it, cheeks streaked with wet, sticky tears. She sniffed and closed her hands over the remnants of Tía Catrina. She brought one fist to her mouth, the other to her heart, and held what was left.

"Oh, mi hermana," she whispered, barely squeezing out the words. "Oh, how I wish. How I wish."

31
The City of New Hope

For the first time in days, we watched the sun rise.

The brides of El Sombrerón, Santos and his police officers, the stragglers of Tierra del Sol—they stood with the freed army of criaturas, stood with me and my familia and my curandera and criatura friends, as the brilliant gold light crested the cerros. We all watched it over the desert, and above us, the moon's crimson color healed back into a cool, calm white. Blue skies carved through the storm clouds, and we stood together as life came back into our home.

Tears filled my eyes, and I closed them as the warmth of the summer sun finally touched my skin again. My alive, restored, living, breathing body. And I felt the gods breathe with me.

Well, I heard the whispers of Mother Ocean in the clouds. *You did well.*

I was so glad this long night was over. The sun's light

streaked over my chest, and I could feel my soul, even deep down inside, brighten.

"The dawn has come," Dominga del Sol said behind us. "And just in time, ¿sí? There is so much to do."

She was right; there were a few very important things left to do. Return the gods' souls to safety, somehow restore the Court of Fears, and—of course—figure out where we were going to live now. And what we were going to do with the big holes left in the desert. We should probably fix that.

The adults debated and discussed the last one among themselves while Juana, Coyote, Lion, Kit, and Ocelot noticed Quetzalcoatl beckoning us over to him, where he stood by the base of the broken castle.

He placed a hand over his cloak, where I'd seen him tuck the gods' soul away. "The gods' souls are my responsibility now," he told us. There was authority in his voice so strong that I got chills. But there was no threat in it. I just—believed him. "As the guardian of death and rebirth," Quetzalcoatl said, "I am also the guardian of life. This makes their power my responsibility."

"Where will you put them?" Kit asked. "They should probably be somewhere safer than a cloak."

Quetzalcoatl offered a sliver of a smile. "I will not keep them in my clothes, I assure you, Kit Fox. But I will be the only one who knows their resting places." He looked to me. "The gods' souls are meant only to continue to power their bodies—to bring fresh tides to the seas, new dawns, new phases of the moon, and seasons to the land—and to guide the curanderas. They are not to be misused as Catrina did, and this, I promise you, I will attend to with all prudence."

I smiled and nodded. "I trust you, Quetzalcoatl." It's pretty hard to argue with the guardian of life and death, after all. Especially when he's just helped restore your life.

He bowed before us, and we bowed deeper in return. When he straightened, he placed a hand on Coyote's shoulder. Their eyes met.

"Today," Quetzalcoatl said, "you have made me proud to be your familia, Legend Brother."

Moisture filled Coyote's eyes. He smiled, cleared his throat, and nodded. "Gracias," he managed.

Quetzalcoatl offered us all one last smile before leaping into the air—and transforming into a feathered serpent. He twisted and glittered like a diamond in the sky's low light, before taking off over the montañas. He vanished into the horizon.

Juana's voice called for us. She stood a few feet away, by a puddle left over from the storm.

"Well?" She pointed at it. "Time to bring the Court of Fears back, ¿sí?"

Yes! It was finally time! I sprinted over and opened up a portal to the mountain river as quickly as possible. Lion was still wounded, but Jaguar noticed our flurry of activity and leaped over. She nodded to him.

"I'll help," she said.

Lion and Jaguar disappeared only for a few seconds before they popped back up out of my portal, carting the Court of Fears' combined statue to our desert. They rested them down gently, or as gently as they could, in front of Coyote. Coyote stretched out his arms. He'd been resting for about half an hour. It wasn't a lot of time to recuperate from everything he'd just done, but he didn't look on the edge of dying anymore.

"Time to bring back our friends," Coyote said, and placed his hands back on their stone arms. "Not as dark criaturas"—white tattoos shot out from his hands and began to cover their four frozen bodies—"but who you really are."

White tattoos curled around his skin and wrapped first around Tzitzimitl's bones, hovering around her soul like a net of stars and stories.

"I give you back your Name," he said, and the air rang with it, with drumbeats and rumbles, a chorus of wind instruments and tender whispers. "You were, and are, and always shall be, not Tzitzimitl the Devourer and Protector of Progeny, but Tzitzimitl, the daughter of the Moon, the protector, the star."

White light encompassed Tzitzimitl's frozen pose, and cracks burst through the stone. It shattered off her like a shell and revealed something burning bright inside. Coyote stepped back as the glowing ball rose into the air. I watched her bones and flesh and headdress fall away—and the form of a glowing star take its place.

It hovered through the rest of the frozen Court of Fears, toward me. I outstretched my hands, insides tingling, to receive her. She was so—beautiful. She came to rest, a glowing light, above my hands.

I will forever be grateful, Tzitzimitl's familiar voice rose from her new form, *for the day I met you. The day you trusted me to bring you home.*

My bottom lip quivered. And even though I wasn't sure if it was possible, I couldn't help myself—I flung my arms around her light, and held her close. She felt weightless and warm as the first dawn.

"Thank you for saving me," I whispered. "Back when I was seven, and again when Rodrigo stole my soul. I know that's probably what got you stuck in prison in Devil's Alley. I'll miss you so much, Tzitzimitl. But I'm so happy you finally get to go home to the sky."

This will not be the end of our friendship, Cecelia, Tzitzimitl whispered. *For though Naked Man might not remember, they once communed with stars.* She pulled back gently, and I released her, so I could stare into her light. *I hope you may be part of bringing those days back again.*

I smiled. That felt like a promise. And I'd cling to it, delighted, determined, ever hopeful.

For now, the star said, *Farewell, my dear friend.*

"Hasta luego," I said, "mi amiga."

Tzitzimitl shot into the sky with speed and grace. I watched her comet's tail streak behind her as she rose into the dawn—and vanished, embraced by the sky.

The wind left behind in her wake whistled through my jacket and sent me stumbling into Coyote. He steadied me. Once the air settled, and Tzitzimitl's laughter faded, we looked to her friends. Coyote rolled his shoulders.

"Now for the rest," he said.

The tattoos still glowed across his arms, and when he placed his hands back down on Bird King and La Lechuza, the light exploded through all three of the remaining figures in the statue—and the stone shattered off their bodies instantly.

The Bird King had been a magnificent bird who hunters had made it their goal to slaughter, legends said. No one had seen such a bird in centuries. But my mouth dropped open in awe as he took flight, with brilliant red feathers, bright blue and yellow and gold lining his wings. He cawed, loud and joyous, as he fluttered over our heads.

"He's back!" Juana laughed and waved. "You look beautiful!"

Kit grinned. "It's been a long time since I've seen the Bird King as—well, the Bird King!"

Lion and Jaguar waved too as he took flight. The Bird King let out a magnificent call from his golden beak, soared overhead, and went his way into the horizon. We cheered for him and laughed, and eventually, turned to the two people left standing there.

La Lechuza was a handsome woman. She was about as old as Consuelo had been, with deep wrinkles, fluffy eyebrows, and narrow, warm black eyes with thick lashes. She wore a rebozo de luto, the black shawl of a widow in mourning, and sweet smells of orange and cinnamon hung in the air around her. She chuckled when we all looked at her in amazement. I reached out my hands. She took them.

"I am Chipahua," she said. "I am the widow who protected the harmed and the unprotected. But now—now I would like to live again. Being mortal will be different indeed." She winked. "I look forward to finally being able to join my familia in the Great After when it is time."

I beamed. "Welcome back, Chipahua."

She smiled, and all her leathery wrinkles were muy hermosas.

Juana stepped forward and smiled down at where Alux once stood. "And what's your name now?"

Alux was still short, only about four feet tall, but his eyes were no longer a mottled brown, and thousands of years of being a vengeful, powerful being had fallen off him like fruit from a cactus. He stared at his hands, turning them over and tracing the veins, before smiling up at us. His eyes were large, rich and brown. And though he was no longer a man, he also wasn't a child. He was somewhere between.

"I am Huemac," he said. "I was Renamed when I was just a vengeful boy," he had a strong voice, and he grinned. "I had wondered, if I ever got my Name back, whether I would still be a child or whether the centuries would have turned me into a man." He laughed and looked down at his teenage body. Then he looked up and smiled at Coyote. "Gracias, Great Namer. You've given me the chance to grow up on my own terms now."

Coyote shook his head with an aching smile. "Whatever I can give you now, it is only repayment."

Huemac looked at me. "You will let me live in this new world, in this new city you've all been dreaming of, won't you, Cece? So I may recapture a life I never had?"

Huemac and Chipahua each looked hopeful. They were

both similar to who they'd been. But so new, so fresh, so ready to be themselves after a long time away from that truth. I smiled. My heart surged. It was just like El Silbón. And this new world could be their home.

"Of course!" I said. I looked around at everyone, at the remnant of the battlefield, the carved hole in the ground, the widespread emptiness. "This place—we'll make it somewhere all of us can live."

A feeling, big and true, swelled up my chest like a geyser. I placed my hand on Coyote's shoulder and faced the chasm left in Mother Desert. It didn't happen often, but right then, I knew exactly what to do. All the newly warm and hopeful colors of my friends' souls, of Huemac's and Chipahua's, spurred me on.

"We'll take what's broken," I said, "and repair it."

I lifted my hands to the sky. My nails lit up in a bright, triumphant flash of brilliant turquoise. I felt the water rise up in my soul, a song, a trumpet, calling out to the sky. The tattered rain clouds gathered over the hole, rumbling with thunder, cracking with lightning. And I beamed as the water fell in a wild rush down into the hole.

Coyote and Kit and Lion began to laugh. They ran forward as Juana threw her head up to the sky, spreading her arms with me. The sun was brilliant, bright, and as Juana sucked in a strong breath, the light poured through the raindrops until we were soaked in rainbows. Damiana gasped nearby, watched what we were doing, and ran to join us.

My water began to fill the broken edges of the cavern. It rose higher and higher as Coyote and my friends rushed to its edges, waiting to meet the rising tide of a new, grand lake. An oasis in the desert. Damiana stopped beside it too, overlooking the sun as it danced across the surface. Ocelot strode over to her. Damiana looked up.

"Use your voice," she told her. "It's time you had that home."

Damiana's brown eyes lit up. Ocelot smiled and nodded. Damiana stepped forward.

"Sí, this place will be a home," she said. The words reverberated through the ground. She lifted her hands, and burgundy light flickered through her nails. In a great rush, the land swallowed up the remnants of the broken castle, the rubble tossing around as the soil rolled. The broken bricks jumbled and clattered as Damiana moved them, sorted them—and let them fall in stacks. In houses. Two starter houses, in fact.

We all stepped back and looked at what we had made: the beginning of a city, all surrounding a new sparkling lake.

"What should we call it?" Damiana whispered.

Santos and Black Bear and Mamá looked to us. Coyote and I looked at each other. Behind us, the army of Tierra del Sol, the remaining and returned brides, and all my familia stared across the land that would be our own. And I could tell, we were thinking the same thing.

"Ciudad de la Nueva Esperanza," I said.

The City of New Hope.

The Epilogue of Esperanza

Most people had a last name, but I didn't. All my life, it had just been me and my one first name: Esperanza. No one had given me one when I was born, so I'd picked it out myself when I was four yours old, in the orphanage of Costa de los Sueños. And when I'd heard that there was a city with my name, I knew I had to see it for myself.

And, if I was lucky, maybe I could even make it my first real home.

"Ey, chiquita!"

The wagon I was riding in suddenly lurched. My propped-up feet slipped off the hay, and I squashed into the wooden wall. I spluttered, and the farmer craned his neck to look over his shoulder and clucked his tongue at me.

"This is as far as I go," he said. "You'll have to walk the rest of the way if you want to go into that strange place."

I gasped and stood to peer over the side of the wagon. Ahead of us, the road pointed like an arrow to the city rising up before us. Its walls were painted in bright, beautiful murals with a gate opened wide and only a few people to guard it. Beyond those walls, I could just barely see a lake shimmering at the center of the city, surrounded by adobe buildings of all heights fanning out like petals on a flower. I squinted and stretched. Was there a tiny island at the center of that lake too? For some reason, it called to me.

"Ciudad de la Nueva Esperanza," I breathed. "I finally made it."

"They say humans and criaturas live together in that place," the farmer said. He made a disparaging grunt. "I heard from some merchants that the place is haunted. Suppose it's because of humans and criaturas mixing. Brought about strange spirits and mutated humans." He shook his head.

But I wasn't listening. Instead, I squealed, toppled out of the wagon clumsily, and started sprinting down the road. This was the start of a whole new life for no-last-name Esperanza.

I waved goodbye to the farmer. "Gracias for the ride, señor!" I called. "I'm gonna go be a scary spirit person too!"

The farmer rolled his eyes before setting off in the opposite direction. I sped up, sprinting for the city. The closer I got, the more I could see. There were guards at the gate. One was lithe and thin with blond hair and eyes like caramels. He was talking to some merchants who wanted to go in. It looked like they asked travelers questions before allowing them inside. Hmm. Not a good sign for me. If they asked me too many questions, they might not like that I was a runaway.

Better to avoid the problem, I decided.

I scurried off the road and ran up to the wall, keeping myself as out of sight as possible among the brush. The guards at the city transformed into animals and sniffed the merchants' supplies, so they were too busy to even notice me grabbing the bricks and scurrying to the top. I was practically a professional at scaling walls by now. That's how I'd broken out of the orphanage.

But when I finally climbed to the top and straightened up—I ended up face-to-face with a coyote.

Its gold eyes flashed. I yelped—and lost my balance.

I tumbled off the wall and slammed into the ground on the other side. There were bushes to cushion my fall, but I still wheezed in pain when I landed.

I fought to untangle myself with the bush and stand up, and that's when things went wrong.

"Tío Kit!" A boy my age stood about ten feet away, nearer the gate. He scowled at me from under his thick head of black curls. "That chica just broke into the city!"

I whirled around. The blond guard from before squinted my way. He laughed, just once.

"That's weird," he said. "Why would anyone need to break in here?"

He didn't look super interested in arresting me, so I quickly steered around and tried to dart away. Emphasis on *tried* because when I turned around, I smashed into a brick wall of a person. I yelped and stumbled back, clutching my nose.

"Tío Lion!" the same boy cried. "Grab her!"

Hands gripped my arms. I looked up. A stocky man with arms as big as tree trunks and red burning eyes glared down at me from under a sweep of jagged black hair.

I grinned as pleasantly as possible. "Oh, hola. I, uh, didn't see you there."

"And breaking into the city?" he asked, voice rumbling.

"I didn't . . . see it there either."

I'll admit, it wasn't a good lie. And I paid the price because he just looked at me deadpan, picked me up under his arm, and started carting me down the street. I yelped. Atop the wall I'd just scaled, the coyote turned its head to look at me. Its eyes flashed gold again. I stared, transfixed. Its tail swished across its body, and when I blinked, it'd disappeared.

"Stop wiggling," the man carting me said. He sighed. "You know, I'm a black lion, and chief of police, and now I'm somehow reduced to arresting a child."

"Wait, no!" I wriggled. "I'm sorry, don't arrest me!"

"Oh, don't worry. I'm not actually arresting you. I'm doing something far worse." He grinned down at me with sharp fangs. "I'm taking you to the *mayor*."

"I've got a suspicious girl here," Chief Lion said, as he plopped me on the ground.

My butt stung a bit when I hit the red tile floor, but I was hardy. So I just rubbed my pompis and grinned up at the lady looming over the desk.

Chief Lion had taken me to the town hall near the center of the city. He'd carted me up three whole flights of stairs before dumping me here, in the mayor's office. And the mayor herself now stood over me like a pillar of fire.

She wasn't tall, but she was still pretty good at looming. She had long, thick waves of dark hair, almond-shaped eyes that were dark as night, and wore a red dress with ruffles that looked like it would be really fun to wear. I'd never had a dress that nice. I was busy considering how pretty I'd look in red when I suddenly remembered everyone was glaring at me.

"What's your name, chica?" the woman demanded. Her

voice was like a combination of roses and thorns.

"I'm Esperanza," I said. "And you?"

"I'm la Señora Juana Rios," she said. "The mayor of Nueva Esperanza." She crossed her arms and tilted her head. That's when I noticed she wasn't really glaring. She was more like—evaluating. The way other kids looked at their lotería cards when we played games together. Before they eventually got frustrated and tossed them, anyway. She pointed at me. "What's your last name?"

"Don't have one," I said, and bobbed up and down on my feet.

I glanced around the office. It was pretty nice. Not as nice as the mayor's office in Costa de los Sueños was when I broke into it to find a map, but pretty all the same. The curtains on the windows looked hand-stitched, and the center window behind Mayor Rios's desk had a stained glass depiction of the four gods on it.

"Ah," Mayor Rios said. "You're an orphan, then?"

I nodded. "No parents, no familia. But you named your city after me, so I figured I should at least come pay a visit."

I grinned. Mayor Rios's mouth quirked for a second, but then she shoved it down, like she didn't want me to know she thought I was funny.

Behind me, though, Lion snorted. I grinned up at him. His red eyes sparked a little. I had a feeling he liked me. I'd definitely have to lean into that. Having the chief of police and Criatura of the Black Lion on my side could only be a good thing.

"That's very magnanimous of you, Esperanza, to come visit," Mayor Rios said. She sat back against the desk and raised an eyebrow at me. Her face softened a little, but she looked no less fearsome. "But tell me. Why are you really here? It's a long and dangerous way for a chiquita with no familia to travel all alone. Did you run away?"

"If you don't have a familia, you can't really run away, can you?" I asked.

She narrowed her eyes. Okay, she didn't like evading. Honesty wasn't usually my first tactic. But I had a feeling it would finally be useful—and welcome—in a city like this.

"Actually . . ." I shuffled my feet. They looked so muddy and embarrassing against the tile. "I heard the stories of the curanderas. Of Cece and Juana Rios, who saved the desert years ago. And I—I just wanted to see if maybe . . . I have dreams sometimes, and . . ." I lifted my head and took a deep breath. "Can I please meet la Señora Cece? Can I visit the Academia de Curanderismo at least once?"

Mayor Rios's face fully softened then. She looked rosy as a sunset like that, and she shot Lion a look. Lion smiled back.

"Well, if that's all," Mayor Juana said. "You should have

led with that, silly chica." She gestured forward, and Lion opened the door. "Go on, then. Chief Lion will take you there himself."

"Does that mean you think I'm really dangerous or really special?" I asked, but quickly met Lion at the door.

"Maybe it means she thinks you're really annoying," Lion said, but I could tell he was teasing.

"Lion," Mayor Rios berated all the same. We made to leave, and she called out, "Ey, Lion! Make sure you're home for dinner on time tonight, mm?"

Lion grinned back at her. "Sí, mi amor."

She folded her arms, satisfied.

"Come on, little wannabe curandera." Chief Lion marched forward, and his broad back led the way out the tall building again. "Cece would never turn away anyone who wanted to see her. But it's a long walk—the Academia de Curanderismo is on a small island in the central lake, in the daylight district."

"So you've got the city split up by time zones or something?" I asked. "How does that work? Like, people can only get into one part a certain time of day, or—"

"Not exactly," he cut me off. He propped open the front door of the town hall, and I wandered back outside. He pointed to a turn in the road that led to a different section of town. A sign hung over that street, and its words were just visible: "Now entering the nighttime district. Shh. Your criatura neighbors are sleeping."

"Oh!" I pulled on his arm. "That's because lots of criaturas are nocturnal, right? Are all of you?"

"No," he said. "And children of criaturas, shape-shifters, even less so. See?" He pointed with his free hand.

Just a few yards ahead of us, a small coyote weaved between the people on the street. It trotted ahead and darted out of sight.

"I saw a coyote like that earlier!" I gestured after it. "Aren't they supposed to be nocturnal?" I gasped and dropped off his arm so I could grab at his leg. "Is that *the* Great Namer?"

"You heard what I just said, right? She's a shape-shifter, so she's half human." Lion brushed off my hand, but I didn't let go. He let me cling on after that.

"Wait, who was she, then?" I asked.

"Dulce," he said simply. "You'll probably meet her later."

There were all kinds of beautiful things in my city as we wandered through. Merchant stalls, with criaturas, curanderas, and humans all selling their wares and people of all kinds and shades browsing them. Yards of hand-woven fabrics, embroidered clothes. Tools and delicious foods and spices. We even walked past a large library, and the librarian, a pink-haired woman Lion said was named Axo-lotl, waved to us from inside. It was like walking through a rainbow.

We finally reached the lake, and it was bordered with long stretches of floating gardens. They were lush with foods, crested with tall, golden maize, and some even had colorful flowers. A fence separated the walking paths from the waters, and an older couple leaned against the wooden slats together, gazing out at the sun-dotted surface.

"Hola, Lion! Buenos días," the woman called. She was wide and strong-looking, with long black-and-gray hair. Something about her smile reminded me of Mayor Juana.

Lion waved. "Hola, Señora Axochitl, Señor Santos. How are you doing?"

"Muy bien. We were just visiting mi hija." The woman gestured to the building across the lake.

"She's doing very well," the man called out. He had a nice beard with flecks of gray in it, and a wide build. "She says she's waiting for someone though." His eyes dropped to me with a twinkle of curiosity.

I looked up at Lion. "Who're they?"

Lion just smiled a little and gestured me toward the wooden bridge that spanned the lake, to the centermost island. "That's Cece's mother, and her husband, Santos."

So cool! I waved to the woman. She and her husband waved back.

I turned slowly and stared as a large, blue building with stained glass windows stretched high above us, several floors tall, with murals painted on some of its adobe walls. The sun caught on its gold-painted dome. I had to shield my eyes to see it better—and then I noticed an animal perched atop the dome. It was a coyote. Not the small one we'd seen in town, but larger—the one I'd seen atop the wall coming into the city. I bounced on my toes. For a second, it looked like the coyote's gold eyes sparkled. Then it turned with a flourish of its long tail and leaped away, out of sight.

I gasped. Lion smiled, just a bit, and stopped me at the end of the bridge.

"Is this—really the place?" I asked. The island spread on either side of us, and directly in front of us were the wide wooden doors of the building. Just waiting for someone to knock and enter.

"Why don't you go find out?" he directed me forward.

I tiptoed closer, excitement rumbling inside me. Wow. Was this really it? I edged toward the stairs—and someone yelled.

"Hey! You!"

I turned and found the boy who'd told on me earlier marching toward me. Now that he was closer, I could see he was about my age, twelve or thirteen, and had a strange spot on his neck. Is that why he was so mad? I dropped my arms and sighed really loud, so he knew I wasn't happy to see him either. His black, curly hair bounced as he stopped a foot from me and pointed accusatorily at my face.

"Why's she here, Lion?" he asked and scowled. His shoulders were up so high, I couldn't see the splotch on his neck any better. "She was trying to break in earlier!"

"Because she's dumb," Lion said. "Not because she's dangerous."

I frowned at Lion.

"She *could* be!" the boy insisted. He circled me, narrowing his eyes. "What're you really here for, huh? What're you up to?"

"Ugh, nothing! I just wanted to see the academia!" I scowled and stepped back. "Señor Tattletale."

The grumpy boy quickly grumped himself to a new level of grumptitude, folding his arms, dropping his dark, straight eyebrows into a hard line. He folded his arms and glowered. Obviously, that look was supposed to make me uncomfortable. But I was distracted by the fact that he had the softest, roundest brown eyes with the thickest black lashes I'd ever seen. They were really pretty. In fact, he would've been cute, if he hadn't been so annoying.

"The Academia de Curanderismo is a special place, so if you've come here to hurt anyone, you'll have to go through me." He narrowed his eyes, but even that didn't make them look less soft. "What's your name?"

I offered my hand to him and purposefully ignored the whole first part of what he said. "Esperanza."

"Esperanza what?"

"It's just Esperanza. No last name."

He scowled. It wasn't exactly an unkind expression. Half concern, half suspicion. "You don't have a last name?"

"So?" I asked. "What's your last name then, Señor Grumpy?"

He folded his arms. "Rios. I'm Paz Rios."

Something clicked above the stairs. He turned his head to look back at the large doors—and I could finally get a better look at the splotch on his neck. But it wasn't a splotch at all. More like a birthmark, or a tattoo. And it was in the perfect shape of a howling coyote.

I gasped. He jumped and looked at me in a mixture of discomfort and concern as the doors behind him opened.

A hush fell over the area. From between the large entrance doors, a woman stepped out into the bright daylight. She was curvy and smiled gently, with broad shoulders, a round face, and eyes like river stones. A braid cascaded down one side of her head like a waterfall, and turquoise jewelry dangled from her ears. She wore a blue coat over a pair of what looked like gardening pants and a plain white shirt with just a little embroidery around the collar. She smiled down at us. And it was so warm, I felt all the fear around my muddy toes disappear.

"Buenos días, compadres," Señora Cece called. Her eyes were so deep and warm, I felt like I could sail away inside them.

If there was anything I usually wasn't, it was at a loss for words. But I couldn't find my voice as I stared up at Cecelia Rios, the ocean curandera, one of the founders of Nueva Esperanza. The one who'd stopped the end of the world—*and* helped make a new one.

Lion stepped up. "Buenos días, Cece. This is—"

"I've heard," she said, with a wink.

Lion chuckled and folded his arms, resting back like he wasn't surprised.

She looked at me again. "My husband told me a spunky chiquita wanted to see the Academia de Curanderismo so much she broke into the city. Unnecessary, but I appreciate the eagerness. It's a beautiful quality in a curandera."

She pushed the door open a little wider. The coyote from the gold dome sat next to where she stood, and an even smaller coyote sat beside him. My heart beat faster. Both animals shivered, and with gentle, changing lines, they began to morph. I held my breath as I watched sweeps of charcoal edges straighten up and expand. Gentle colors wrapped around their shapes, assembled into human limbs, and then suddenly, and quietly, they were just two people standing there, watching us.

Coyote was tall with gold eyes and curly hair like Paz's, only his was multicolored instead of jet-black. He had a close-shaved beard too, and he smiled, and it was a warm, mysterious smile, like he knew something I didn't.

"Good to see you again, chiquita," he called out.

The little girl beside him was about seven years old, with short-cut black hair that stuck up like a cactus. She had a black coyote birthmark just like Paz's, only hers was on the back of her right hand. She giggled and ran down to Paz. His whole face melted as he wrapped his arms around her. She peeked out at me, and though her eyes were brown, there were little golden flecks dancing through the irises.

"Papá said you were extra grumpy today," she said to him. "Is it because of her?"

"I'm not grumpy, Dulce." Paz made a face sideways at me. "It's just that she's suspicious. And weird."

"Maybe she's good weird," the girl said brightly.

I nodded proudly at "good weird." Footsteps trailed down the stairs toward me. I looked up, and Señora Rios stopped before me, her turquoise earrings swinging. She went to say something—then paused. The air sparkled, and a strange pressure, a push and pull, moved in the space between us. It felt strange—but good. Her eyes widened slightly as she looked at me. The same round, rich brown eyes Paz must have inherited filled with a sparkle of blue light.

"What's your name?" she asked, intent and breathy.

"Esperanza," I said. "Just Esperanza."

She smiled and shook her head. "No. You are Esperanza de la Luna, a moon curandera. I've been waiting years to meet you," she whispered.

"Me?" I whispered.

Señora Cece's eyes melted into warm, deep puddles of river water. She stepped back, reached for my hand, and gestured me up the stairs.

"If you want it, this is your new home, Esperanza de la Luna," she said. "Por favor, come inside. We've been waiting for you."

I'd been waiting my whole life to hear that. To have a last name. To have a home. To have people who'd be excited when they'd see me arrive. My mind tingled with all the future I'd never been sure I'd have. My heart soared, and my fingers prickled with joy, delight—possibility.

And as I followed them all inside, I was absolutely sure everything that had led to this day had been 100 percent, totally, and completely, worth it.

Glossary

Academia de Curanderismo—The Academy of Healers.

Bienvenido de nuevo—Welcome back.

bisabuela—Great grandmother.

cálmate—Calm down.

Don/Dona—Originally titles used for nobility, in more modern times, they are honorifics that go before a first or full name, indicating respect for someone's higher social class, education, or other great endeavors.

dulce—Sweet.

el sol—The sun.

Encantada de verlos a todos de nuevo—Very nice to see you all again.

escapa—Escape.

esperanza—Hope.

idiota—Idiot.

La Abuelita—Grandmother.

La Dama—The lady.

león—Lion.

lotería—A traditional game of chance, sometimes called "Mexican bingo."

mi vida—A term of endearment that literally means "my life."

montaña—Mountain.

novio—Boyfriend.

órale—A common interjection in Mexico, this Spanish exclamation is usually celebratory or encouraging, but has multiple connotations.

paz—Peace.

pero—But.

perro—Dog.

pompis—Butt.

¿Qué pasa?—Literally means "What's up?"

Quetzalcoatl—The feathered serpent. This powerful deity's role in Aztec religion evolved with its people, but he was often known as the god of rain and then as the god of death and rebirth. He was said to be an important part of creating the world and its people.

Río Fuerte—Strong river. In Cece's world, this is the largest body of water near Tierra del Sol, located in the cerros.

tlalpanhuehuetl—A cylindrical, vertical wooden drum usually carved with symbols of war and other mighty iconography. Played by the Aztecs during war rituals.

tu—You.

zorro—Fox.

Acknowledgments

There are almost too many people to thank for the creation of this book. It was written and revised during one of the lowest points in my life, while I had mono, then COVID, then all the repercussions of both those illnesses. There were nights where I dripped sweat and tears on my keyboard, and it was because of the loving strength of others that I made it through it all.

First, to my mother, who found ways to care for me when I couldn't move, and who made sure I still ate and slept and had clean clothes when I was too weak to do any of the basics. Thank you for everything.

Second, to Serene Hakim, my agent, for championing me and my work. To Stephanie Guerdan, Jessica Berg, Catherine Lee, and many more wonderful, kind, and helpful team members at Harper. I'm so glad you've come out of your strike victorious, and that we got to keep working together to finish this trilogy. It's an honor to have had your skill and support on this series.

Next, if it is not too indulgent: to my past self, because even though I know you thought you were doing a terrible job, I'm so proud of you for pushing forward (or perhaps crawling), even when you were unsure whether you were going to make it. You did. Thank you for enduring and hanging on to the light.

And a big thank-you to the wonderful members of the writing community who have offered their support, guidance, and insight. Laura, because you are clear-sighted and striving, thank you for seeing potential in the first draft of this third book where I, at the time, couldn't. J. Scott Savage, for being a supportive and kind influence who gives me courage and inspiration. Dan Wells, for sending the elevator down to me and so many more. Celesta Rimington, for your knowledge and kindness and willingness to share both. Heather Clark, for your infectious enthusiasm and dedication. And all of Writers Cubed, for your fantastic work and love for children and literacy.

And for all the teachers, librarians, parents, and readers who have supported Cece since the first volume. I was only able to conclude this trilogy because of your support, and I hope that I have offered some light back for yours. Thank you y muchas gracias.

And last but never least, always first, to the Light of the World. Thank you for saving mine again and again.